A LADDER OF BONES

ESSENTIAL PROSE SERIES 233

Canada Council for the Arts / Conseil des Arts du Canada

ONTARIO ARTS COUNCIL
CONSEIL DES ARTS DE L'ONTARIO
an Ontario government agency
un organisme du gouvernement de l'Ont

Canada

Guernica Editions Inc. acknowledges the support of the Canada Council for the Arts and the Ontario Arts Council. The Ontario Arts Council is an agency of the Government of Ontario.

We acknowledge the financial support of the Government of Canada.

A LADDER OF BONES

BUNMI OYINSAN

GUERNICA EDITIONS

TORONTO—CHICAGO—BUFFALO—LANCASTER (U.K.)

2025

Guernica Founder: Antonio D'Alfonso

Michael Mirolla, general editor
Kulamrit Bamrah, editor
Interior and cover design: Errol F. Richardson
Front cover image: *Not always, but every time*, Soji "Shakes" Oyinsan

Guernica Editions Inc.
1241 Marble Rock Rd., Gananoque, ON K7G 2V4
2250 Military Road, Tonawanda, N.Y. 14150-6000 U.S.A.
www.guernicaeditions.com

Distributors:
Independent Publishers Group (IPG)
600 North Pulaski Road, Chicago IL 60624
University of Toronto Press Distribution (UTP)
5201 Dufferin Street, Toronto (ON), Canada M3H 5T8

First edition.
Printed in Canada.

Legal Deposit—Third Quarter
Library of Congress Catalog Card Number: 2024945680
Library and Archives Canada Cataloguing in Publication
Title: A ladder of bones / Olubunmi Oyinsan.
Names: Oyinsan, Bunmi, author
Series: Essential prose series ; 233.
Description: First edition. | Series statement: Essential prose series; 233
Identifiers: Canadiana (print) 20240457013 | Canadiana (ebook) 20240457021 | ISBN 9781778490088 (softcover) | ISBN 9781778490095 (EPUB)
Subjects: LCGFT: Linked stories. | LCGFT: Novels.
Classification: LCC PS8579.Y56 L33 2025 | DDC C813/.54—dc23

PART ONE: MIRY BURR

Burr: "A rough edge remaining on material, such as metal, after it has been cast, cut, or drilled." —*American Heritage Dictionary.*

Canada — 1997

Enilolobo

AH, VICTORIA DAY. That illustrious long weekend when Canadians prematurely summoned summer—because, evidently, anticipation trumps the Gregorian calendar. Once celebrated as Empire Day (how retro) it now serves to honour the "official birthday" of Canada's monarch—though the relevance to the actual birth date of the reigning sovereign is, amusingly, nonexistent.

The day pays homage to Queen Victoria, the monarch under whose rule Canada cobbled itself into a federation. This homage is, of course, in spite of Newfoundland's leisurely eighty-year hesitation before it hopped onto the unity train. Imagine the confederation party, waiting awkwardly, checking its watch, wondering when Newfoundland would finally show.

Yet, despite the enduring reverence for the crown, many Canucks remain blissfully unaware of the historical quirk that almost had them exchanging snow for sand. They would rather not remember that had it not been for prevailing negrophobia, the sunny Caribbean isles might now be sporting the maple leaf flag, transforming Canada's image from the staunch "saltfish bastion of the North Atlantic" to perhaps the spirited "rum capital of the Americas." Now, wouldn't that have been a glorious twist in the national identity tale?

In the good old days, rich Canadians—giddily claiming themselves to be British—went to their cottages and fastidiously got drunk for three days of Empire Day revels. These days, their not-so-rich offspring, who cannot afford cottages because of the "precarious" state of the economy, host frolicking barbeque parties—all booze, burgers, and bikinis. There are few fireworks now. They've almost fizzled out along with the empire. Still, some people who do not quite see the sense in downgrading a celebration as "rich in meaning" as Empire Day to the nondescript Victoria Day cannot resist lamenting the fact that most so-called new Canadians completely ignore the rich British traditions of Canada. As such, "patriots" who choose to hide under the Hudson Bay blanket of traditionalism ruminate loudly on the need for more citizens to focus on Canada's "European heritage." They are confounded by the "new Canadians" who seem quite content to remain blissfully ignorant of Canada's roots even if it has been at the expense of the indigenous people. To such ideologues, it is deplorable that, even in Great Britain, British identity is allowed to atrophy, to disintegrate into Scottish, Welsh, and Irish nationalisms and is unfortunately contaminated by the hordes of new immigrants.

All the same, the Victoria Day long weekend allows the nostalgic to indulge their worries that Canada might soon end up a part of the third world given what they deem to be the massive onslaught of immigrants from the shithole regions of the earth. They believe that immigrants do nothing for the economy other than milk social services. Those who believe they are custodians of the "real Canadian heritage" eye Quebec with a quiet, secret envy for what they see as the province's ability to sustain its sense of white wool nationalism and loyalty to Europe, the "mother continent." They yearn to harness the conservatism of like-minded suburbanites, the joie-de-vivre of the French in Quebec and other francophone enclaves (such as in Acadia). They value the law and order of the British and crave to unite the white-flight suburbs of cities like Kingston, Peterborough, and London in Ontario; Halifax in Nova Scotia; Fredericton and Saint John in New Brunswick; St John's in Newfoundland; Victoria in British Columbia; Edmonton in Alberta; and all those illustrious small towns dotting "the real Canada." They credit that only such a "progressive force" can propel their great country through the new millennium, and save it from being sucked into the hellholes of the Third World alongside Africa, most of Asia, South America, and especially the sordid neighbourhoods in the Caribbean that tourists do not dare visit.

Nowadays, Victoria Day weekend in Nova Scotia is when people who are still privileged enough to own a cottage open it for the season. It is also a time when folks flock to garden shops to purchase compost and mulch, or hang baskets and trays of transplants for their gardens. A time to watch blossoms explode and fireworks explosions blossom.

Thus, as their police car cruised northwards on Barrington Street in Halifax on Victoria Day in 1997, Officer Gordon Scott and his partner, Keith Dale, expected to find lots of people heading home after having watched the fireworks display in celebration of Dead, Dread Victoria. They anticipated a few overzealous spectators, one or two drunks, perhaps, but they did not expect any major-league criminal to rock the peace or disturb their watch.

But approaching the area known as the Grand Parade, it was Gordon who first noticed that there was a large crowd gathering a short distance away and all seemed to be peering down at something on the ground. He pointed at the group, and Keith, who was driving, quickly stopped the car at the corner of Argyle and Barrington, so Gordon could leap out. Reaching for his radio, Keith watched Gordon plod through the exponentially swelling crowd.

"Excuse me. Please make way!" Gordon squeezed past the last two women who were blocking him from seeing what it was that fascinated so many and was amazed by the sight before his eyes. It was a child, a girl. She looked about six, and naked as the day God made her. Even though her skin did not quite make the onlookers think of onyx, she was brown enough to make them think of cinnamon and nutmeg, and some even thought of mahogany.

The girl had several scars on her body. Some around her wrists formed a thick band of keloids. Her thick, long, coarse hair had a hint of silk, but it was dishevelled and seemed to stoop down her head and sag her surprisingly thin neck. Her eyes were wide-set and huge, like minuscule saucers. They looked too big for her face. The whites around her deep ink-coloured pupils looked as if they were about to spill, as fear pranced, splashing tears. She sat on the ground, shivering with her hands flat on the concrete next to her bum on either side of her. She kept looking up, unblinking, terrified by the unblushing, motley observers staring down at her scrawny, brown-girl-child nakedness.

When Gordon reached down to touch her, the girl flinched, and a woman's squeaky voice from the crowd tried to reassure her. "Don't be scared, sweetie. It's the police." She enunciated the words as if she did not expect the girl to have all her faculties intact. She definitely didn't expect her to understand English. Another woman, spaghetti-skinny, handed Gordon a small pink and white shawl, too inadequate to cover the quivering pickney.

"Where did she come from?" Gordon asked no one in particular.

"No one knows," the thin woman said. "I just saw her running from the direction of the Citadel, and then she slumped down, out of breath."

"Well, she couldn't have simply surfaced from nowhere. If you ask me, it's another one of those child abuse cases. I bet the perpetrators aren't far off," another person said, and then several people joined the hubbub.

"Yeah, that's what you need to do, officer. Find the blasted, cock-sucking parents or guardians."

"She might have been abducted for all you know."

"See how terrified she looks. What's your name, love?" a stocky-looking woman with two front teeth missing asked, stretching out a passably charitable hand to the girl.

But the girl simply turned her face to look at the ground, giving no indication that she could comprehend anything that was being said.

"See, she's a foreigner, I'm sure," a man said, thus domesticating xenophobia.

By this time, Gordon, who was trying to wrap the shawl around the odd chit, noticed that she had two flat navels shaped like jagged stars. He almost shuddered at the sight of the two identical marks on her perfectly round stomach. But either none of the onlookers saw them, or they did not think anything of them because no one commented.

The scene was a freak show. Gordon was relieved when Keith joined him, and together they managed to wrap the skimpy shawl around the skin-and-bones local mystery before leading her to the patrol car.

When they got to the vehicle, the girl looked up, and her eyes seemed to catch a glare around the spire of St. Paul's Church. She raised her right hand as if to shield herself from the brightness, but the hand stopped mid-air as she became momentarily transfixed, then collapsed onto the back seat of the car. Keith nudged her, then gasped. "I think she's passed out!" He quickly slipped into the driver's seat as Gordon got in beside him, then reached to work the radio. The cruiser turned onto Sackville Street, then blitzed—with siren blaring—toward the Izaak Walton Killam Hospital. Revels interrupted, the citizenry could only continue to trade speculative gossip about the mysterious waif.

***

Gordon was relieved at the IWK Hospital when the paramedic who came with a stretcher to take the girl noticed her two navels and exclaimed. Gordon had been beginning to think he was the only one who noticed the anatomical feature or found it strange. He followed the girl's stretcher into the huge hospital complex and saw that she was wide awake.

"How are you?" he tried to ask in his most paternal voice, but her eyes stayed staring and she laid shivering in a fetal position on the stretcher.

Gordon returned to the police car after completing the necessary reports.

"I think we should start looking for her parents around Uniacke Square," Keith said when he entered the car.

"Sounds like a plan. It's close enough to where we found her. I also want us to stop at St. Paul's Church and all the other churches around the spot where she appeared. See if anyone knows anything about her."

Keith agreed. He had also noticed how the girl reacted when she looked up at the spire of the church. Though neither of them said anything, they were wondering if a church in the neighbourhood was harbouring refugees, like some other churches had been known to do in the recent past.

But their trips to the churches turned out to be as futile as their attempts to find her parents in all the places from where they thought she might have been fleeing.

That night, when news of her strange appearance broke on TV, residents of the deceptively quiet NATO naval base that is Halifax could not help contemplating the girl's origins. Though the news report did not have a picture of her, the fact that she was described as being of African descent led some to conclude that she was from somewhere around Dartmouth or one of the less reputable areas of Halifax. After all, Uniacke Square was essentially the remnant of

Africville. That blot in the face of the otherwise postcard-perfect, harbour city was not far from the spot where the child was found.

Recent African immigrants held their breaths, hoping she was not one of theirs. Not a Sierra Leonean, Somalian, Sudanese, Ghanaian, Nigerian, Zimbabwean or Liberian stowaway. Very few members of the fifty-two historic African Nova Scotian communities—including Shelburne, East Preston, Annapolis Royal, Cherry Brook, Sydney, Springhill, North Preston, and Beechville, to name a few—wondered if she could be "Africadian." Most were not quite concerned when they heard the news because they would have known she was missing if she had been one of theirs. If the centuries they had spent as outsiders in their own homeplace, surviving all kinds of obstacles thrown their way, had taught them anything, it would be to have one another's back. Someone would be related to someone who owned the child. They would not need the TV or radio to tell them one of their offspring had been found in the state the child was when she was discovered—naked and scarred and as scared as any slave girl of yore.

When Gordon went to see how the waif was doing the following morning, he was taken to her room by a doctor. He smiled, pleased to see her lying in bed, sleeping peacefully like any child her age. The two navels, which made her look so mysterious to him, were logically explained. "One of the navels is nothing more than a scar. We think the original navel must have healed badly as well, which is why it looks similar to the other wound, making it look like she has two navels," Doctor Ira Protowsky explained in what Gordon suspected was a strong Eastern European accent, even though he could not quite decide which country her distinct way of speaking came from. He decided it could have been any one of those ex-iron curtain duchies being ironed out by star-spangled capitalism.

"We think she's not as young as she looks. She's probably about nine years old. She's still not talking, though. I can't find any reason why not. She's seriously sleep-deprived because she can't seem to stay awake for more than a few minutes before dozing off again."

"Water, please!" A voice emanated gruffly from the girl.

"Ah, she speaks!" Gordon exclaimed, and Doctor Ira Protowsky moved excitedly to the bed. She bent to peer closely at the patient. Adrian, the nurse, went to fetch a glass of water.

"How are you feeling?" the doctor asked, and the girl looked surprised at her question but said nothing. Doctor Protowsky placed her stethoscope on the girl's chest and then lifted the skinny wrist to count the pulse. Looking satisfied, she asked, "What's your name?"

The girl pondered this for a few seconds, then looked puzzled.

"Where are your parents?" the doctor asked, bending over her bed.

"Do you have brothers and sisters?" Gordon asked from beside the door where he was standing. His curiosity was boundless. Then, while tears streamed down the sides of her face, the girl shut her eyes. She began breathing evenly as if she was fast asleep again.

"At least we know she talks and speaks English," the doctor said, looking pleased as she straightened up.

"Did you notice if she had an accent?" Gordon asked, a fourth generation Newfie.

"Of course. Everyone has an accent," the doctor, a Polish immigrant, said.

"I was just wondering if you think she's from around here." Gordon's suddenly pink face betrayed his tongue's faux pas.

"Let her rest for the night. We'll try again tomorrow to see if she's ready to say more. It's, of course, possible that if she's been traumatized, she might not want or be able to say anything." The doctor snubbed his query because she was still peeved by his comment about the girl's accent—as if everyone isn't exotic to others elsewhere. They exited the room as Nurse Adrian entered with water for the bedside.

That evening, when Adrian stepped quietly into the girl's room to check on her, the TV was on, the volume very low, and the girl fast asleep. About to leave the room, his eyes caught a breaking story he had been following, and he stopped at the foot of the bed, squinting at the muted TV trying to read the newsfeed subtitles because he had left his glasses at the nurses' station. Unknown to him, the girl's eyes had popped open soon after he'd entered the room, and she too was staring at the TV, entranced by the shots of a police-dog hunt. Led by two boisterous German Shepherds, three policemen were searching a wooded area of North Preston, seeking evidence on a case.

"My farm back yonder," a shy voice said.

Adrian was utterly startled. The voice was coming from the girl but it was completely different from how she spoke earlier, when she had requested water. He looked around the room quickly. They were alone.

"I grow greens and yams and squash, what Walks-Far-Woman tell me thrive on that them there scrap of a land." Its contralto continued, unhurried, thoughtful, as if rising from a deep-down place.

"Walks-Far-Woman, she like no other person I know. She knowed the language of the leafs and the trees and even some beasts."

Adrian fled the room as if pursued by the strange voice, which seemed to track him out into the corridor.

Returning with another nurse and Dr. Schultz—who had relieved Dr. Protowsky—Adrian was even more perplexed to find that the waif was still talking, wholly oblivious to her surroundings. She seemed to be addressing an invisible, enraptured audience.

"That first winter for claim more of we, if not for Walks-Far and her folk. When she talk to the leafs in their language, they listen and do as she want because they knowed she respec' them and for every one of them she pluck, she plant another. She the one what show me and Maud and Mattah and Congo woman and some of the men who refuse to be broke how to plant that there hard land. She telled us which plant will not mind to be planted in winter so that we not starve when the cold bite fit to kill us."

Adrian was so unnerved by the girl that he stood just inside the door, ready to bolt, while the other two men took posts on either side of the bed to study the patient as observantly as possible.

"Walks-Far, she knowed the names and the manner of all crop. People say she done birth all her eight children by herself and when my time come to birth my twins, she the one what hep me because my time come on the farm far from my own folks. But she say, in this here place, we all kinfolk given the White people don't want none of us." She sighed and promptly fell asleep again.

"Who was she talking to?" Adrian asked in a whisper.

The doctor swivelled his head and scratched on his notepad. "I'll give her something to keep her calm for the rest of the night."

"Do you think … she's safe?" Adrian, though quaking, managed to convey what he really meant: Was the child safe to be around?

"Was she violent at any point?"

"No, but … it's hard to imagine what to expect."

Adrian wished to skirt the bizarre child.

As the doctor began to inspect the child's pulse again, he seemed bemused. "I don't think we'll have any more trouble from her tonight." He made to leave. "I'll check on her in the morning. But call me if she wakes up again before the rounds." The doctor left, followed closely by the other nurse.

Having made up his mind never to be alone in the same room with the strange creature again, Adrian, too, left the room quickly, quietly shutting the door. Gone!

By morning, all the nurses on duty had heard various versions of this Haligonian, Jimi-Hendrix-style, "Voodoo Chile's" behaviour.

One attendant, Iyin, a Yoruba ex-Nigerian woman, found the tales profoundly upsetting. She quickly damned the child as the Devil's spawn. Soon after Iyin resumed duty that morning, she had to accompany Dr. Protowsky, Dr. Shultz, and a female psychiatrist to examine what Iyin had concluded was a "daemonic" patient.

"So, how are you today?" Dr. Schultz asked, taking the girl's hand, but she looked flummoxed again. "I know you can hear and understand me. So, please, I want you to try and answer our questions. It's alright if you don't know the answer." His voice was patient, kind, but coaxing. "Can you feel pain anywhere?"

The girl pursed her lips. Her head pivoted from side to side.

"Very good. Can you tell me your name?" the psychiatrist asked.

Left-to-right and right-to-left, the child's head indicated no.

"What's your name, dear?" Dr. Protowsky asked.

From the bed, the mysterious patient only stared.

"Where do you live?" The psychiatrist now tried coaxing.

"In the box, I … I … think," the girl said calmly in an inscrutable, yet oddly familiar accent.

"Box?" the psychiatrist asked, and Dr. Protowsky shrank back from the bed to favour the insurgent shrink. "Where is the box?"

The waif shrugged; her head turned very slowly from side-to-side as she conveyed the question, "How should I know?" without opening her mouth.

"Who else lives with you … in the box?"

"All of me."

"What?"

"Me."

"How did you get here?"

Mute, the child sat up on the bed and started to make slow, wavy, languid movements, as if practicing a stationary yoga pose. Now, Iyin gasped, configured the sign of the cross, and excused herself.

As she sped to the door to leave, a chill ran through Iyin's body. Instantly, goose pimples sleeved her arm. Iyin was now even more convinced that the girl was no ordinary child. She hurried to her post, mumbled a prayer, and only regained her composure after consigning the disturbing thoughts of the girl to the farthest reaches of her mind. By about eight in the evening, when she had to deliver the girl her vitamins and medication for the night, Iyin felt sufficiently strong enough to venture back into the room, having fortified herself with the anointing oil from a tiny bottle always ready in her purse. Iyin was pleased to find the girl—to her, the "creature"—lying in bed enjoying a TV cartoon.

"I need you to take these," Iyin said, studying the girl's chart to avoid any eye contact. The chart boasted the name "Victoria" to honour the day the waif was found, and to avert labelling her ominously as Jane Doe.

"O seun, Iyabo Ifasanmi. Omo Awo, Opele i'se igi …" An intimate voice sang Iyin's old name and the start of her family praise song in flawless Yoruba. In shock, Iyin dropped the plastic tray she was holding and jumped back from the bed. The girl smiled faintly.

Iyin drew herself up to her full height and, aiming her index finger at the creature—for she was now fully convinced this was no human child—and commanded her in Yoruba: "In the name of Jesus! If you have been sent, return to whoever sent you and tell them you have not found me at home." To be sure, she added in English: "Return to sender!"

"Ha wu! You stare at me, but you do not recognize me. How come?" the girl's voice said in Yoruba. "It is I, Enilolobo. Was it so long ago since we were together in Ife O'd'aye, where the day dawns? The place where we spoke to the earth in a language it relished?"

"I bind you in the name of Jesus!" Iyin was almost screaming. She felt compelled to speak to this daemon in English to ward off the lure of the creature's tongue.

"You forget that God is but one, residing deep inside all of us." The child sighed ruefully, then chanted in the Ife dialect of Yoruba:

Suddenly, like the snapping of a strap,
The fetter snaps.
It happened even to their Ifa Priest in the city of Itori,
When Akantanpo snaps, it loses its strength
It lies loose and powerless on the earth.
Ifa divination was performed for Orunmila
On his way to mend the life of the Oni of Ife
As if a life is the same as a calabash.
To whom then shall we turn to help mend our lives?
Jin wini jin wini,
It is up to those of us who are living to mend this life.
Mend our lives, Mend lives, mend life …

The voice petered into a murmur as the girl kept swaying, slowly shifting back-and-forth and side-to-side.

"I say, I bind you in the name of Jeeeesus! Back to sender!" Iyin shouted as she stepped backwards out of the room before turning to slam shut the door. Unlike the ram, which paws backwards only to muster the strength to dash forward in attack, Iyin's gait lacked confidence or purpose. She crumbled in front of the door where Adrian, who also dreaded the girl, ran to Iyin's aid when he heard her slam the door.

"What did she do?" he asked as he helped Iyin to her feet.

"That is not a child in there," Iyin whispered, shaking her head sadly as Adrian led her away. Suddenly, Iyin slumped, passing out into a world not quite of nightmares, but of remembrances that she had once banished into what she believed was oblivion.

In that unconscious state, her father, wearing a rich agbada made of etu thread, ornately adorned because he had just returned from a long journey, tried in vain to explain where he had been. Instead of bearing gifts, the way he used to when he returned from forays to sell his farm produce, he tried to give her charms and amulets, which he said were to fortify her. When he left her embattled mind, disappointed by her spurning of his gifts, her grandmother, too, surfaced to urge her into a battle, which Iyin had long conceded.

While Doctors Protowsky and Schultz conferred in a corner, Iyin awoke to find herself a patient. Dr. Protowsky was the first to notice she had regained consciousness.

"Are you alright?" She stretched her hand to restrain Iyin, who was trying to rise.

"I'm fine," Iyin said, her voice falsely breezy, falsely lilting.

"Good. Can you tell us what transpired between you and the girl?"

Iyin harrumphed. "You people don't know what you're playing with. That girl's more devil than human." Once again, Iyin tried to lift her torso. This time, both doctors pushed her gently back onto the bed.

"Okay, if you won't tell us what happened, we need you to hear what we think. And hopefully, you can help us figure her out." Schultz could hardly hide his excitement. "You're Nigerian, aren't you?"

Though Iyin refused to answer, he pressed on. "I am quite sure you must be familiar with the phenomenon of Abu-iku or Oba-ni-je. A belief in reincarnation. A complex concept based on the idea that some children are born as part of an endless cycle of birth, death, and rebirth. Which I—"

"It is an evil and pagan belief! As medical doctors, you cannot believe in such rubbish." Iyin cut him short without even trying to correct his mispronunciation of Abiku and Ogbanje.

"Please be patient with us. We've not studied the phenomenon. But major research into reincarnation is the domain of the eminent psychiatrist, Dr. Ian Stevenson, whose research, thanks to studying children in various countries, reveals evidence that some remember a previous life," Dr. Protowsky explained, while sounding apologetic.

"Although the prevalence is frequent in countries and cultures with a strong belief in reincarnation, there have been cases found amongst Caucasians, in Europe, and North America," Dr. Schultz said.

"We think this girl might be an Abu-iku or oba-ni-je or what have you. It might be why her parents abandoned her," Dr. Protowsky explained.

"Or she might simply be an unusually prescient child ..." Dr. Schultz said.

"She is not!" Iyin exclaimed. And, noticing the addled looks on the doctors' faces, added: "For I myself am one."

The two doctors were more amazed by how she said it than by what she said. They had started boning up on studies about the reborn dead since Adrian reported his encounter with the girl. What Iyin disclosed was not alien to them. What was surprising was the emotion behind her words. The turmoil within her gave her words a life of their own. A strong, proud, commanding life.

Upon realizing how her words sounded, Iyin covered her mouth as if to throttle them, but the words had grown wings and flittered away. Her words floated around the room and then wafted across the hall to the sleeping form of the mysterious girl, where they announced themselves to the child in her sleep, eliciting a smile and a low chuckle from her worn face. The smile might not have been completely visible, but the chuckle was audible enough, if sotto voce.

"She told me that her name is Enilolobo." Iyin began recounting her encounter with the waif. "In Yoruba, it means 'The one who had gone has returned'."

The two doctors exchanged discreet looks, pleased. They were thrilled because they believed that they would soon be able to fathom the child.

"The name is similar in meaning to my old name, Iyabo, which means 'Mother has returned.' I was born soon after my father's mother died, and my parents believed that I was her reincarnation." Iyin hung her head sorrowfully. "I can't believe in abiku anymore, but when I was a child, I could remember my past life, but I stopped when I was about seven." Her voice lowered as if she was about to admit a most shameful secret. "The name was a curse, and my parents should never have encouraged such devilry. They gave it to me not only because I was born after my grandmother died, but because they believed that I stayed this time because I am my grandmother who came back. They said I had been born three other times before." She avoided making eye contact with the doctors. "It's all nonsense, of course. Satanic pagan rubbish." Her unsure voice was lacking the sureness of Christian dogma. Iyin took but seconds to relate her life story, but it felt like hours. What really scared her was that a sense of foreboding had gradually crept up on her over the three days prior to her encounter with the girl. It started with a dream about her dead father. Since his demise, she'd never dreamt of him. Then, suddenly, a few days earlier, she'd dreamt that her father had come to visit her, bringing her a gift: an Agidigbo drum. The pleasing part? Her father's gift of the talking drum in her dream made her recall joyfully her carefree childhood.

The morning after that dream, she found herself humming songs that she had made up for her girlhood dancing group. Two nights later, she dreamt of a friend who had died when they were young. Then, only the night before she met the exotic, female child, her maternal grandmother, who'd died when she was a teenager, invaded her dream, urging her to get up, make her bed, so that she would not be late for work.

To crown it all, her mother, who still lived in Saki, her village, and who had made herself the bane of Iyin's life since becoming a Christian, called her that very morning. The ever dutiful Christian daughter, who regularly sent money home for her mum's upkeep, Iyin dreaded speaking to the woman who insisted on calling her Iyabo, a name Iyin shed when she became born again. Whenever her mother called her by her old name it was as if she was trying to overrule Iyin's newly acquired Occidental faith. Being a staunch member of one of the most prominent evangelical churches globally, Iyin would rather die than continue answering to such a pagan name.

Although Iyinoluwa was born into a family of stiff-necked Yoruba Baptists, she realized that her parents were nothing but pagans masquerading as believers. As far as Iyin was concerned, while avowing their belief in Christ, her parents' superstitious beliefs in Osun, Orunmila, and even Esu—and their acknowledgement of all the other over-four-hundred Yoruba deities—was sheer mockery of authentic Christianity. Her folks continued to participate in traditional festivals and pageants, and had cursed her from birth with a name like Iyabo. They never even renounced the family name, Ifasanmi, a tribute to Ifa's benevolence. They were convinced that it was Ifa who had eventually favoured them by allowing her to survive. Her mother always reminded her by singing her special song. Her mother had made up the song to remind her that it was only after she had made a sacrifice by carrying a rich ebo, made to appease ori, her spiritual head, that abiku ceased hounding her womb:

Eyele lo koko tele Ife odaye,
owun lase mu
Eyele meje,
Pelu atare meje,

Ati orogbo meje
Pelu osan meje,
Ati abata meje
Pelu igba oyin meje
a tun wa gun ako isu meje,
lawa ko po
la ta epo si lori,
la wa gbe logan jo yen
lo si ori omi tin san.

By the time her mother finished enumerating the precious items in this song, starting with seven live pigeons, Iyabo, whose head always expanded with pride at how much she was desired whenever she heard the lullaby, would be up, singing and dancing along. The seven pigeons marked how highly esteemed the sacrifice was.

The seven pigeons were the most prized items out of all the other things offered in sacrifice so she could be born and not die a fourth time. Each item in the offering signified a prayer. The fact that Ifa had recommended seven live pigeons to appease the deities was nothing short of exceptional. As a child, Iyin had learnt how the pigeon was the first animal to inhabit Ife when it accompanied the deities from heaven to touch down there. She, therefore, knew that the pigeon was the most efficient courier of messages to the spirit realm because of its close association to all the orisa and Olodumare even before Mitochondrial Eve cast the first human shadow. That seven live pigeons were required to make her stay and not die used to infuse Iyin with an uncommon sense of self-worth.

The seven pods of alligator pepper symbolized healthy longevity. Unlike most other kola nuts, the seven bitter kolas, which remain fresh perpetually, signified she would live long and stay relevant. Seven kola nuts represented the favourite food of Ifa, who will always help to repel evil from her demesne. The seven calabashes of money and seven oranges signified that her life would know only sweetness and joy, happiness without any bitterness. The seven large yams that were pounded would ensure that she would never know hunger. The generous dollops of palm oil made the offering attractive to the deities and ensured that she would enjoy a smooth and easy life, a life filled with love without friction.

All these were then taken in the dead of night to be laid carefully on a flowing river. Since water is everlasting and has no enemies—because everything in life needs water to survive—she will, therefore, never know enmity. The flowing river will ensure that no enemies will ever catch up with her, and she will travel far and near with ease. All the sacrificial items in the ebo were significant in elevating her parents' prayers so the gods would nod in concord and act accordingly. This would realign the universe so that she could stay alive and not return as an abiku.

As a much-cherished child, she loved to be regaled by a lullaby that was hers alone. She was the envy of other children who had been born only once. She would wail and sulk whenever she wanted to get her way until Iya Iyabo, her mother, an accomplished akewi, whose mellifluous oral poetry enjoyed a high repute in their town, would burst into her song.

The only other thing that could make the young Iyabo yield whenever she wanted to have her way was her oriki, the praise poetry of her family. The invocation of her oriki would always start with her praise names, which her mother would string together and link to the laudable triumphs of her ancestors and the sterling prowess of her family's totemic animal, ekun, the dauntless and energetic tiger that growled down every challenge.

As a child, whenever Iyabo was ill, her parents massaged her with a little of the leftover aromatic palm oil from the sacrifice placed in the flowing river to usher in her birth. The oil was kept in a pot underneath her mother's bed, and it was rubbed on whatever part of her body that Iyabo felt was ailing. Her parents would then pour libation to her Egun, her paternal grandmother, who was also her guardian spirit. They would always anoint her head with sprinkles of the oil. They then poured libation to her ori, her right-hand divinity.

Esu, of course, would never be left out, so the trickster, imbued with both elements of right and left, would not play mischief. Instead, Esu would dutifully ensure that all the divinities of the right, as well as those of the left, were appeased, by ensuring that they got their fair share of the sacrificial items, so they would always play their part in reordering the universal elements to restore Iyabo to good health.

After Iyabo cast her lot in with a modern Pentecostal Christian fold, she was warned that her pagan upbringing was responsible for all the insidious and toxic events that had plagued her and her family. Iyabo did not need much persuasion and hastily abandoned her cultural traditions. She grew up in Nigeria in the eighties when structural adjustment programs imposed by the IMF had started making the lives of most Nigerians unbearable. Like other Africans under the tyranny of the Breton Woods system, Nigerians did not know it at the time, but the loss of their ability to dream of a future, any kind of future at all, was just the tip of the iceberg of misery that awaited them. Iyabo's adult life did not fulfil her girlhood expectations. Still, she was not one of those radical young Africans who denounced the IMF as "Imperial Mother Fuckers," the World Bank as "World Bandits," or NATO as "the North Atlantic Terrorists Organization."

After taking stock of her life, Iyabo decided the Pentecostals were right. She had never come to terms with what she had concluded was too long a streak of misfortune. For instance, her father's early death from a heart attack. Whoever heard of a man as strong as her father slumping dead amid his cocoa crop after only a mild chest pain? As far as Iyabo knew, the man had never even suffered from any serious bout of malaria that could not be cured by agbo, the foul smelling herbal concoctions that were a mainstay in their home for curing all ailments. He had never darkened the doors of the village's primary health care centre—which was shuttered the year before he died. The closure was part of the austerity programs that the olive-drab-garbed Prez'dent enforced to placate the IMF, World Bank, and the NATO-backed greenback.

Also ill-starred was her only brother's involvement in cults at university. It led to his rustication. When he first signed on to the cult, the boy had confided in Iyabo that his poverty mandated ingratiating himself with literal snake-handlers. He said the cult protected him from lecturers who augmented their skimpy salaries by compelling students to buy pricey handouts. Indeed, students who refused to purchase their faded photocopies of copious chapters lifted from obsolete textbooks were stricken with an F no matter their brilliance or industry. He insisted that expensive handouts were the only sure way to get a passing grade, which was why, as an indigent male student, he needed the cult to smooth his path to graduation. Looking her dead in the eyes, he smiled knowingly at Iyabo. "Sista mi, I know that for you female students, things might not be so tough."

Iyabo lashed out playfully to slap him, but she knew that if she had not played "the game," she would still be struggling to pass her nursing exams.

Other curses? Her younger sister's teenage pregnancy, yes, but also her own inability to find a proper husband. Then, even after clawing her way through nursing school, Iyabo went years without a job.

But what truly convinced her of her parents' erroneous lifestyle was how quickly her life changed as soon as she embraced the true faith—like millions of other Nigerians were doing. All she had to do was step up and answer the call to the altar during a Sunday service, inviting all those who had not accepted Christ as their Lord and Saviour to do so. That same day, Iyin turned her back on her pagan past, including her heathen names—first, middle and last. She replaced them with the explicitly Christian ones of Iyinoluwa Oluwasanmi. Less than six months after committing her life, her Canadian visa application got approved! Had she known that the Occident was truly the Holy Roman Empire gone transatlantic, she would not have wasted six years after graduating from nursing school.

Years wasted indulging in magical thinking, black magic cussing, only for her pious, Christian prayer to turn her dream of leaving Nigeria into reality. Just like that.

Indeed, Iyabo had first tried for a British visa. The rumour then was that nurses were in high demand in the UK. She was not one of those Nigerians who suspected that, since Britain became a veritable trail mix, professions like nursing had lost their genteel quality. After getting turned down three times, having wasted money getting three passports with three different names, she turned to the US Embassy. She was forced to give up that effort after her second attempt. Although she used a new name on a new passport for that second US visa application, their computer system recognized her picture and placed a five-year ban on her. She then turned to Saudi Arabia and Kuwait. It was while she was contemplating taking an Islamic name to improve her chances of getting to the Middle East, even after she learnt about the many casualties of the Kafala System, that a friend invited her to her born-again church. She became what some haters called a "Jesus Freak" by embracing the fastest growing born-again church in the country, but her life changed.

After committing herself, the pastor of her new church asked her to bring all of her documents for sanctification before going to any embassy. Although the Saudi Arabian and Kuwaiti Embassies both turned her down (being a de facto "infidel"), the Canadians granted her a student visa! Still, her mother insisted on calling her by her birth names. But for her Christian charity, Iyabo—now Iyin—would have renounced the obdurate woman for trying to push her back into impoverishing paganism.

As if to further compound all the other ominous signs of the days that preceded the evil child's arrival at the hospital where Iyin worked, her mother's voice was the first she heard that morning. "Karo oko mi, Iyabode Durosinmi …" Her mother's singsong voice grated on Iyin's nerves when she answered her phone. After Iyin ended the call as politely as possible, her first inclination was to go back to sleep and start the day again. She wanted to do over her prayerful waking into a new dawn and thereby cancel her mother's voice, which assaulted her by uttering her forsaken first and middle names, therefore potentially jinxing her day. Unfortunately, her duty at the hospital started early, and she could not afford the luxury of returning to bed. So, she said a second prayer, a more extended prayer than her usual one, thereby technically restarting her day. However, despite taking that precaution, the mysterious, double-navel'd girl had blasphemed her day.

As Iyin picked up her bag to leave the hospital, she could not stop thinking about the demon waif. Something about the girl, a pithiness, threatened to drag Iyin back into the abyss of all the old places and things that she had forsaken to arrive where she now was. Her personal new dawn. After she admitted who she was to the doctors, Iyin felt naked, and her nakedness made her ashamed. She knew that they, too, sensed her discomfort at having to bare herself when they hastily excused themselves before vacating the room where she was convalescing from her parley with the wild girl.

In Dr. Schultz's office, the two doctors agreed that they did not know what to make of her story. Dr. Schultz, who secretly fancied himself a psychiatrist, felt he could read some signs of self-loathing in Iyin's statements. How shockingly indoctrinated by Christian fundamentalism Iyin seemed!

"What name did Iyin say the girl called herself?" Dr. Protowsky asked.

Ira Protowsky, who had been raised in a predominantly Jewish suburb of her old country, was a little put off by Schultz's judgmental outlook, but chose to dodge confrontation. She made an exaggerated show of concentrating on her notes as she searched for the girl's name.

"Here it is. Eni-lo-lo-bo ..." She broke the name down syllable by syllable, mispronouncing the letter "o" the first and third times.

"It's too long. People will never be able to wrap their tongues around it. What's wrong with continuing to call her Victoria, in honour of the day she was found?" Dr. Schultz asked.

Exasperated, Dr. Protowsky shook her head. She thought, then exclaimed, "Eni! We can call her Eni for short." She was so pleased with her brainwave that she completely missed the fact that the way she pronounced it, "Eni" sounded very much like "any." "As soon as she's strong enough, if she still doesn't remember where she's from, we should arrange for her to be taken around to places like North and East Preston to see if her memory will be triggered."

"Yes, or maybe someone will recognize her. We should start where she was found, though," Dr. Schultz said.

"I hate to think that she might end up with the Centre for Child—"

"I agree." Dr. Schultz did not let her finish. "Certainly not before we've tried to find her family."

A thrill caused his spine to shiver. He could hardly conceal his excitement even though he could not quite admit even to himself that there was something to be gained by determining the girl's origins. He tried to visualize himself on the local news or in newspaper headlines: "Doctors decipher the mystery behind the waif found on the street of Halifax."

The following morning, the two doctors were at the girl's bedside almost as soon as she awoke.

"So, how are you feeling now, Vic—?" Ira Protowsky stopped herself then, read from the transcript of their session from the previous day. "I mean Eni-lo-lo-bo."

For his part, hawk-like, Dr. Schultz surveyed the girl for any sign that the utterance of the name might elicit a significant response. No. She just continued eyeing Ira unblinkingly.

"Later, if you're feeling up to it, Dr. Schultz and I will take you out for a drive to places which might help jog your memory." Dr. Protowsky paused to gauge the girl but she was inscrutable.

"You know, so you'll be able to tell us who you are and where you come from," Dr. Schultz said, smiling.

When the child turned to fix him with the same focused stare, he felt compelled to offer further explanation.

"What I mean is that we think we can help you tell us your story."

Enilolobo sighed slowly and then answered. "You want my story?" she asked in bewilderment. "But it is my story."

Excited by the girl's speaking, Dr. Protowsky pulled up a chair and slowly took the girl's young, bony hand. Gently, she stroked it. Then she tried to probe her mind. "Are you a-b-u-i-ku?" she asked, stressing every letter of the unpronounceable word.

Enilolobo looked puzzled.

"O-b-a-nni-je?" Dr. Schultz interjected.

Enilolobo almost smiled, then made him vanish by turning her head.

"The scars on your body, how did you get them?" Dr. Schultz asked.

Now the child flashed him a questioning look.

Pointing to her own stomach, Dr. Protowsky clarified: "The wound on your tummy … ?"

Lifting up her hospital gown, Enilolobo pointed to the two navels, then looked up at Dr. Protowsky, who nodded enthusiastically. "This is the road to the old world, and this one is to the new one. I am both. I am the road crossing the river," Enilolobo said. Her mien was suddenly surreally striking. She spoke as if she carried within her the vision, memory, knowledge, and the pain of a worrisome past. Her soft voice sounded old, thoughtful as if she was delving deep into herself until she found a morsel of insight, which she could share, not self-assuredly, but demurely as if she feared the listener, the world, would disagree with her tendering.

"Like a bridge?" Dr. Schultz asked. Metaphors discomfited him.

"Yes!" Enilolobo exhaled her reply. She seemed surprised by their ability to comprehend her. "A road with two ends across the water, each end planted in two worlds."

"What about the other scars on your body? How did you get them?" Dr. Protowsky tried to repress her joy in this breakthrough—feeling a bit like Francine Patterson soliciting intelligent signs from Koko the gorilla.

"Oh, they are nothing. The wounds are inside me." Enilolobo lowered her eyes. Those internalized scars were somehow still fresh, painful, and shameful.

Dr. Protowsky was captivated as she tried to imagine the source of the wounds. But the memory of how she got them was too hurtful for Enilolobo to excavate. Still, unable to nix the urge to get her to talk about them, or the compulsion to get her to begin healing, Dr. Protowsky pressed on. "Do you know what, Eni? Can I call you Eni?"

The girl shrugged. Did she care what she was called? Did it matter what new name she was given? After being called so many different names, what difference did one more make?

"Good. Eni, it is then. If you really don't feel up to going on the drive today, we can do it tomorrow. I also want you to … to …" Unable to complete her thought, Dr. Protowsky posed a question instead. "Do you know when you are about to go into a trance? The nurse who was here yesterday said …" Dr. Protowsky stopped herself.

The girl looked perplexed.

"I mean, do you know when your old self is coming on?"

Eni's answering glance informed Dr. Protowsky that her query sounded quite daft.

"Okay, I'll tell you what. The next time you get the urge to talk about yourself, anything at all, old or new, can you let me know?"

"Why?" the child whispered.

"Because I need to record it so I can help you make sense of it."

Suddenly Eni opened her mouth. Words began to spill out. Just drops at first. As she spoke, her face became radiant, "No! … My words … They are my own … They are me, all of me …"

"No, No!" Dr. Protowsky tried to arrest the onset of the trance. Both doctors scrambled for the door when Dr. Protowsky, eager to find a tape recorder, paused and yelled at Dr. Schultz to stay and scrawl the girl's "rap," her rapture. Then, she rushed out, muttering, "If she'll just hold on for a minute!"

Eni was unstoppable. Her words slowly, gradually started to pour out in a transfixing flood. She did not seem conscious of Dr. Schultz, who was scribbling away as if his life depended on it. When Dr. Protowsky returned, they fiddled with the recording equipment, desperate to capture as many of the onrushing words as possible.

"Where are the words of my despair when I turn on myself and them Fulani people tear my pickaninny from my back in the farm in Osogun and throw him on the groun' and carry me for sell? And when my word turn to wailing and the smell of my other dead bodies and our shit and vomit kill my word and turn them to sigh inside Potogese ship and Dutsh ship and French ship and English ship and American ship? What you do with them words I cry? And my words, as we walk inside the water to go back home for Ibo Landing? Where was you to hear my words I scream out at wharf side of Louisville, when, massah Clayton and him men tear me from Blackburn and sell me down river? My words, they the road to myself. If you take them I will never find rest. I will just continue to journey without no end in this here world, gathering more of pain, blood, and sweat, turning on myself and wounding others too as I go along. And my words? The ones that turn into wind, which fly aroun' my bones which lie shamelessly in Biafra, Zaire, Congo, Liberia, Sudan, Sierra Leone, Rwanda, for months just inside the door of the Church in Nyarubuye? That wind, standing still by the sight of my hip bones lying there, spread out, without no flesh cuddling me. Or my pickaninny bones which done become part of me between my legs. My empty chest, ribs, and backbone poking out refusing to agree that the hands that lift the machetes that slay me and the thirteen other people of my family are the same hands that done shake our own as friends and sometimes brothers before? Hands, stretching from bodies that once stand and clap in the same church, sometimes praying in the same mosque and all the other times where our mind become waste instead of soft and strong as any good books suppose to make we …"

For what seemed like hours, Enilolobo recited an epic of torture, lynching, betrayals, and loss. As the words surged out, she slapped, scratched, and pinched her body. As if to destroy it, to spare herself the pain of recollection. At times, the rememberings ran into one another. At some points the doctors couldn't tell if she was speaking a mishmash of English, Arabic, French, or millennia-dead tongues.

Finally, exhausted, she curled up into a fetal position, sucking the middle and index fingers on her right hand and occasionally whimpering like a baby. She lay like that for long after the tape in the recorder ran out.

Mumbling, grumbling, muttering, stuttering.

An agonizing poetry.

Canada — 2005

Enilolobo

THE WEEKEND THAT Professor Akpa Tira landed in Halifax en route to presiding over a Modern Language Association confab in Chicago, Eni could not help but notice how different her adopted mother, Ira Protowsky, behaved in his presence. Ira giggled, flittered, and sashayed, just like Eni's teenage, boy-crazy classmates. For a start, she could not figure out why Ira hung on to each word that came out of Akpa's mouth as if it were a precious gem. When Ira rushed into her room one morning, a few weeks before Akpa Tira's visit, to announce that they would have a house guest who was a former professor with whom she had studied at university, Eni concluded that this was, at last, the love interest of the until-then celibate Ira. Ira spent hectic days fixing up the house, ordering the most exquisite wines and groceries in anticipation of the scholar's arrival.

And the moment he stepped into the heritage house with its cute, white, pink, and blue heritage plaque in the South End of Halifax, nothing else existed for Ira. She seemed enthralled by the pitter-patter of Akpa's tiny feet shod in brown pigskin, Bridgeport Hush Puppies loafers. Eni was bemused by how Ira became so totally infatuated with the bespectacled gnome. She seemed to read his thoughts and rushed to meet his every need even before he became aware of them.

However, less than five minutes after the professor's arrival, it was apparent, even to the pubescent Eni, that the only love affair that the professor had was with himself. Thus, Eni felt protective of diminutive Ira with her silky jet-black hair, which she was forever pushing away from her bony face.

That first night, after suffering through the five-course French meal the loafered gourmet dished up, and which Ira kept proclaiming was like a taste of Heaven, Eni excused herself. She'd barely left the dining room when she heard an irritatingly mellifluous voice dissing her in a posh English accent.

"So, is there more to her or have I seen it all?" The disdain in his Oxbridgian voice compelled Eni to linger just beyond the threshold.

"Oh, she's an adorable girl."

"Your bias is understandable. I dare say motherhood sits well on you. Remind me, what's the final verdict on her being preternatural?"

"Oh, she's become as normal as any girl her age …"

"Just as I suspected after reading through the transcripts of the sessions you sent me."

"If only you had seen her when she was first brought in. Her total lack of self-awareness whenever she went into a trance. Her perfect mastery of so many languages at such a young age … At least that was how it seemed to me."

Eni winced when she heard how apologetic Ira sounded about her adopted protégé.

"She must have learnt those things by rote," Akpa said. "She simply memorized those lines in the various languages that she rattled."

"But why?"

"She could be from one of those travelling theatre families you can still find all over Africa."

"Wow! You know, that never occurred to us!"

"The validity of my hypothesis about her inauthenticity as a reincarnated entity is buttressed by my recent work on a postmodern approach to the question of race. Some of the scripts you sent to me of her ranting reflect the influence of half-baked ideas that you find Afrocentrics trying to peddle. As if we're all recycled Egyptians!"

Ira found herself struck once again by the sheer beauty and elegance of this man she had loved almost since she first met him as a pre-med at Harvard. Born in Cambridge, England, at the time of Akpa's birth, his father was a prince of Ipeja in Ile Ifa, a small, natural-resource-laden country. Ile Ifa was a major port of embarkation for human cargo during the transatlantic slave trade. It was nestled in West Africa just off the coast of Nigeria. At the time of his birth, Akpa's father was at Cambridge University, studying law in preparation for ascending the throne of his ancestors as paramount ruler. His family ruled most of the country and controlled its resources, both human and otherwise, until the country's independence in the mid-sixties. Also at the time of Akpa's birth, his British mother, she too a student at Cambridge, was a rebellious heiress. The only surviving relative of a wealthy Dame who, like her, descended from a rich tea-and-sugar-trading clan. For over a century, their ancestors dominated these products in India, East Africa, and the Caribbean. The Dame was the widow of a scion of the Chancellor of the Exchequer in Britain during the peak of that country's mission—conducted in the name of Sanctimonious Widow Victoria—to enlighten the Dark Continent.

Although he spent three years attending elementary school in Ile Ifa, Akpa lived most of his life in Great Britain—other than his stint as a young professor at Harvard. Irrespective of Akpa's love of men, his round, bun-like face, crowned by a graciously receding bald head, supported by a deceptively short, rotund figure, rendered him, for Ira, the epitome of virility. Here was a man who, by the sheer coincidence of his birth, straddled two extremes of the world and had inherited the kind of wealth that only a Midas or an Ali Baba could command. In Ira's eyes, before Akpa, less fortunate mortals had no recourse but to remain pale in obeisance. After all, he could have spent his life basking in the glories of his illustrious, transatlantic ancestors. But due to his father's misrule as the O'yo'fa of Ile Ifa, the kingdom and subjects had come to practical ruin, and Akpa and his two sisters inherited immense, matrilineal wealth. And instead of succeeding his father as a traditional ruler, he opted out in favour of a cousin. He loved his gilded life in the ivory tower, where his well-paid gig was to grapple with semantics, an exclusionary intellectual exercise, simultaneously elitist and worthless.

Thus, Ira was forced to settle for being Akpa's "best friend" after she accepted that the gent couldn't care less for women. Not because of his queerness or that he was an ascetic like Gandhi, but because he solely adored himself. In a way, she could not fault him for that. She was that much in love with him that she understood. How could he not be in love with himself? What was there not to love? Even after over twenty years of knowing him, she still found it hard to resist masturbating to images of the erudite Professor who had moved on to Oxford University, where he wrote copiously and published extensively on political theory, probabilistic semantics, moral theory, intellectual history, race and identity theory—all valentines for the intellectually insidious.

Akpa's words about Eni only confirmed what, at first, Ira was loath to believe. With each passing day that Eni filled out, exchanging a scrawny physique for the "phat" look of a Black "ado" gal, with a bubble butt and snippy, pouting lips, the veracity of Ira's previous convictions that the child was some kind of supernatural prodigy wore prodigiously thinner.

Gradually, Ira began to believe that it was not the medicines that she and Dr. Schultz had administered to calm the girl down that had stemmed her words. No, apparently, Eni had exhausted whatever residual script her mind had fixed upon during whatever trauma she'd encountered before she was found on that auspicious Victoria Day.

The only thing that continued to intrigue Ira Protowsky about Eni was her ordinariness. She endured all the intricacies of adopting

Eni after falling in love with what she presumed was a spirit child or, perhaps a protégé, or failing that, a polyglot extraordinaire. Still, she remained a doting mother even after she conceded that she had brought home a dud. Her purse bottomed out to expose Eni to high culture—music, art, and language courses—at high cost. She assured herself that she did this not necessarily to try to rekindle some idling spark in the child, but just to edify Eni. In turn, Eni demonstrated no exceptional talent at all, but was unenthusiastic about all. Nor did any spark of evident genius result from all that lavish exposure.

Over the years, Ira watched Eni laugh, giggle, talk, and walk like any girl her presumed age. Every trace of the paranormal that had fostered Ira's love for her seemed to recede daily from her charge. Eni's transformation from angelic mystery to teenybopper was depressing for Ira. Her grief was similar to Humbert Humbert's distress in seeing his pre-teen "nymphet" mature into a gum-chewing bore. Eni's former precocity was now easily explained away: Though she was about nine when she was found, she looked no older than a child of six. Even the recordings of strange and ancient-sounding languages she had voiced spontaneously, which Ira Protowsky and Dr. Schultz sent off to experts to be deciphered, turned out to be nothing more than a coherent combination of English, French, Arabic, Portuguese, Spanish, Swahili, and several African languages. Polyglot? Maybe. Prodigy? No.

Totally confused but enjoying the frenzy excited by this gem of a character who had practically fallen into their psych and medical labs, Protowsky and Schultz had also couriered off several copies of their recordings to various experts on reincarnation. Crushingly, one by one, they all returned a nullifying verdict. The child did not fall within their area of expertise. She "seemed" to "remember" not just one life, but many—across several centuries and continents.

Finally, at the suggestion of one reincarnation expert, Ira also tried to tape—for analysis—some interviews conducted when Eni was not entranced, but Eni could recall "nada." She could not even recall the session in which she termed herself a bridge, which baffled Ira, for Eni seemed fully conscious at the time. Even Eni's medical examination to check for sexual abuse was inconclusive. Her broken hymen could not be unquestionably put down to sexual activities.

After months of futile probing, police could only theorize that Eni must have been snuck into Canada. There was no missing person's report on any child matching her description. No one was looking for her in any of the provinces.

Yet, sometimes, while peeping at Eni's sleeping form or seeing her concentrate when watching TV, Ira could not help noticing a shadowy depth on her face that seemed alien in one so young.

For her part, Eni took to writing down her dreams and so-called trances a few years after she was found. It was soon after Ira played her some of the early recordings that were made when she was first found. She sat quietly, listening to the strange yet uncomfortably familiar voices, yet unable to associate them with herself. Although she continued to experience trances, they became infrequent, then seldom. Still, she was as perplexed as Ira when she did not understand any of the many languages emanating from the recorder. She was perplexed beyond measure, since Ira insisted it was her voice saying all those things. Black magic troubling the ivory tower?

The night after Ira debuted the tapes, Eni had one of her recurring dreams. She was flying to faraway places and faraway times, all exotic yet recognizable. When she woke up, she decided to write down her dream because she suspected that it was somehow linked to the recorded voices. Since then, she'd entered her dreams into her notebook every morning before greeting the world. Writing down her dreams helped her stem the feeling, which she sometimes got, that a flood was washing over her. She also carried the book everywhere she went—in case she felt the "urge" coming on.

Wild were some of the things that came to her during sleep or sometimes when she was awake. It was like being transported to another place, another time. Eni would struggle to remember when she tried to write them down. But she forced herself to write anyway, having accepted that these remembrances, dreams, trances, or visions (she could never quite decide what they were) were precious gifts entrusted to her care. She also believed that writing down her visions enhanced her ability to live a normal life.

The few times she resisted writing, she found her dreams hounding her even during the day and separating her from her peers.

She had to unravel where she came from and how she came to be found on a street of Halifax. To be so strung out metaphysically, to be tethered to a mystery.

She was resolute to put together the scraps and pieces that kept coming back to her.

That night, after overhearing Akpa discussing her, Eni went to her room to pen a paper on the Middle Passage for an African history class. She sat at her table in her room, which Ira had decorated with an ornate wallpaper in various pink tints. She powered up her desktop and googled: "What is the relationship between the trans-Saharan trade and the transatlantic slave trade?" She was soon engrossed in reading:

The trans-Saharan slave trade was at its peak between 1450 and 1900. During this blip in human history, which implicated the Sahara, the Red Sea, and the Indian Ocean, millions of Africans were transported for slavery to the Middle East and the by-then predominantly Muslim-Arab controlled areas of North Africa.

Africans were sold throughout the Middle East. This trade, also known as the Arab slave trade, was multi-directional and changed over time to meet the demands for menial labour in Northern Africa, Arabia, the Persian Gulf, India, European colonies in the Far East, and the Indian Ocean islands. The transatlantic slave trade, the equally heinous sibling of the trans-Saharan slave trade, was perpetrated by Europeans and built around pre-existing forms of African slavery crafted and sustained by Arabs and their African collaborators. The transatlantic slave trade could not have thrived without the networks established by the trans-Saharan or Arab slave trade. The Atlantic slave trade, also known as the Middle Passage, was the capture and forced transportation of Africans across the Atlantic Ocean to the New World (the Americas and the West Indies) for enslavement between the 1500s and the middle of the nineteenth century. The trade was a triangular one that involved a first leg during which goods such as knives, guns, ammunition, cotton cloth, tools, brass implements, etc. were sent from European countries to Africa. The second leg, or the Middle Passage, saw Africans who had been captured all across the African continent shipped to work in the New World as slaves. This axis of the evil triangle had raw materials which were produced through slave labour in plantations in the Americas and West Indies—such as sugar, rice, tobacco, indigo, rum, and cotton—and transported back to Europe. Millions of African women, men, and children were callously transported on the twenty-one-to-ninety-day voyage aboard grossly overcrowded sailing ships operated by crews mainly from Britain, the Netherlands, Portugal, and France. All European countries benefited from this evil and inhuman trade. The transatlantic slave trade contributed to the economic activities of Europe and through redistribution markets. It enabled the creation of large fortunes that were invested in highly diverse activities and forms of consumption …

As Eni read, she began to feel drowsy, but did not fall asleep. She saw the image of a familiar-looking girl.

A girl rinses her hands in dirty dishwater. She had been washing a clay cooking pot before standing up. The image of the girl is distinct—she is only about eight years old—yet Eni feels that she is looking at herself. This is not the first dream or vision that she has had in which she is both participant and spectator. The girl is glad she doesn't have to go to the stream that day to fetch water. Four girls from the neighbouring village had been abducted only three days before. The town crier had been going around the village twice a day, morning and evening, to remind everybody to remain vigilant against bodysnatchers. It was the reason why her parents had decided that she and her twin brother should remain in their family compound, like the other children in the hamlet. The hamlet elders had agreed that the young children could not run fast enough to escape being captured in the event of yet another slave raid, either on the farm or on the way to or from a redoubt. An able-bodied young man, Oga, son of the Baale—the chief of the village—had been left with a machete to protect the young ones. They had been drilled to raise the alarm and run into the nearest bush in the unlikely event that the slave raiders had become bold enough to venture into the hamlet in broad daylight. The girl began to mutter:

> *"Suddenly, like the snapping of a strap,*
> *The fetter snaps.*
> *It happened even to their Ifa Priest in the city of Itori,*
> *When Akantanpo snaps, it loses its strength;*
> *It lies loose and powerless on the earth.*
> *Ifa divination was performed for Orunmila*
> *On his way to mend the life of the Oni of Ife*
> *As if a life is the same as a calabash.*

To whom then shall we turn to help mend our lives?
Jin wini jin wini,
It is up to those of us who are living to mend this life. Mend our lives, Mend lives, mend life ..."

"Henh Taye! What are you saying?"

She is startled by Kehinde, her twin brother, who had come out from the hut on his way to the small, thatched shrine at the back of an adjacent small mud hut. He is holding a flat black dish containing some boiled yam and palm oil, the day's sacrifice to the family God, Ogun.

"What did I hear you saying just now?" Kehinde rephrases his sentence.

"Is it any of your business?" Taye asks defiantly.

"It is my business, if you were saying my Ifa verses again."

"Your Ifa verses? How are they yours?"

Kehinde puts the dish he is holding on the ground carefully. He touches the earth in front of him with his index finger and points to the sky.

"Swear by Ogun that you were not just reciting the Ifa verse that Baba said I should memorize."

"And what if I was?" She cuts her eyes, attempts to push her budding breasts forward, her arms held akimbo. She clenches her hands into fists at her waist, just above her loincloth, swaying swiftly from side to side, taunting him, haunting him with her indomitable girliness.

"Did Baba not tell you that you should face your own work and leave the things of awo to him and me?"

"What is my work?"

"Are you not supposed to be training with mama to be a midwife like her?"

"And so?"

"Do you want to pretend that Baba did not tell you so?"

"He just said that you are to learn Ifa, and I am to learn how to be a midwife."

"So why are you learning the Odu Ifa? You, an ordinary girl."

"And you are an ordinary boy. Is it my fault you don't have the brains for instruction?"

"Are you calling me a dunce?"

"No, Baba did. But if the cap fits—"

Suddenly, Kehinde bends, reaches for her left leg and pulls her down. The noise of a Dane gun erupts. They let go of each other and are about to dash into the largest of the three huts which dot the compound when three men, including Oga, rush into the compound.

"Don't run!" Oga shouts in a reassuring voice. "No need to run or shout!"

The twins stroll toward the men. As they approach, one of the men motions to Oga to tie them up. He goes first to Kehinde, who looks at him questioningly as if wondering why they had to be tied up. Taye cannot help noticing that Oga is avoiding eye contact. After tying up Kehinde, Oga moves toward where Taye stands. He rolls his eyes from side to side as though he does not want the two men to see that he is trying to communicate with her. He then mouths something. Taye thinks he is telling her to fear not. She is confused, but gives him her trust. Extending her hands, he binds them together. Another man approaches her, and she thinks that he looks familiar. She wracks her brain, trying to recall their previous meeting.

The man leads the twins out of the compound and onto a narrow path that runs beside the hamlet. As they progress, other children are led out from other compounds by other armed men. When they reach the edge of the village, Oga calls one of the men aside. After they confer in whispers, the man hands him a bag of cowrie shells. Oga then goes into a nearby bush and emerges a few minutes later without the bag. Taye immediately figures out that Oga has sold them to slave raiders.

The man with whom he talked then ties him to a tree before the children are led into the bush through a path that leads—sociopathically—away from the hamlet. Some kids cry at first and call for their parents when they see that they are being marched away from the hamlet, but the raiders strike them down, pushing and shoving them. Every time one of the children slacken, they are beaten with thick ropes.

When they are some distance from the village, they come to a cleared place. Two more men with a herd of cattle are camped there. Seeing the herd helps Taye recollect why she thought one of the slave raiders looked familiar. She had seen him several times before, leading cattle through their hamlet. After making the children sit beside an old anthill, their captors go into the tent. About a half-hour later, the men emerge to look over the cattle. After more deliberations, a man they had met at the camp approaches. He gestures to them to get up. They are then corralled toward the herd of cattle. A man they met at the camp passes around a calabash of coarse millet mixed with a bit of cow milk that most of the children gulp greedily, but which Taye will not swallow when it's her turn.

"Drink it!" Kehinde, who is standing next to her, mutters. "You need it to survive."

"Yes, do as he says. Or else ..." The man passing it around warns her to consume the "bush" breakfast.

She manages one or two gulps before the man passes it to Kehinde, who drinks until it is wrested away from him.

When Eni awoke after the rather long vision, she was physically and emotionally drained. She dragged herself off the chair and, too tired to even change into her nightie, collapsed into her bed. She had barely pulled her duvet over her body when she blacked out. However, the sleep she fell into was not the dreamless, restful one that her aching body craved. She was not even sure if she was asleep because she was suddenly assailed by an overpowering odour. A nauseating blend of urine, sweat, feces, and vomit.

T*he thick, thick smell envelops her like a dark cloud, through which she begins to make out a shadowy image of a man carrying a limp form over his shoulder. Eni feels herself cringe as the image of the boy who is being carried becomes clearer. It is the boy twin from her earlier vision, Kehinde. Eni tries to shift on her bed, but she cannot move. Her hands, cupped together in front of her, seem stuck together as though fastened by an invisible rope. When she tries to move her legs, they are also bound tightly. Momentarily she finds herself levitating until she is floating above her body. Except, when she looks down, it is not her body that she sees but that of Taye, the girl twin who is crying as she lies on a coarse plank floor. She is muttering and invoking every Odu Ifa that she knows and calling out to all the Orisa to save her twin brother. Eni's floating form follows the man carrying Kehinde up a narrow flight of wooden steps.*

When the sea wind hits Kehinde's limp form as he is brought onto the deck of the swaying ship, he realizes what is to become of him. He tries to rouse his limp body to resist, but the many days of diarrhea and vomiting within the bowel of the ship render him incapable. He moves his lips, trying to plead for his life as he feels himself being propelled across the man's head over the side of the ship.

When his body hits the cold water, frigidity animates him. His bound hands and legs begin to flay, warping his body into the most awkward, fish-like postures. When he opens his eyes, the sea around him is indigo-dark. He might have even considered himself momentarily comfortable. Although he is sinking really fast, the sensation he feels deludes him into believing that he is floating. Still, he is unable to relax because he had started holding his breath just before hitting the water. The feeling of comfort makes him open his mouth to release the air he has been holding, but when the water hits his throat, it contracts very sharply. So intense is the pain, it knocks him unconscious. As his body grows limp, his ears register an ethereal, familiar voice howling his name: "Kehindeeeee!" Suddenly, Eni's floating form is sucked back into the bowel of the ship. Eni is thoroughly confounded because she has become one with Taye. For a long time, Eni finds herself paralyzed still in the belly of the ship. Her soul despondent.

When Eni's eyes finally opened, it was morning. She was tucked comfortably under her duvet in her room in Halifax, Nova Scotia. However, she was unable to shake off the leaden burden in her heart, and she mourned for her lost twin and too many lost lives. She roused her aching limbs, reaching under her pillow for her dream journal.

She was still trying to shake off the torpor in her spirit when she joined Ira and Akpa in the kitchen that morning. Akpa was sitting at the small round dining table with a newspaper open, but he was not reading. Instead, he was holding the remote control of the TV, whose screen was flickering from war to woe to war.

"Hi honey, did you have a rough night?" Ira said. "I thought I heard you moaning. I came to your room, but you were deeply asleep. You didn't even wake up when I practically lifted you so I could get your duvet to cover you." Ira poured some cereal into a bowl before handing it to Eni.

"Oh," Eni replied noncommittally, turning to open the fridge door. She did not want to discuss her night in front of Akpa. She was glad when he distracted Ira.

"I don't know why people persist with this nonsense." He was talking about a TV program, a slavery documentary.

"What? Is there something wrong with the documentary?" Ira said.

"This whole Black History Month is rubbish dressed up as gibberish. It doesn't make sense. People need to stop making such a big deal about race. Scientifically, there is no such thing."

"Be that as it may, is it possible that your position on race is because your privileged antecedence and status protect you from an experience that has led others to fixate on a phenomenon they can only describe as racialization?" Ira's tone was placatory. She did not want Akpa to think she was contradicting a view so central to his grant-gilded research.

"The whole concept of race is nothing but an illusion peddled by the likes of Du Bois, who was nothing if not a racialist. Race does not exist. Acting as though it does is scientifically indefensible and morally dangerous. People need to discard the idea completely in order to arrive at a rational and just worldview." He enunciated every point as though talking to a child. He'd forgotten her thesis that he'd okayed.

"So how do you explain the persistence of racialized and race-based practices that continue to affect people's lives? I mean, the legacies of slavery, the slave trade, and colonization …"

"That's something else that people fail to address. Slavery and colonization have been practised everywhere at one time or the other since time immemorial. Look up all the major civilizations. There was slavery in Africa long before the transatlantic slave trade. Slavery is not a uniquely African experience, nor is colonization. Why do you think none of the Abrahamic religions, or any other major ones, condemn slavery outright? They all attempted to modify it, but they did not denounce it!"

Ira was not irate. "But, surely, race complicated the way slavery was practiced in the Americas and the Middle East. It was rancidly racist, not just an economic praxis."

Eni did not care to hear the end of this argument as she rushed out of the kitchen. She slipped into her room and locked the door behind her before slumping onto her bed. She had felt herself falling into a trance as she audited the argument between Ira and Akpa.

She is now one with a figure that moves away from a door into a room with eight men sitting around a dining table. She moves as stealthily as she can. She will do anything to avoid triggering her master's explosive anger. She places first the wooden tray containing the large pewter jug of ale and then a small decanter containing Madeira wine on the card table beside the dining table. The men are bunched up together. Her master had explicitly told her to serve the Madeira for the gentleman, Mr. Jefferson, the special guest. He had come all the way from Virginia to meet with her master and other local gentry. She carefully arranges the large silver platter containing roasted pigeons, some ragout of cucumbers, thinly sliced fried ox tongue, some mince pies, and the frothy, sickeningly sweet dessert syllabub—so truly foul—to which she has never understood why her master was so addicted.

To provide extra seating for her master's guests so that they may dine more comfortably, she moves the tray to the edge of the dining table next to her master. She then returns to the elegant and sensuous curves of the antique French walnut game card table that her master had brought back from Paris on a trip with her mistress two years prior. A table handcrafted with an inlaid top section of matched parquetry in a geometric pattern. Her master is fanatical about card games, and all the house slaves have been trained to revere the game table. She avoids unhinging the two sections of the top when she pulls the back legs away from the table front, which conceals the interior containing playing cards and dice that her master stores there.

She is careful to pick the card table up completely off its four cabriole legs joined by a shaped apron. The joining gives the impression of a seamless line from the floor, up each leg and across the lower edge of the table's apron.

She makes a show of skirting the top with a raised lip around its perimeter, using a kerchief that she carries tucked into her apron pocket. She notices a lull in the conversation. She unhinges the folding top, revealing a flat, almost new green baize. She had no way of knowing that centuries later, one of her descendants, a psychiatrist and political philosopher, Franz Fanon, would espouse theories on the political chicanery operative around a "green baize table" just like this one.

She then proceeds to move toward the china cabinet, which is sitting prettily on the northern wall of the room. It stands to the right of the domineering mantle. She takes out the crockery. She wipes her right hand with her kerchief before placing the silver on the escutcheon plates and willow mounts with bail handles on the glass door of the maple chest of drawers. She grimaces when she remembers how excited her master and mistress had been when they first saw the design of the escutcheon bearing the newly commissioned family emblem with a matching coat of arms. The bail handles are exaggerated, oversized with a top that exposed the wide dovetail joints with cut lines. The joints are framed by trim mouldings with mitred joints at the front corners and a bevelled underside edge with more yoked moulding, forming a crown.

Again, very slowly, she proceeds to carefully take out china from the five graduated panel drawers below the top of the dresser. She then begins to lay the china in front of the men, who remain uncomfortably silent. Adjacent to the plates, each spoon is a shovel, each fork a pitchfork, each knife an axe.

She lays a place for her master's childhood friend, the ruddy-faced, rotund Master Tucker, who grows barley a few miles east. He has doffed his grotesque, antiquated cap, made of lace with a wig at the sides and set it on the table. She curtseys and smiles at him demurely, and he swiftly makes room for her to arrange her service by transplanting the wig from the table to his knees. She then approaches Mr. Jefferson, who is wearing a fashionable, padded wig, which rises steeply from his forehead in an exaggerated toupee. Standing next to him, she observes the wireframe of the wig where the hair has shifted. Mr. Jefferson hands her his tiny hat, and she goes and places it on a hanger behind the door. She then increases her pace, having concluded that whatever the potentates want to discuss deals with slavery and Negroes. Why else would they be so reluctant to continue talking with her in the room? She completes her service, then exits, shutting the door firmly behind her. She drags her shod feet loudly as she walks away from the door and then stealthily tiptoes back to the door to eavesdrop.

"Phillis? No … she is to be trusted completely. I would not have assigned her to tend to us otherwise. The mistress of this house raised her like her own child ever since I rescued her from an auction in Boston. She was barely seven or eight when I bought her nine years ago. She could barely speak. Her mistress schooled and nurtured her. She is devoted to my wife," she hears her master say.

An unidentifiable voice then warns: "Still, the matters we are deliberating upon here tonight are grave."

"I know, Mr. Jefferson. You need not impress upon us just how dire. As Sons of Liberty, my friends and neighbours here appreciate the need for utmost discretion. We are even warier now since the agitators started roaming the streets—"

Her master is cut off by another voice that snorts and says, "And Loyalists tortured and terrorized."

"Precisely! The political climate is intensely polarized. As many as a third of the people of these colonies are either pro-British or opposed to our take-no-prisoners methods as Patriots," the voice that she is now certain belongs to Jefferson says in a warning tone.

"We have also been targeted. 'Tis not only the Loyalists to the Crown who have had their properties burnt, been smoked out of their houses, or had their flesh tarred and feathered. Some of us Patriots and our brothers, the Free Masons, have also suffered great losses," a different voice says, bemoaning the cost of political action.

"Still, we have to be wary about how we air our views. There is no doubt that God is on our side since we are doing only what is right and just. However, we must continue to be clandestine as we meet, recruit supporters, and plan raids, such as the Boston Tea Party."

"Yes. Even the Negroes are on our side. I have heard it said that the riot in Boston was triggered by a Negro: One Crispus Atticus."

"That is something else we need to be wary of. The etching by Paul Revere does not indicate the participation of any Negro at that august event. Too many rumours making swift rounds."

"But I was present at the event. T'was indeed a Negro who first fell—"

"It matters not whether t'was a Negro martyred. We must be master of the uprising lest it gets the better of us. We must muster Patriotic militias to prevent citizen degeneration into mobs."

"I am aware that some free Negroes want to be a part of this. They are enthusiastic because they believe that, once we are rid of the British, they will be rid of slavery. A good number of them back the rebellion because of their personal desires for emancipation," a voice not heard before says.

After an elaborate throat clearing, another voice begins to speak in an unsure tone. "God in Heaven knows that the practice of slavery is a most confounding thing. True, logic and the Bible condemn slavery. Yet, our duty as members of the civilized race compels us to treat with compassion the Negro race. For one thing, we must admit that they are creatures without souls. Therefore, we are compelled to accommodate them as a race that is immanently inferior to ours and deserving of our devotion. It is indeed a conundrum, this question of whether or not slaves ought to be granted their freedom. It is the greatest contradiction of our times."

Phillis imagines this speaker sounds thoroughly confused.

"Friends, I freely admit that I am contradictory. As their owners, are we guilty of shirking in our duty if we free them, or do we concede their right to liberty and equality?" Jefferson states gravely.

"So, what is the current situation in Virginia since that insane Dunmore's declaration calling on even slaves to help him defend the colony?"

"Well, the situation has been desperate since the governor's proclamation in my homeland. Hundreds of armed rebels now camp

in the streets and fields of Virginia. However, Dunmore has been forced to flee Richmond," Jefferson says.

"In your estimation, is Williamsburg now safe for … "

"Yes, we Patriots are completely safe in Williamsburg. Dunmore's forces have been reduced to no more than about three hundred men."

"Is it true that many of his forces are Negroes?" her master asks.

"Yes, some who claim to be free. However, while very few slave owners are coming forward to claim them for obvious reasons, 'tis apparent that Dunmore is desperate enough to accept runaways," Jefferson says.

"I hear tell that he accuses most like you, Mr. Jefferson, who are slave owners, as nothing but hypocrite rebels."

"Lookit! Remember that Dunmore is desperate. He will say anything to further his cause."

"Why do the Negroes flock to join him? Even those belonging to masters who care for them—like your good self?"

"Well, he has promised the Negroes freedom in exchange for service in the army. 'Tis clear that Dunmore has gone stark raving mad."

"Mad, he might be. I have been reasonably informed that about eighty Negroes have since signed up with him."

From where Phillis stands eavesdropping, she senses the uneasy silence.

"No doubt the numbers are exaggerated. We're not simply wringing our hands out in Virginia. We have issued our own declaration. We have denounced Dunmore's offer of freedom by pointing out that it beggars Virginia's society. We have also warned the Negroes that Dunmore is peddling false hope, which will end up causing them greater suffering. We have also issued a death penalty for escaping slaves."

There is a long pause, and because Phillis does not hear the scraping of plates or cutlery, she quickly picks her way through the dark corridor, past the wooden staircase to the back kitchen.

When she steps quietly into the kitchen, she leaves the door ajar just as she found it. Because she has been so engrossed in auditing the parlour conversation, she realizes that the three slaves in the kitchen pause as she enters. She is relieved when they pick up their gossip as she goes about preparing her mistress's nightly tea tray, conscious that she is taking it later than usual.

"So, you will throw your life away because Master does what is most natural to his race?" Sally, Mr. Jefferson's slave, whom Phillis had seen leaving his room looking dishevelled earlier, sounds near tears.

"Joining the Ethiopian regiment is not the same as throwing my life away. Besides, how can you describe Mr. Jefferson's meddling with you as natural?" a young lad who looks like Sally says—his skin so light he can almost be mistaken for White. He has a round face and silky but curly hair. Clearly, he is her brother.

"I belong to him. And he's White, ain't he?" Sally replies.

"You belonged to his late wife, who was sired by the same man as you and me. Being White is no excuse for what he did to you and—"

"I told you, 'tis well with me. Please do not lose yourself over this foolishness."

"Signing up with Lord Dunmore as soon as we get back to Virginia ain't foolishness. Leastways, I'll get my freedom."

"Begging your pardon," Scipio Grafton charmingly offers. The burly Negro with a scar on the side of his forehead had come in with his master the day before and had introduced himself to Phillis. Though drawn to his good looks and chivalric compliments, Phillis has resolutely rebuffed him. He is not the first man to pay her attention, but she knows that her mistress will never let her go. She had noticed Scipio occupying one corner of the kitchen when she came in from serving in the parlour.

She suspects that Sally and her brother had either not noticed him sitting at the other end of the large table or forgotten about him when their argument erupted.

Scipio smiles spectacularly before opining: "Don't be so sure."

"Sure of what?" Sally's brother asks, sounding gruff.

Scipio shrugs. "You cannot be sure of either side of this conflict. The Patriots want their independence from the Crown, alright, but we have no assurance of what that means for us. The Loyalists invite us to help them fight, and offer us freedom without any guarantee—"

"What kind of guarantee do you want? Freedom is freedom, ain't it?" Sally's brother is definitive.

"I'm just talking from the perspective of a man who's escaped slavery twice."

"Twice?" Sally, her brother, and Phillis—who had been pretending to ignore the spat—all echo Scipio in various degrees of disbelief. Phillis abandons her tea tray and joins the trio around the worktable.

"How?" she asks.

Scipio smiles again. He's not sure if she means how he ended up in slavery a third time—or how he escaped the first two times. He starts by narrating his first escape. "The first time I escaped was not even planned. I went to check on my mother at a plantation not too far from the one I had been sold to when I was no more than ye tall." He uses his hand to indicate a point slightly higher than the table.

"I borrowed a horse from the servant of a friend of my master to visit my ma. Didn't know that he took the horse without permission. I was on my way back from visiting my ma when I ran into another slave who warned me of my peril—that I'd be accused of being a horse thief."

"Was the horse stolen?" Sally asks.

"No, he'd been sent with it on an errand and should've returned it several days before. I knew that a terrible beating was waiting for me, and so I ran away to Charleston."

"Charleston?" Sally's brother doesn't believe his story.

Scipio continues because, being a born raconteur, his story is enthralling the two women. "In Charleston, I joined the Patriots. An officer's servant, I travelled with his regiment. Once, I got separated from the regiment and met another officer who promised to transport me back to my original officer. After two days on the road, I realized that he had no intention of reuniting me with the regiment."

"How?" Phillis asks.

"He aks't me if I'd likes him to be my master."

"What did you tell him?" Sally's brother asks.

"I had no choice because he threatened to put me in irons and give me a dozen stripes every morning if I didn't agree to be his slave. So, I grinned and grinned, said 'yes sah, masah.' But I bided my time until a good opportunity arose and made my escape again."

"And you were not caught?"

"Nay. This time I found my way to the Royal Navy."

"And?"

"I wasn't treated any different from when I was with the Patriots. But I suffered the misfortune of being captured by a slave catcher who was hell-bent on frogmarching me back to my master to claim the bounty on my head. Strangely, he was really kind to me, and took the trouble to explain that his actions echo Bible teachings."

"All sides tout their favourite Bible verses," Sally says with a harrumph.

"I escaped from him one New Jersey night by wading across the Hudson, but then got pinched by my present master."

"Well, I wouldn't be so foolish as to end up on the wrong side," Sally's brother quips, unimpressed.

"For us, there really ain't no right or wrong side," Phillis says. She recalls the parlour chat of the slaveholding, libertarian Patriots. "Thank goodness we always have our smiling faces on ..." She stops speaking because she feels a sensation at the nape of her neck, which compels her to look at the door behind her through which she had come into the kitchen. She is struck dumb by the sight of her mistress, standing there in her nightdress; her visage displaying disdain and contempt.

"Begging your pardon, ma'am. I was just bringing your chamomile tea up—" She stops mid-sentence when she sees her mistress turn—snubbing her—and exit the kitchen.

"Lord God, ha mercy!" Sally wails. "She heard everything. On my mother's grave, she heard it all!"

"Uh huunh," Scipio grunts.

"It don't matter to me," Sally's brother says. He tries to sound nonchalant, but his words funk like a sulk. "It just means I won't wait till we get back to Virginia. I'm out of here before first light."

"Don't you care what that will do to the rest of us? To me?" his sister asks, admonishing him.

"Now, now, let's not get ahead of ourselves. I will take my mistress her tea and find out if she heard prattle … or sedition." Phillis sounds more confident than she feels.

"What if she has not gone up to her bedroom? What if she has gone to the parlour and told the men that we are here plotting a rebellion or a ruction?" Sally whispers fearfully, almost choking.

Phillis goes to the door, opens it. Standing just inside it, she listens. "She's gone up to her bedroom. She will not go to the parlour—I mean among men—in her nightdress."

"Thank goodness for mercies—"

"Hush up, Sally! Let's not get carried away again!" her brother says.

Phillis clinks together a tray of tea and plated cakes, then climbs the stairs, turning left at the landing. She hesitates at her mistress's door before knocking. Not hearing anything, she turns the knob. "Ma'am?" She offers tentatively before she crosses the threshold. "Begging your pardon, ma'am. I was delayed cause I was tending to master and his guests …" She feels relief to see that her mistress is back in bed.

"Just lay the tray down." Her mistress sounds mildly impatient. Phillis does not allow herself to dwell too long on whether it is because she had overhead things downstairs or because she has brought her nightly tea tray up a tad late. She places the tray down on a stool

beside the right- hand side of the canopied bed. She then goes over to the dresser, which dominates the southern wall of the room. She pulls out one of the drawers of the upper section of the white chest decorated with raised gold and green lacquered chinoiserie figures and landscapes. The chest also has a moulded cornice. She takes her mistress's neatly folded satin, taffeta, and linen bonnets from a laundry basket standing to the left of the chest, and she places them inside a drawer. She pushes back the drawer and bends down to open another in the bottom section, with three graduated drawers resting on Chippendale bracket feet, to take out a small pile of dirty clothes when she hears her mistress snigger. The sound? Like a razor ripping a throat.

"Are you going to put on your smiling face for my benefit and deny what I heard you saying to those confounded, ungrateful niggers?"

Phillis's back remains bent a few seconds before she straightens up with the pile of undergarments that she is holding.

"Begging your pardon, ma'am ... "

"Begging my pardon? For what? You heard me, and I heard you. You ingrate! Have I not always taken care of you, tended you even when you were sick like my own bairn? Have I not always treated you right?"

"Yes, ma'am. You have been nothing but good to me."

"Then why would you collude so spitefully with those good-for-nothing niggers against our noble charity? You two-faced ... two-faced hussy!"

Knowing that smiling will not appease her mistress this time, Phillis dons instead her innocent, no-secrets, childlike face.

"Forgive me, ma'am, I don't know what all came over me. May God almighty strike me down for being so ungrateful after all you've done for me, ma'am." She keeps her voice pleasing. Honey, not bile.

She puts the pile of clothes that she is holding beside the bed. Bending with her back toward her mistress, she pours some chamomile tea into a teacup, adds two pinches, not just one, of the sleeping powder that Dr. Shaw supplies to nurse insomnia. She is praying the tea will help her mistress slumber quicker than it usually does.

"Have I not seen to it that you're fed, clothed, and kept warm or cold as the elements demand?" Her mistress still gives Phillis her back.

"Yes, ma'am. I have no cause to complain."

"Have I not even taught you to read and write at great risk to my life?" The mistress's voice is, as normal, whiny.

"Yes, ma'am. You even sent my poetry off to that publisher." Phillis gives her a placating smile as she tucks her into bed. "All the way in Boston."

The mistress sighs, then yawns loudly, turning to project her tea-and-sedative-and-cake-sweet breath into Phillis's face." You should never let those other tiresome, patience-taxing, good-for-nothing niggers mislead you. You're better off than all of them."

"Yes, ma'am, I know just how lucky I am to have you as my mistress."

"Don't you ever forget it. I shall have to tell the master not to let his visitors bring their niggers into the house. Don't matter if they're supposed to be house niggers. Most of them are trifling ... good-for-nothing, trifling ... nigg ..." Her voice peters off as she begins to doze.

Phillis remains standing beside the headboard of the canopied brass bed. She watches the sleeping woman like a mother watching over her child. She recalls how she had looked up to this same woman when she had first been gifted to her by the master after he purchased her from the slave block. It was several months after she had been captured from her village in Ile Ifa. The recollection of her life in her homeland? Just scraps of memory and figments of visions which haunt her quiet wakeful moments and restless nights.

After watching to ensure her mistress is sleeping, Phillis picks up the pile of clothes to take downstairs. She then returns to the kitchen, where the others await her decisive news. Yet, bickering still are Sally and her brother.

"For the love of God! Do not—" Sally stops speaking when she sees Phillis. All turn to her, nervously expecting doom-and-gloom alarms.

"I am sure we are safe till morning. She's fast asleep now, but ... I ..." Due to nerves, Phillis stutters.

"But what?" Sally's brother is impatient.

"I cannot vouch what dawn will bring. She will tell the master whatever she remembers of the conversation she overheard here."

"Gracious God in Heaven!" Sally is apoplectic with fright.

"That's it, we're leaving." Sally's brother reaches for her hand, but she backs away, distances herself.

"Quit playing the fool, Sally! Do you think sharing his bed will shield—"

"I don't know, Caleb. But I'd rather stake my chance with Master Jefferson than out there in an unknown world."

"But you heard what she said. Her mistress overheard us ..."

"I'm not sure how much she heard or how much she will remember in the morning. Moreover, I am not sure what the master will make of whatever she says, for she is ... well, addled and dotty," Phillis said.

"Do you mean she is insane?" Scipio asks.

"No ... I don't ... but she's ..." Phillis stumbles over her words. How can she explain her mistress's condition?

"Well, what then?" Caleb asks.

"My mistress is not like other grown folks. She's stuck in girlhood."

"So, your master might not believe her?" Sally sounds relieved.

"He might or mightn't. I can't say," Phillis says.

"'Tis best not to take a chance then." Scipio gets up.

"Truer words have never been said." Caleb looks at his sister appealingly.

Sally shakes her head. "Go if you must, Caleb, but I will stay. Master Jefferson is heading on to Paris from here, and he needs me. Besides, I will convince him that I did not know about your plan to run away." She looks at her brother, then sighs. "I'll find a way to let you know anything I find out that may put you in jeopardy." Caleb walks back to her, and they embrace as Scipio strides for the door.

"Wait!" Phillis says. The strident monosyllable arrests Scipio and breaks off Sally and Caleb's embrace. "Please, let me come with you!" Phillis surprises even herself as she appeals to Scipio.

"Come with me? I am not even sure where I'm heading. All I know is that I have to get out of here before cock-crow."

"That's what I want, too. Put space between myself and this place. I ..." She falters because she is unable to put her emotion about the years she has spent with her mistress into words without sounding like an ingrate. She hates her situation—a poet, a pet.

By the time Phillis had been with her mistress only a few months, she knew that, though a fully grown woman, her mistress possessed the mind of a dolt and the intellect of a child. Phillis's suspicion was confirmed by Martha, the old slave, who had known the master's first wife. Martha reported how desolate the master had been when he was widowed so young. However, by the time Phillis joined the household, he was besotted with his kindergarten-variety second wife. Perhaps it had to do with the fact that he had no children. He seemed quite content with his wife whom he treated as both wife and beloved child. Her mistress was too much a girl in her mind to be a mother, in fact.

Although she wants to run away with Scipio, Phillis is genuinely grateful for the life her mistress has given her, knowing she could have ended up working on a field or in a household to be whipped or raped or both. She knows that, demeaning as it was, being treated like a plaything is a unique kind of blessing. One is cuddled, not cudgeled. But the "blessing" was bestowed at the whims and caprices of an irrational mistress who will coo to her as if she were a baby one minute, but berate her the very next.

Scipio approaches her, peering at her face.

"Are you sure?" He is thoroughly puzzled. He had taken a liking to her the moment he cast eyes on her tall, shapely figure. Her ebony-black hair was covered by a kerchief, but he could see a few unruly

strands around her ears. Her round face looked determined, with eyes that pierced—like two spears—his heart. However, his is a nihilist world for which no future exists. So, he allowed himself to admire her but not entertain any hope for a relationship. Not even for a quick roll in the hay. There is something about her. Solid is the only word that fits her. Suddenly, she nods her head vigorously in response to his question.

"I can make you no promise ..."

"I ask nothing of you. Only your company to get us out of here."

He moves closer to her. "I hear there is a safe house not too far from here ..."

"About nine miles east!" she blurted.

What doesn't she know? He wonders.

"I know the farm. We can make it there before light if we leave now. We'll go through the woods off Payton's farm," Phillis says.

"So, how come you're only leaving now?"

"There is safety in numbers." She smiles before she begins to rifle through her mistress's laundry that she had brought down with her. She picks out a shawl and a bonnet.

Caleb, eavesdropping, clears his throat. "Can I join you?" Embarrassed, he glances from Scipio to Phillis. Scipio shrugs.

"We'll need some provisions," Scipio says to Phillis, who nods as she trods toward the pantry. She's suddenly not so confident about running off.

"Nothing too heavy. Just enough to sustain us for a day or two, in case ..." Scipio's voice drops off. He'll not announce his fears.

Sierra Leone – 1997

Siaka

THE FIRST TIME Siaka lost his brother, he thought his own life was forfeit.

One minute, they were lying down, side by side on the floor, telling stories, in a half-finished building. Outside, the night was a dead-zone. It was as though the birds, animals, and crickets that ordinarily provided the village with a musical backdrop had taken one look at the desolation and abandoned it, taking their song with them. In their absence, the night didn't settle into true silence; rather, it was filled with a different kind of auditory texture: whispers of the wind, the distant creaks and groans of the building, and the subtle, yet pervasive, rustling of leaves—all conspiring to create a haunting, albeit less familiar, nocturnal chorus.

Tejan, one of the three other boys in their pack, was recalling a story his grandmother told him about the wily, slow-footed tortoise and his quick-witted wife. Bursting with joyous laughter, Alamin and Moses, the other two boys, vividly reminded Siaka of the delight he found in the colourful tales of the trickster tortoise's numerous adventures. Their laughter filled the air, ringing with genuine amusement and infectious mirth, drawing Siaka's gaze. As they recounted their favourite episodes, their animated expressions and lively gestures painted vivid scenes, bringing the tortoise's cunning escapades to life before Siaka's eyes.

At that moment, it was as if the boys had finally succeeded in vanquishing the alien quietness that engulfed the village, and the war seemed an illusion. They had started by teasing one another, reluctant as they were to admit to themselves that they missed the click-clicks of crickets, the rustle of bats, even the distant yowling of stray dogs, hunger-mad, or the meowing of wild, scrawny cats out to taunt the bony, disowned canines. For the moment, they were ordinary kids again.

Given their forced levity, they could even pass for boys who were carefreely enjoying a sleepover in the secure home of one of their parents.

The boys had chosen their refuge for the night because the roof looked new. It was as much a home as is the word itself. It did not matter that the place reeked with damp from the rain three days earlier—which had swept in through the gaping holes left for windows and the gaps between the cheap, shoddily laid, corrugated roofing sheets, more like paper than tin. A heap of sodden leaves interrupted the large room's dirty—no, muddy—floor. At least, the building had not been burnt like others in the small village. One unfortunate unknown to the boys? That shining new roof was one of the things that had attracted the militia faction that had attacked the village the day before the children sought shelter there. Initially meant to be a primary school to serve the village and its now equally devastated neighbours, the site had become dilapidated. Three years before the "liberation" war began, the government contractor responsible for the project abandoned it. He pocketed the money, then jet-rocketed to London. When the villagers could not get anyone in the government to either force the builder to complete the job or assign it to another contractor, they taxed themselves for materials like rocks and sand to continue the construction. The corrugated tin roof had only been installed a few months before the village was sacked by a horde of murderous jackals who fancied themselves rebels.

Siaka lay closest to one of the bare windows in the dim room. His attention was focused on the naked, unglazed moon, whose pallid nonchalance struck him once again as it dawned on him that life had not stood still despite all the paralyzing horror they had known. He stretched, removing his aching right hand, a bad cushion for his head. When he moved, he felt Bobo nestle closer to his side. Siaka extended his hand, and Bobo placed his tiny warm left hand inside Siaka's right one. Instinctively, Siaka cupped the little hand in his, amazed by how easily Bobo picked out his hand even in that shadow-mugged room. He felt himself drawing as much strength from his brother, as he knew the boy had come to depend on him since the day they came back from his uncle Khalifa's farm.

The five boys had left that morning for the cornfields, which Moses's father had allowed him to plant for himself near his cassava farm. They planned to roast the corn as soon as they returned home. Upon reaching the farm by early afternoon, they were delighted to see the green-clad, gold spears of corn jab at a light-grey sky ready for them to harvest. When it started drizzling, the boys were not alarmed. They hoped the teasing drizzle would turn into a less bashful downpour so they could frolic and splash about. They knew that, back in the village, a real soaking would be a welcome occurrence for other children and women, for it promised a day's supply of clean water, cancelling a trip to the stream. The boys groaned when the drizzle spat to a stop. They collected as much corn as they could carry and started heading back to the village in the afternoon, but kept straying en route, trying to rustle up bushmeat.

They eventually got there, just as evening gelled, only to find the entire village torched; dead bodies strewn everywhere. The first corpse they found in the village square? Siaka and Bobo's mother. When he first saw her charred carcass, Siaka just stood, hypnotized. He was about to crumple into a heap beside his burnt-up mother, but he felt Bobo's hand slip from behind him into his. He was compelled to turn quickly, to shield the six-year-old Bobo from glimpsing the godawful remains. In that instant, he became an adult with the responsibility for his brother's survival resting—like heavy piles of lead bricks—solely on his shoulders. He did not bother helping the other boys find or identify the bodies of their other close relatives.

Far too many lost in a blink. His Uncle Khalifa, who was Alamin and Tejan's father, their aunts, Abiba and Tai, their step-grandmother ... When the three boys started running frantically from one blackened or hacked-up body to another, screaming and wailing, Siaka plunked on an upturned trestle bench cradling Bobo's head on his lap, rocking from side to side to soothe and shush his wails. Sitting there, overwhelmed by the smell of burnt flesh, Siaka recalled how the roast-goat aroma had wafted to envelop them in a macabre welcome—almost a half-mile before they reached their village. They had walked faster upon first inhaling it, hurrying to get back home, for someone must have slaughtered a goat. They were hungry, and every single one of them had drooled, dreaming to eat roast corn with seared goat. It didn't matter whose family had slaughtered the animal. The cluster of huts was small enough, and everyone was so related to everyone else, the boys could feel assured that they would soon be feasting on the shared meat.

Sitting on that trestle table, Siaka spied ears of corn lying in a puddle of blackened blood where Tejan had dropped his basket. It was hard for Siaka to come to terms with the fact that this was the same village that had greeted them with dancing and large trays of steaming fufu, rice, and cassava-leaf stew made with goat meat a few days prior. He and Bobo came with their mum from Freetown to stay with his uncle Khalifa's family in the village in Koinadugu district to dodge their addled father just a week before the annihilation.

That night, concluding that they were the last of their village, the boys decided they could not stay there because they feared the raiders would return. The five boys started what they all agreed would be a long trek to Freetown to reunite with Siaka and Bobo's father.

Siaka and Bobo had come to the village because their parents were always feuding. They started having problems soon after David, their father, a geologist, lost his job at the head office of the British mining company. They'd decided to replace him with an Oxford-trained, twenty-six-year-old expat contract worker.

David had been with the company since he graduated from university. He had worked close to ten years at the company when the British brought their own people to take over the top jobs, leaving behind a handful of Sierra Leoneans to oversee manual labour and lower management positions, irrespective of their qualifications. Over the years, he had also seen his expat-dominated company grow and thrive while the rest of the country struggled with political instability and corruption.

But David was not the sort to think too much about things that he could not change. Long before he was retrenched, the rumour in the company was that the British owners had ascertained that the political problems in Sierra Leone would end up as a long, drawn-out, internecine bloodbath. Therefore, the Brits imported more of their own people to consolidate and protect their interests before the country imploded. The local mining company employees disdained to use the word "war," but its whispered synonyms were apocalyptically omnipresent. Its shadow permeated every conversation, an ever-present spectre of destruction and chaos.

When first unemployed, David was not so bad. He was just very often sullen. The drunken snits and physical lashing out at Miriam, the boys' mother, only started after his car caught fire near the Cotton Tree on one of his fruitless forays downtown to dredge up income.

The minute David stepped into their apartment on the day his car got baked black, Miriam, who was folding laundry in the living room, took one look at his stricken face and her heart skipped several beats. His eyebrows pulled up and looked scared frozen. She resisted the urge to rush up to him and ply him with questions, an act of self-preservation that would postpone hearing whatever had happened to him. So, she bit her tongue. Her ability to sense that there was something amiss had nothing to do with her being a woman or his wife. Had the boys been home, they would have sensed it too, just from seeing his face.

The old jalopy surprised David when it seemed to have spontaneously combusted rather than continue ferrying him from one office to another to get rejected after offering his services for even the lowliest positions. But it was not the fact that his car was incinerated that upset David. Yes, he would miss having a car, but he had been spending so much on maintaining the pack of metal that the car had become, it was almost a relief to be rid of it. No, it was the fact that it caught fire at the roundabout circling the concrete fence that surrounded the regal Cotton Tree that unnerved him. David had been raised by stories about how the Old Cotton Tree, which was indeed several hundreds of years old, had offered refuge to the first group of formerly enslaved people from the Americas when they arrived in Freetown after gaining their freedom by fighting for the British against the Americans. As their descendant, David felt that it was ominous that he should have suffered such a misfortune at that sacred spot.

When unbidden, David blurted out what happened to the car. Miriam got up and lugged the laundry into Siaka and Bobo's room. She was thankful that the boys were playing in the yard. She rested her head on the closed door of the room and counted from one to ten, willing herself to remain strong. She opened the door and stepped back into the living room, where she found David fiddling with their small battery-operated transistor radio. The electricity had been out for about three days, and the room was clammy, even though all the louvre windows were open. She found herself once again regretting her choice of a glossy royal blue paint for the room's walls. Not only did the oily tint make the room a sauna, but the garish hue emphasized the imperfections in the plaster job, so unnoticeable before. She had selected the colour and the oil paint—which cost twice as much as what the regular water-based paint would have cost—because the paint seller told her it would last a lot longer than water-based emulsion. She had smiled at the fast-talking paint seller as she paid his charge. She told herself that, hopefully, this was going to be the last time she would paint the flat. Her husband would get another job, a better paying one than his last one, and they would move into a more commodious, better finished flat.

When she opened her mouth to address David after she emerged from the boys' room, and he reported that his old jalopy had simply burst into flames, even she found her voice too breezy. But it was all she could do to keep from allowing herself the luxury of joining him in his soul-corrosive despair. She smiled soothingly.

"Don't worry, we have lived without a car before—"

"Uman! Wetin yu de du me so? You de happy?" He screamed acidly when he saw her smile. She stood still as his words spilled walloping out of his embattled soul. Never before had he accused her of somehow enjoying seeing him diminished.

After that day, as their circumstances worsened, he progressed to damning her as a witch. She defended herself by reminding him that she was the same girl he wooed at Fourah Bay College. At first, she would shriek back at him: "I be the same uman you don marry for twelve solid years, why I kin start winching you now?" At first, her questions seemed to have the power to placate him, and she would let go of the tears that she had been fighting to hold back. And unable to stand her tears, David wept too, and then they would hug, clutch, and console each other.

A light sleeper who always woke up as soon as voices were raised in the tiny flat in Kissy, Siaka was not sure which he found more disturbing: his parents' bickering or their sobbing helplessly together. However, come one morning, there was quiet. His mum, noticing that his eyes were insomniac-red, tried to reassure him: "Sia, no allow your fada vex worry you. You hear me so? He is a good man, and losing his job is what is making him so angry all the time. He feels he is not a man if he cannot provide for us."

"Will he find another job soon?"

"He will continue to try. If not, we will try and survive with my salary." She stopped, stared unblinkingly at him, then reached out her right hand and started rubbing his newly shaved head. But her touch was not so comforting that morning. Anxiety insisted on sabotaging hope.

Then the ministry where she worked laid her off, along with three hundred forty six others, after a coup that ousted the army-fatigued-uniformed "Prez'dent," who had stupidly allowed his wives to multiply and his palace guard to dwindle. Now, Miriam's shrieks lost their power to soothe David's drunken outbursts.

"Maybe you just became a witch!" he shouted, hurling a dining chair at her one night. It struck her left shoulder, stabbing out blood. Siaka, who was taking some plates to the kitchen, let them clatter and shatter, the last of his mum's treasured bone-china. He found himself propelled to rise to his mother's defense. He charged, his head lowered like a ram's, aiming for his father's stomach. He butted into David's groin instead. He was amazed by how easily his father fell. Luckily, Miriam came between them, throwing herself over Siaka to shield him in case David meant to retaliate. She did not need to worry. David was too dazed to even lift himself off the floor. When he finally dragged himself up, he strolled out of the house.

That night, when Siaka heard Miriam open the door of his room, he shut his eyes, feigning sleep. When he felt her slight frame perch on the edge of his bed, he had to open his eyes. She said that she would be taking him and Bobo to her village at sunrise. He nodded, relieved that even though her voice sounded laden, her eyes were not wet. Yet, he could not trust himself to speak. After she exited, he got up and walked to the other side of the room, where Bobo lay sleeping on a narrow wooden bed. He reached under Bobo's bed and quietly brought out an old school satchel, large enough to hold a few of their belongings. He felt morose but did not realize it was from guilt at having charged into his father. He thought he was sad because of the tension between his parents, which was now making them leave home. As he began to fill the bag, he wondered how many clothes he should pack since he forgot to ask his mum how long they would be gone.

Siaka, Miriam, and Bobo snuck from the apartment at dawn. Unfortunately, their bus did not leave the Freetown area early enough to avoid heavy traffic entering the city, so their driver opted to take the mountain by-pass.

They wheezed past Grafton, but as they approached a one-lane bridge, they found that traffic was beginning to get backed up because another passenger bus, three vehicles ahead, was struggling sluggishly up an incline. Their driver ordered all to alight so he could ascend the slope without so much weight on the bus's rickety frame. The passengers all clambered back after the bus had croaked its way up the hill. A mile or so after their vehicle successfully manoeuvred the slope, it stopped. When some passengers started to complain, the driver asked them to thank God that he was a cautious driver because the brakes felt wrong. He got out of the bus and lifted the bonnet. He then laid on his back to look under the bus. He came up almost immediately to announce that the brake fluid was leaking. Some passengers wasted no time thanking God loudly that the brakes did not fail when they descended the treacherous incline.

It took three hours to fix the brakes. After they were finally free of Freetown's suburban shanties, Miriam nudged awake the dozing Siaka. She needed him to see the beautiful adjacent hill and rocky outcroppings of the picturesque Kabala nestled amid the Wara Wara mountains. Bobo tried to whistle when he caught sight of a monkey swinging through some trees overhead, but his lips were too dry from the cold morning air. The sky was incredibly hazy because the Harmattan season was poised to birth an atmospheric Sahara. The road was dusty, rugged, and rough. The land stretched out on either side of the road, sloping high and low, erratically. The morning wind swayed with the grass as though to a jagged tune, twisting here, sashaying there, humping and bumping around the branches and trees. Siaka did not allow himself to become overwhelmed by the road ahead, which seemed to go on and on—except where shifting sand blunted and stunted its reach. He tried to cast his eyes as far as they would go, and every so often, he picked a lone tree or palm out of the dust-engrossed highway to mark the distance.

They had to change vehicles at Kabala, but were fortunate to hire a battered pickup willing to ferry them onward. They drove out of Kabala and onto Freetown-Bo highway again. They soon turned off and onto a bumpy dirt road that ran smack into a small river that the pickup—suddenly turned hippo—miraculously waded.

Although Miriam kept telling Siaka and Bobo that they were only visiting the village briefly, until their father found a new job, Siaka was not deceived. It was 1997, and the war in Sierra Leone was electric-chair-hot, crematoria-hot, blast-furnace-hot. He knew far too many kids like him whose parents were out of work. He did not expect David to draw another paycheque soon.

The trip to the village was Siaka's first one since he was a baby. Bobo, who was four years younger than Siaka, had never been there. Their father, David, a Krio, was a typical Freetownian. He liked to boast that his mother's ancestors were from Granville Town. He said they were some of the original four hundred who were sent from England, the first settlers in Freetown in 1787. "My mother's people came under the auspices of Granville Sharp, the British abolitionist," he would say and beam proudly whenever he had to explain his origins. Siaka, who did not know what the word "auspices" meant, concluded it must have been a grand way to flotilla into Freetown. For him, "auspices" conjured up grand men and women dressed in regal clothes disembarking gingerly from a ship boasting shining white sails. Perhaps the women wore brightly-coloured flowing gowns and the men stood stiff and upstanding in tight suits and pants that clung like socks to their thighs and legs—the kind that Europeans sported in history books. These grand ancestors of his all wore elaborate white wigs. The men as well as the women. David also claimed that on his paternal side, he was descended from the Nova Scotians who built Freetown on the former site of the first Granville Town, which had been destroyed in 1789. "Nova Scotia"! The way David said those words made Siaka dream about the place. He could not help wondering why any set of people would want to leave a place with such a fancy name.

In reality, there was no way David's claims could be substantiated without a thorough DNA analysis. His claims were just as fanciful as Siaka's imaginations about their ancestors' grand arrival in Freetown. In terms of ethnicity, he could have been a veritable mishmash like most other Krios who could have equally traced ancestors from among the Nova Scotians, Maroons, Shebro,

Temne, Limba, Aku, Igbo, Hausa, Akan, Fullah, Tyra, and even the Mende. Like some other Krios, David only held fast to his assertions about his ancestry because it was prestigious to do so.

***

Life did not end on the day the village was destroyed, Siaka thought as Tejan concluded his story about the tortoise in the boys' unglazed, unfinished, unprotected sanctuary. Alămin and Moses started arguing about who should next tell a story, when suddenly, unmistakable bursts of gunshots riddled the night. Unknown to the hapless boys, the soldiers who had only a day before destroyed the village where the boys were taking refuge had come back to make it their base after ransacking other neighbouring villages. They chose to return to this one because it had the uncompleted—derelict—building with the contradictorily brand-new, shiny, corrugated tin roof. The very thing that attracted the boys to the building when they stumbled on the village.

Siaka's first instinct when he heard the gunfire was to grab Bobo's hand. Turning toward the window, he picked him up and flung him out, shouting, "Run na the bush! No wait for me, oh!" There was no sign of Bobo by the time he jumped after him, but the rattling shots chinking through the shallow building were closer and propelled Siaka to take to a path between two huge tallow trees. With the rat-a-tat-tat sniping at his heels, he was spurred on by fear as much as he was driven to disprove the alarming possibility that Bobo was lost for good.

Siaka stopped running when the zip and zing of bullets finally dissipated after what seemed like several hours. Exhausted and trying to cease gasping for air, he collapsed in a clearing when he realized that the voices of the other boys sounded close. He mustered enough strength to whisper hoarsely, "Bobo? You dey yonda?" Hearing no response, he rephrased, "Any of una see my brother Bobo?"

Silence.

Siaka's breathing became louder because something in his chest rasped violently. Was it due to a lack of air or from his acute pain at the loss of his brother?

"I done die oh!" he wailed, flinging himself onto the moist earth. He dug his hands into the muddy ground on either side of him and grabbed hold of a clump of slippery grass with his right hand. The grass slithered out of his grip even as he pulled at it. Anguish, which he was unable to unleash at the sight of his dead mother's immolated body, resembling a goat fresh-charred for skinning, rushed out of him, threatening to drown him. He whimpered like the child that he indeed was, surprised by the fleeting relief he felt. For an instant, he allowed himself to stop trying to be a man and was the boy he was before he turned to shield his brother from the offensive sight of their mother's gruesome spitting. The image of Miriam's remains now flummoxed his senses. Unable to conceive the grisly death of his procreator, he could only allow himself now to heave, grieve, and weep for her. Suddenly, a tiny warm hand touched the side of his face like the kiss of a furtive ghost.

"Sia, I dey yia." Bobo's voice came at him from the swaddling darkness. He sat up quickly, donning the mask of manhood again even before enfolding his brother, who threw himself into his open arms. He was surprised at how much he suddenly felt weighed down, not only by the boy's slight weight, but by the burden of the charge to shield this one life. Every cell in Siaka's body ached for his own lost boyhood.

Siaka's second loss of Bobo occasioned no reflection. He knew now that the power of death, of losing one's loved ones, resided in the irreversibility of the occurrence; and that first separation somehow delegitimized any necessity for grief. It completely knocked the teeth out of losing his brother. He believed he could never again feel the intense pain he felt that night when he first lost Bobo. Several days later, when the motley group of boys was swimming in a stream and found themselves scattering when bullets began to rain again from everywhere they turned, Siaka, disregarding Bobo, fled toward a hill.

He had no trouble remaining calm. As a matter of fact, it was impossible for him to even imagine the complete vanishing of his brother. So, about an hour later, when the area was safe again, he found Bobo with a group of other boys on the other side of the stream. Bobo ran toward him, his now painfully skinny arms flung wide as he made to embrace Siaka. The gesture seemed somewhat superfluous. Siaka had to stop himself from sidestepping to avoid Bobo's hug. Abruptly he urged him, "Oya, waka!" A small part of his mind reproached him for sounding so brash in the face of Bobo's relief at their being reunited. Siaka told himself that he wasn't uncaring, but only anxious to reach the next village before nightfall.

He should not have been in such a hurry to reach that village, which Tejan remembered from a visit he had made there with his grandmother the year before. Tejan's grandmother sold fabric from village to village and she sometimes took one of her grandchildren to help carry the large sacks containing her wares. On nearing the destination, Siaka and the others ran into two women carrying empty baskets on their heads, walking away from the settlement. When the boys accosted them, the women simply turned on their heels and ran back toward the makeshift gate of their village. The boys ran after them, calling out, "Mami! Mami!!" Only to be met by a group of men who emerged from the village wielding machetes and cudgels, who urged them to return to wherever they were coming from. No respite here!

Alamin and Tejan wailed, begging and appealing to them to let them sleep the night under the protection of the villagers. Moses pushed Bobo, the youngest of the group, forward, and Alamin began to explain what happened to their own village. All they needed was some food and a night of refuge.

"Refuge? You think to say we no know who una be? If we let una stay, then for night the people wey send una go come kill all of we, not so?" one of the men screamed at them.

"No, no, not so. We just dey hungry and we no wan die." Alamin had snot dangling from his nose as he blubbered heartrendingly. Bobo, too, joined in the plea, rubbing his stomach and gesturing with his other hand toward his mouth, pleading for food.

"If una no clear commot for yia we go machete una and throw una for bush," a second man said.

"Look, I done see una face well, well. I don't care whether una be government soldier or RUF, make una tell una commandant say if anything happin for dis village we go find una and deal with una well, well," the first man threatened.

All this time, fear held Siaka captive. He was spooked by the fear he heard in the voices of the fully grown men who were accusing him and the other boys, mere children, of being soldiers. Peering closer, he spied the dread in their eyes. The incongruity of the situation stirred hope in his heart. At that precise moment, Siaka realized that their survival—collectively and individually—depended not on the hospitality of any village—they had passed through so many desolate villages that their group's survival necessitated—but upon joining an army. Any army! All soldiers were hunters, and all civilians prey.

Two days later, starving and exhausted, they walked into a group of rebel soldiers, most of whom were children like themselves. Between the time they'd left that village, whose terrified men had repelled their entreaties, and when they encountered this army of brats with machine guns, something had changed in the other boys as well. Without having to articulate his thoughts to the others in his group, Alamin, the oldest lad, had come to the same conclusion as Siaka upon their being chased from that last village. On meeting the young soldiers, Alamin, Moses, and Tejan, too, proved themselves as desperate as Siaka was—to belong to a community of other powerful human beings. They all prostrated, pleading not for liberty, but to be accepted into the rebel ranks.

The fact that his final dislocation from Bobo came from Siaka's own hand was really no big deal. If anything, it seemed natural and offhand at that time, in that place. When the rebels gave him a gun to shoot his brother to prove his manhood, what a small price to pay! He and Bobo had lost and found each other so many times; he was as immune to the pain of losing him as he was to the no-longer-so-joyful reunions. In his mind, Bobo had died too many times already. If anything, Bobo's eyes seemed to urge him to comply with the order being barked at Siaka by Augustus Caesar, the one-eyed leader of the ragtag thugs.

Siaka had also seen so many dead people, he welcomed the peace that their breathless visages mirrored. It did not matter how they came by their end—gunshots, burning, or open gaping wounds chopped into them by machetes. Death delivered peace. He came to this conclusion when they ran into a woman who was beside her own entrails, in the last throes of bleeding to death. The five boys gathered around the dying woman, watching her shudder until the convulsions subsided, and she was still. Siaka was enthralled by her eyes, which remained open, and her teeth, which stayed set. He was mesmerized by the contrast these two parts of her body made compared to the rest of her cadaver, which now lay dishevelled. By that time, he no longer tried to shield Bobo's eyes from such sights. No longer startling, also, was the similarity between human remains and goat carcasses, a fact which had upset him when he'd observed his mother sprawled out like a charred carving.

That sunny day when they ran into Augustus Caesar's pack, Siaka and the other boys laid on the clayey ground with sparse clutches of grass, cringing and crying to be inducted into Caesar's troop. Caesar looked them over, then pointing his gun at each, he barked, saying they were mad to think they could survive as soldiers. The boys chorused their affirmation that they could. He then proceeded to hit and kick them where they lay. "Just for the fun of it," he explained calmly to his troop, before commencing his show of might. Eyeing Bobo, he guffawed.

"And this one, wetin e be?"

Siaka raised his hand and whispered, "Na my brother."

"Stand up!" Augustus Caesar barked. They all scrambled up.

"So una wan to be soja, like we?"

"Yes sa!" they sang out, even though Augustus Caesar was no older than sixteen or seventeen himself.

"Una fit to kill?"

"Yes sa!"

"And shack?"

"Yes sa!"

"And fuck?"

"Yes sa!"

Pointing at little Bobo, chorusing "Yes sa!" along with the brother and cousins, Augustus's posse bust their guts laughing. Augustus stalked toward the tiny boy and punched him to the ground. He stood over him dismissively, then pointed his gun at Siaka.

"Come yia!" He signalled to one of his soldiers to hand Siaka his gun.

"You wan be soja? Then shoot him." The gun snout daggered at Bobo.

Siaka took the offered firearm and brooked no second thought. Thinking was a luxury he could not afford at that time, in that place. Now aiming the weapon at Bobo, he was convinced that his brother's sunken eyes, already nothing but skull sockets, were urging him on. He was certain, too, that Bobo was sick and tired of the running, of having to eat raw lizards and rats, of the vomiting and diarrhea, of his scabies-covered skin, of sore lips and tiny blistered feet, of ...

Siaka pulled the trigger. Eyes wide open.

After several weeks of scooting and skedaddling from all sides of the war, Siaka's liberation came when he slew his little brother. He felt unfettered, even by his own body, freed from fear, from the burden of a filial link to Bobo or any other creature. He was free to become a soldier, and in his mind, soldiers needed weapons, not baggage. He did not look back at the tiny body that he knew would be lying still as his group fell in step with Augustus Caesar's ragtag pack when they jogged from the scene. Neither Tejan, Moses, nor Alamin eyed him as they high-stepped away. Past, present, and future ended in graveyards. Let the dead rest in peace.

Sierra Leone – 2000

Siaka

Two and a half years after Bobo's death, Siaka, who had lost track of his cousins—Moses, Alamin, and Tejan—was one of thirteen boys handed over to UNICEF as part of a pacifying parley between his RUF commandant and the United Nations. While the UN were not always good guys, aggressive rapists in Haiti and passive bystanders to Rwandan genocide, they lodged Siaka and other boys at a Freetown rehab centre.

At rehab, the ex-child-soldiers were under the care of Angela Simcoe, a middle-aged psychotherapist from Canada, who was part of a team of nurses, doctors, and social workers, whose mandate was to help the boys navigate back into the human race. At first, there was little anyone could do to coax Siaka out of his child-killer's shell. He was unlike some of the other boys who were thrilled by the jeans, t-shirts, and shoes, all made in China, received upon arrival. Some shifted quickly to just being kids. Others could not break free from demonic addictions.

Although Siaka was unresponsive at first, Angela realized that he was unlike two other recalcitrant boys, suspicious of all conversation. Indeed, this tandem would violently assault their peers and some of the local staff, without any provocation. There was something about Siaka—the eerily self-contained teenager he now was—which made Angela believe him when he declared that he loathed all booze, all narcotics. Studying him, she saw a startlingly handsome, five-foot-eleven-inch, gangly teen with the open face of a child and a most winning smile, which could only be caught when he did not think others were watching.

He also had dimples so deep that it seemed as if he was smiling when he talked.

About his family, Siaka provided only his father's name and last known address in Freetown. What puzzled Angela the most about the lad was how agitated he got every time she told him that no matter what he had been forced to do as a conscript soldier, nothing was his fault because he was a child. All he did was obey the adults who commanded him. Then one day, he rose angrily and hissed, "You stupid cunt. What if I really wanted to be a soldier? What if I really wanted to kill, rape, and chop off arms and legs?" His voice was as level as an assassin's aim.

Still, he looked surprised when, without moving from her seat, Angela calmly replied, "It still wouldn't be your fault. It was an unnatural situation, and you did what you needed to do to stay alive." She was pleased because she saw that he was conflicted between sitting back down and leaving the room. He then slowly exited. She watched him go, but felt that she had scored a major breakthrough.

That night was sheer misery for Siaka. It was not because of his recurring migraine—he had learnt to live with that. It was because, for the first time, he was invaded by dreams of Bobo. They were not dreams of the six-year-old baby brother whose round, dimpled face, so like his own, he had resolutely compelled himself to forget. He had so succeeded in forgetting what Bobo looked like that he had no problems peering into any mirror. That night, Siaka dreamed of Bobo's disembodied eyes and tiny rows of teeth that danced and chattered noisily, forcing the surviving boy to lash out at the unkillable poltergeists. Siaka awoke with a blinding headache, desperate to, for the first time, talk to somebody, anybody, about Bobo. He was suddenly sure that the burden of not confessing to his murder would kill him at last. Come morning, he raced to his weekly one-on-one session with Angela in her office, but found her looking flustered at the sight of him.

"I've been waiting for you. Please sit down." She gestured for him to sit in front of her instead of on the couch, his usual perch. "I'm afraid I have to give you some unpleasant news."

He noticed how she kept studying a nearly blank sheet of paper. "Yes?"

"We traced your father to one Anita Sankey. Do you …?"

"His younger sister." He was surprised that he remembered her. He had utterly forgotten she even existed. Anita did not get on very well with his mum and was living in Guinea when the war first erupted.

"Well, she told us your father died about two years ago." Angela stopped to observe the effect of the news, but his face was a mask. She inhaled deeply. "Normally, our procedure here is to try and reconcile boys with family members, but Mrs. Sankey, who seems to be your only surviving relative … em … she … is unable to take you in."

Angela noticed his shoulders drop, and he bit into his lower lip even before she started to explain that, though Anita was glad to hear that he survived the war, she could not take him in because her husband was worried about their own children. He believed that, as an ex-soldier, Siaka would be a handful. And there was no telling what would happen if their neighbours found out they were harbouring a former child soldier, i.e., a trained rapist, torturer, and mass murderer.

Angela gasped when she saw blood trickling down from the right side of Siaka's mouth. He had bitten deep into his lower lip to stop it from quivering. He sat silently facing her. She picked up a tissue paper from the box on her desk and was going to hand it to him when she changed her mind. Going over to his side of the desk, she hesitated, standing there beside him, feeling awkward in her strappy brown leather sandals. She was suddenly conscious of her ultra-white, ankle-length linen pants under a plain brown t-shirt that matched her hair. She willed herself to gesture for him to get up. To her surprise, he complied. She then stepped closer to him with her bare sun-browned arms stretched out to see if he would step toward her. When he did not, she moved even closer and seeing that he did not flinch, she broke all the rules of her training and wrapped her arms around him. She closed her eyes to stop the tears that had welled up as she felt him quivering from the sheer effort of trying to stop himself from crying. Though shocked by his animal-like sobs and howls, she held on tight. Gradually, he let himself go, weeping, mumbling incoherently—just a baby. Futilely, he tried to find words to unload himself of the things that had been done to him and the things that he had done to many others, most of all to Bobo. His heart burst open, but tears were his sole vocabulary.

Later, reflecting on that moment in her office, Angela was convinced it was pivotal. Not only professionally because it marked her finding rapport with a patient whose condition she'd thought was beyond her expertise, but personally too. Cradling the man-child in her arms, she was shocked to realize that she would rather die than leave him stranded in that camp in Freetown. Until that moment, she had no inkling that she was capable of the kind of emotion she felt from clasping him as he bawled: Maternal fulfilment and loving attachment.

"Don't worry, none of this is your fault. Your auntie's family don't know you like I do. Would you like to come and live with me if I can arrange it?" She found herself cooing and rocking him even after his mumbling stopped and his tearful sobbing began to subside.

In that instant, the words Siaka was struggling to find died inside him, and he nodded his consent vigorously. How could he even think of jeopardizing his chance of a home with this kind woman who was offering to take him on when no one else cared? How could he relate to her the god-awful secrets marring his heart, sullying his conscience?

After that day, the nightmares and migraines stopped for several weeks, and he was sure he had made the right decision by not dwelling on how Bobo died. Angela, so impressed by his progress, was spurred on in her pursuit to adopt and fly him to Canada. She noted his speedy progress in rehab, unlike some backsliding boys, and convinced the authorities that he was ready to live with her in "civilization."

After he settled into Bowmanville, a sedate suburb outside Toronto, with the saintly Angela, Siaka was too charmed by the comfort of his new life for his migraines and occasional nightmares to matter. That was until Angela's longstanding beau, Luigi, a hack of a writer, returned from a trip to Uganda, where he'd gone to research the kind of psychosis that led to Idi Amin's horrors. Returned, he deemed the trip life-changing.

At the welcome-back dinner Angela organized for Luigi at a local Italian restaurant, the scribe offered an elaborate explanation about how Africa changed his psyche—his very shallow soul. "It was all so sudden, a surreal 'aha!' moment. I was standing in the market in Kampala, surrounded by thousands who were bargaining over goods worth only pennies, when I suddenly realized that with the poverty and diseases—the least of which are AIDS and Ebola, believe you me; anyway, it occurred to me that everywhere I looked, for untold miles, I was better off than everybody else! And this is irrespective of my shitty life, my middling, unsuccessful career as a failed journalist-turned-writer ..." He paused for the laughter he rightly anticipated would result from his attempt to make a joke of his bleak failure. He paused, to let guffaws subside to titters. "None of it mattered. Not my snot-nosed boyhood as the son of working-class immigrants from Sicily, nor my two divorces. Not even the fact that I only have limited custody of my kids mattered. Compared to the distressing lives of the destitute millions out there, I was better off than everybody for miles and miles around, farther than the eyes could see!" He was as proud as a hunter standing atop a heap of elephant tusks.

While some guests laughed, others teased Luigi by asking if he planned to move to Africa permanently, perhaps to do missionary work.

Though he was not old enough to drink alcohol in Canada (even if he could stomach it), Siaka could not avoid seeing the picture of Africa that rose before his eyes as the joking Luigi spoke. The image of Africa that he saw that night was of a site where even second-rate White people go to make themselves feel better about their own shitty lot.

Later that night, after the laughter of the dinner guests had finally died and been buried in his memory, Siaka found himself unable to sleep because, for the first time in three years, he was almost paralyzed by a blinding migraine. He could also not stop thinking about what Luigi had said. Siaka was disturbed by its truth. Even at the best of times, his parents were hardly ever able to keep the family fed and clothed, despite both being university graduates. He tried to imagine David, his father, broken and jobless and hounded by his fear of being bewitched by his mother, who had become so wearied that she was a shadow of her former self. He could not think of either of his parents that night without flinching. As if their casually brutal deaths could be latently, lethally infectious.

He also remembered how one day, just before school closed for a Christmas holiday and months after David lost his job, he wandered into a street in the heart of Freetown, near the clock tower with some classmates. They stopped to observe several dour, tall Europeans distributing boxes filled with pencils, soap, notebooks, and bibles. He remembered how godlike the White people looked. Lying in his bedroom in Bowmanville, Ontario, recalling how much he envied the street urchins in Freetown who were fighting over the gifts—quite useless to anyone who was illiterate or homeless. He smiled, realizing that those treasures probably came from dollar stores. He forced his eyes shut and eventually drifted into blissful oblivion.

Canada – 2005

Siaka

Siaka's eyes slowly cracked open. He squinted, trying to avoid a beam of light that was bent on smacking his face through a small gap where the panels of curtains met in his window. He shut his eyes—to drowse, to snooze. Preferably a dreamless oblivion. "Have I even really been asleep at all?" he found himself asking aloud. He wrapped the duvet tighter around himself, wondering if it was the air conditioning that made his t-shirt cold against his sweat-drenched back. He felt a slight pounding in his chest as if his heart had been beating wildly moments earlier, and he was now catching his breath following a fast walk. He shifted, resting on his right-hand side as if to help his heart resume its normal rhythm. In his mind's eye, he saw the familiar shell of a face, glaring again through its jack-o-lantern eyes. Sometimes the face appeared to him when he was half asleep as he was now. It would then begin to fade, slowly, eluding Siaka as he tried to make out features that always remained obscure. Yet, Siaka never allowed himself the luxury of wondering whose face it was. He could not allow himself to care, and forcing his eyes open again, he banished the visage from his conscience.

Now, his eyes welcomed the shy morning sun which stole in through a small gap where the panels of curtains met in his window. During the still unfamiliar winter months, the curtains were adequate, blacking out any light. He often had to turn on the light even during the day when he needed to spend time in the room.

This morning, the angle he laid in bed situated the sun to cast its light right on his face. The rays lasered through his eyelids. He turned his head towards his pillow to bury his face therein. His mind became flooded by the recurrent dream which had startled him awake. To dissipate the anxiety triggered, he turned his face back up. He sat bolt upright and scrabbled his hands about to find his phone behind books piled on his bedside table. The phone was dead. It had lain uncharged behind the headboard.

He rose from the bed and stepped into a shadowy corridor to reach the living room of the three-bedroom townhouse. In the open-plan kitchen, he checked the time on the cooker behind the island.

He was surprised to see that the time was already five-thirty-seven AM. *That can't be right*, he thought. He wondered if, for some reason, the power had gone off during the rather windy night as it had done once during his first winter in Canada. He had to smile when, for the umpteenth time, he remembered that, in Ontario, power outages were rare. Through the silent house, he slippered to his room and plugged in his phone. The long, drawn-out nightmare that now plagued him repeatedly had elongated his night—if not his ability to sleep.

He reached out for a book he had left open on his bed but could not bring himself to resume reading. He just lay there and wait for his phone to charge sufficiently for him to turn it on so messages could distract from memories. A mild panic threatened to irritate his subconscious, but he shrugged it off as he always did.

An hour later, he returned to the kitchen, where he found Angela washing a coffee mug. She took one look at his face and, knowing him as well as she did, rushed to his side.

"What's the matter?" the now slightly plump five-foot-five-inch Angela asked. She had to stand on tip-toes to feel his forehead atop his now six-foot-four-inch frame, dwarfing hers. She could never stop being amazed by how tall he had grown since the flight to Canada. He was also so ruggedly good-looking that she was struck anew by this miracle of a man-child she could now call son since his adoption had been legalized. By this time, he was not only much taller, but all his scrawny angles had fleshed out nicely. His presence would astonish any room through which he'd deign to orbit. He talked slowly, thoughtfully—like Socrates shrugging off the fatal hemlock. Did he expect others—benighted—to complete his sentences so as to avail themselves of the enlightenment therein?

"I'm fine. I only have a headache," he said, somehow feeling a compulsion to dodge her scrutiny.

While he was pouring himself a glass of water, she left the kitchen and returned almost immediately with some tablets. "You should have taken these. Remember, Dr. Alao said they will ease your headaches and should help you sleep better."

"I'm fine. I can't go back to bed now."

"You should try and catch up on sleep. That's what the weekends are for." She smiled, urging him to take the meds.

He complied, gulping them down, then went back to bed. The tablets delivered a sleep both long and deep, but also trapped him in a nightmare. He was back in war-torn Sierra Leone. Unlike the way it really happened, he was not scared during those first few weeks of running and being chased away by villagers wherever he sought refuge. He was valiant and wanted to be a soldier—because a soldier had no baggage. Somehow, to start with, Bobo was absent when he found their mother's charred corpse. He was alone when he entered the village and found everyone massacred. He ran into a forest, where he then lived for days, waiting for he-knew-not-what at first. Then it dawned on him that he was waiting to be found by one of the warring parties. Why? Combat meant maiming and murdering "whomever," but it also burnished three infinitives: To feast, to loot, to orgy. During this solitary period, he was conscious of something in him changing, becoming congealed, and something else dying. Yet he was alive, could laugh and cry and function, but he now carried the corpse of the thing that had died in his heart. When he strained, he could even perceive the sickening smell of the thing as it began to rot. Then, suddenly, he was conscious of eyes all around him. They were all Bobo's vivid, livid eyes, surrounding, accusing.

Later, when he awoke in his comfy bed in Angela's house, though he no longer felt a headache, he remained troubled because he was convinced he could still smell the thing he had first smelled in his dream. An old, familiar, almost-forgotten stench.

He set about his day, determined not to care about the dead thing within. He only began to wonder if other people might smell it too. He had smelled it before after Bobo died, but stopped trying to figure out what it was days after Bobo died—when he decided that the other boys smelled, too. He convinced himself that it was because they did not have the luxury of bathing, since they had left their village after finding it massacred and sacked. However, soon enough, he realized the stink had nothing to do with their hygiene.

He became reconciled to the smell because the intensity of the odour of the thing inside him kept him preoccupied enough during the war. It helped him avoid worrying about how children would live once he had lopped their limbs. Or how the girls in the camp felt when—at the urging of the older boys and men—he and his comrades launched into raping them after they'd kidnapped them to be their cooks and caregivers.

Lying in bed that day, Siaka concluded that killing was the easiest part of the war. Then a question he had never before acknowledged crept into his head and made it home. Even if it was easy, how can killing serve a country? Intuitively, he knew that in order to live with the question in his head, he had to learn to live with the stench of the dead thing inside his chest. *To hell with whoever else could sniff out a whiff of the leaking reek!*

The smell remained with him all that day, which was why he was on edge when he made his way to Betsy's house. For about six months, Siaka had been dating Betsy, a blond, blue-eyed, Bible college, big-butt girl, who thought she'd remain a virgin by fucking with her eyes closed. Finally, she was inviting him to dinner at her parents' home that evening. He disliked Betsy's girlish expressions of affection. It was quaint at first, the way she would show him off to her friends. "This is Siaka, my boyfriend. I told you all about him, right?" She spoke of him as if he were an Olympic medallist or a Nobel Laureate.

The friends, of course, would start barraging him with questions: "What kind of weapon did you carry?"

One actually asked, if he remembered how many people he killed.

To the last, Siaka replied, "I'm sorry, but I was too preoccupied with killing to count."

Somehow, he managed to smile his way through that encounter. The four McMaster University students found his retort terrifically amusing.

As Betsy led Siaka to her parents' living room, she slipped her arm into the crook made by his arm because his hands were in his pocket. He felt awkward, having forgotten—in his haste not to be late—to stop and buy the box of chocolates he meant to bring for the hostess.

"Hey, everyone, this is Siaka!" Betsy announced with a flourish. He was surprised to find not just her parents present, but another couple, as well, though Betsy's sister was absent. Siaka felt a faint yellow light flash across his eyes, and he knew his migraine was vengefully back. He smiled, shaking hands with her father first, who introduced himself as Flint, then turned to introduce him to the other couple, their friends, Sue and Robert, just as a woman emerged from the dining room, holding up a clean glass.

"I'm Janice, Betsy's mum. What would you like to drink?" She pointed the glass at him.

He asked for a coke and could feel their questions buzzing in the air even before they started slapping his ears with the infernal interrogations.

"Betsy tells us you were in the war," Flint said.

"Gosh! You must have been so young," Sue said, crooning, looking him over to ascertain his age and puzzle out his sexual exploits.

"Tell them how old you were when you were conscripted." Betsy said.

"Yeah. How old were you?' Janice asked.

"I … well … I was about ten, almost eleven at the time." He flinched when he heard Sue gasp. She was imagining unrestrained rapine—all positions, "no holds barred."

"Poor child!" she said. "How awful it must have been for you."

"But, did you actually see any real combat?" Flint asked. Siaka had been told he was an American Gulf War veteran, which meant he'd survived roadside bombs by spraying bullets at anyone sporting a turban and sandals.

Siaka nodded, wondering when the questions would end. But there was no respite. Robert, who had been slouching only moments before, sat up now to scrutinize the poster-boy lab-rat.

"But did you actually kill anybody?" he asked, yearning for a "Yes."

Siaka nodded, turning to face Robert. Silence stuttered the hospitality.

"What I cannot get over is … how well you've adjusted considering the horrors you must have gone through," Janice, the conscientious hostess, blurted out to defuse tension; not at all superficial, but saturating the marrow and the heart and the lungs.

"Yeah! I saw a documentary on the war in Sierra Leone on CNN. It was a set of particularly disgusting atrocities. Why is Africa so bestial?" Sue asked, sounding childlike, wrapping her right arm—as if suddenly cold—around her left shoulder and across her breasts. Yet, due to her shivering twinges of thrills, Sue's nipples began to poke through her bra and her silk blouse.

"You are missing the point," Flint said, sitting up. He unclasped his hands which had been capping a knee, and started to explain as if he was lecturing cadets. "Why do you think the Colosseum was built?" A rhetorical question. "It's the greatest example of ancient Roman engineering. Now, imagine that colossal space with fifty thousand seats in the form of an amphitheatre so that twice as many people could enjoy the entertainment. And what was the entertainment? Well, Romans turned up in droves to watch gladiators, criminals, and savage beasts shred each other. The Colosseum was a monument to the Roman love of orgiastic gore. Brutality is part of human nature, and war is extermination. How can it be pleasant?" Flint stopped, stood, and sock-footed to the bar. Talk of war always made him thirsty for bourbon.

"But chopping off little girls' hands? Or the clitoridectomies voracious in Africa? That black hole of warlords, robbers, and rapists! What in God's name would make anyone want to do such brutal things? Quite frankly, I don't know how this young man managed to keep his sanity." Sue eyed Siaka. None missed her undercurrent of wanton accusation.

"War is war. No one expects it to be pleasant," Flint said, returning to the table with a generous glass of bourbon.

"Oh, but Siaka's not the same person who did all those horrible things!" Betsy piped up, her words an aria in a Salvation Army hymnal.

"It was me." Siaka heard himself intoning. "And anyone is capable of committing evils. Anyone. If forced or pushed, you'll do it, too. It has nothing to do with being African. At the time, I believed in what I was doing. I couldn't stop to ask ethical questions. I believed in the rhetoric of the moment. That I was doing good for our people. The country was poor, and citizens could hardly eat and go to school—even if there was no significant difference between the government and the RUF. There was no right or wrong … I did what I had to do … It was survival …" He paused when he realized he might not be sounding quite coherent. He was suddenly feeling too exhausted to figure out the correct phrases to describe what he experienced and why he played the part he did. So, he rose and headed for the hallway. He stopped just before reaching for his coat, then turned back and walked into the dining room, where everyone was still seated in silence. He stood facing them, and he tried again. "The one thing I'm sure of is that I'm as human as the next person—despite what I've gone through." He turned now to exit the premises. He did not stop even when he heard the voices trying to explain and apologize as everyone attempted to deny or reduce any hint of war crimes accusations. Then, he recognized Betsy's voice crying above the din, blaming everyone else for driving him away.

"Wait!" she shouted after him, reaching him just as he let himself into his car. "Siaka, I'm sorry, they—"

"It's not just them," he said, rubbing his temple. "I've seen you with your friends. You … you think like them, too … and in a way, I understand. You had to have been there for any of it to make sense to you. You had to …" What words could communicate the currency of sadism essential to an economy of terror?

Sitting there, on the serene, maple-tree-lined crescent in Richmond Hill, carpeted by yellow, red, and tan leaves signalling the onset of the dying season, Siaka was acutely aware that behind those secure doors of the houses about, families were engrossed, putting their children safely to bed. In that instant, his life at the war front seemed totally incongruous, even to him.

There had been many days since moving to Canada when he honestly doubted if any of it had happened. Yet, if it had not, then it would mean that his family, his brother, never existed. As tempting as that alternate reality was, he could not succeed in erasing his lineage, which would have made his life in Canada way easier. So, he pulled back the car and drove into the approaching night, not quite conscious of where he was heading. Trauma is never only a *traum*, the German word for "dream".

Liberia – 1992

Melvin

THAT NIGHT IN 1992 began like any in shot-up, bomb-cratered Monrovia.

To Melvin's nine-year-old mind, normal was seeing trucks packed with fatigue-uniformed or denim-and-leather-clad men wielding guns and sometimes firing into the air as their trucks roared past the window of his parents' semi-detached duplex. Normal was barricaded windows with planks allowing only peepholes. Bullets drilled some of the holes, but that was normal, too. The barricades stayed despite the fact that the peepholes let in little air, and without power to run the dusty ceiling fans, the house became so stifling in the afternoon heat that Melvin longed to play outside even if it meant risking a stray bullet strike. After all, his best friend, Francis, who used to live next door in the other half of the duplex, had been hit by a stray bullet out there, but was merely inconveniently crippled, not bagged and buried in a backyard. Now, Francis only went to school, several streets away, when he felt like it and when his older sister felt up to carrying him on her back all the way.

In the only Liberia that Melvin knew, normal meant being herded out of school at ten in the morning because fighting had broken out on a nearby street—fighting between combatants that belonged in kindergarten rather than on killing fields. Normal was picking his way through a street suddenly chaotic with people scattering helter-skelter, hithering-and-thithering to avoid stepping over the body of a man lying with his brain spilled out, parts of it still pulsating. Normal was trying to avoid sloshing into a slough of human blood, not because he was squeamish but because he knew there was no water at home to scour the stains from his shoes. Normal was being thankful that very same night when the streets became quiet again so that his parents felt safe enough to let him sleep in his bed, in his own room, all by himself, instead of the three of them huddling up in the dusty roof with the rats and bats and God-knows-what else (in spite of his father's chronic asthma). All of that was normal because he had seen it over and over again. It had all lost novelty and ability to shock him.

What was not normal was having rebels barge into the house not long after he fell asleep, ordering his father to hand over his car keys, or the hooligans shouting at his dad, now quivering like a leaf, begging them to "pass us by." It was not normal to see a teenage thug kick his father, and then command him to go and start the car. It was not normal to hear his father wheezing and weeping, trying to explain that the car was inoperable due to broken and missing parts. It was not normal to see a baby-faced boy pump his father so full of bullets his remains looked like Swiss cheese. What was also not normal was Melvin having to keep perfectly still inside the roof where his parents had herded him just before the rebels broke the front door.

And though he had been drilled over and over again to do just that since he'd come into consciousness as a human being, it was not normal to watch quietly—tearlessly—as three of the goons teased and raped his mother at gunpoint, even brushing her vagina with the snout. Then, when the soldier-brats were done, each one having taken his pleasure as the woman screamed and wept, the eldest slit her throat. "Just for the fun of it!" he said gleefully, bowing to the applause of his friends as their victim bled out. Even as a child in war-mangled Monrovia, Melvin knew that it was not normal that he should just stay where he was secreted, curled up into a hunch like a fetus, inhaling the smell of his parents' blood until it was light again.

When day broke, Melvin crept down from the roof. Stepping into the now dark-red flood of his mother's blood, he picked his way into the tiny corridor leading to the living room. To escape the house, he had to stretch his legs over a slumped rag, his dead father, also seeping a red tide. As he sloshed through the mess, he felt okay, because he figured that the sand of their now-dilapidated garden, once his mother's pride, would sop up, scour off the blood. It did not.

He was bent double, determinedly trying to clean his feet in the sand, when his father's younger sister, Florence, enfolded him from behind in an embrace. She lived on the other side of town, in an area that was considered safer than his. She lived with her husband Samuel's family but apparently, they, too, were not spared the carnage this time.

Observing her that morning, Melvin could not see the robust bride whose wedding picture had gotten blasted along with other family photos off the eastern wall of their living room by a too-close-for-comfort bomb, which exploded several streets away earlier that year. In the wedding portrait, Florence had stood smiling, her right arm entwined with her tall skinny groom's left. The moderately large families lined up in rows beside and behind the newlyweds in front of the elegant Providence Baptist Church where the country's declaration of independence had been signed. Melvin, a toddler then, was the ring bearer, but he had no memories of the event other than what that snapshot framed.

Not long after the wedding, and unfortunately for Florence, Samuel, her groom, who had no doubt about the justness of his side of the "rattling good civil war," left her pregnant to go and enlist. Ever the optimist, Samuel assured the hugely expecting Florence that the war would be over in a matter of days, maybe a few weeks. Three months later, he was dead. Florence lost the baby she was carrying the first time rebels raided her apartment. She then moved in with her grieving parents-in-law. They and Samuel's sister were killed the same night Melvin's parents died.

Later that day, Florence told Melvin that he was lucky because the rebels also captured Samuel's thirteen-year-old brother. Melvin agreed that he was indeed lucky because he knew Samuel's parents had persuaded their only surviving son to start cross-dressing when he turned nine to avoid just such a fate. They were sure that he would be spared being conscripted if he went around dressed like a girl. Their plan did not fool the soldiers who raided their home the night that Melvin's parents were killed. One of the soldiers had torn away the "girl's" underwear to effect rape and saw that "she" was a male. They then forced the boy to embrace the knife-hemmed duds of his chopped-up daddy before they frogmarched him away.

Now, Melvin broke away from Florence's embrace because he needed to pee badly. Within her warm arms, he had quite forgotten about his parents' massacre and almost rushed back into the house when her hand restrained him when she saw her brother's corpse by the front door.

"Is your mother inside?" she asked.

He knew that what she was really inquiring about was if she was alive. His head swivel said no.

"They killed her too," he spat, turning away from her to aim his penis at a dying hibiscus bush. As he pissed, he almost smiled. His mum would have smacked his bum playfully from behind, calling him a pig for peeing on the remnants of her precious red hibiscus. Only then did his tears gush. The memory of his mother's voice unlocked a flood so huge, he thought he'd die from releasing so much water from two ends of his body. Florence slumped on the sand next to him covering her face with her hands, her body heaved silently in helpless sorrow.

Soon, the last of the neighbourhood arrived to help bury the dead—to prevent an outbreak of diseases that decaying bodies unleash. Melvin and Florence watched them plant his parents, side by side in the vegetable garden. His parents' graves made Cecelia's look even tinier. His baby sister? A malarial fatality several months earlier.

Afterwards, Melvin found himself perturbed because he could not recall if prayers were said for the repose of his parents' souls or if—as their sole surviving child—he'd poured sand on their graves the way he had seen it done at all the make-do funerals he had witnessed. It was all he could think of for days afterwards during the trek, in a convoy of people who after that night swore that enough was enough, and were bent on caravanning across the Sierra Leonean border. Many Liberians deemed Sierra Leone—still deceptively quiescent—akin to "Canaan" and chose to make it their place of refuge.

Though he was plagued by the urge to ask his aunt if his parents were buried properly, he could not bring himself to trouble her. He was too grateful that she was not also dead. He overheard her tell another trekker that she and Melvin were probably the last of their lineage. If she had allowed herself to get shot or chopped up, he'd be solo on the tortuous journey, like some other children who were utter orphans. Even he knew that was really, really not normal.

Child that he was, he convinced himself that given how he wept for his parents that morning in Monrovia, it was impossible he'd ever again have cause to howl so much. He was wrong, of course. Four weeks to trudge to the border; three years to seek refugee status in God's own country and not once did he cry. It took another eleven years for his tears to finally gush and run out. And getting to America did not stop his tears from running dry. America forced him to, tap afresh, a bottomless pool of sorrows.

USA – 2000

Melvin

"NIGGER, GO HOME!" the shortest one of Melvin's assailants barked out. Melvin, who had been sauntering toward the bus stop near the school, told himself not to freak out. He knew the voice was that of a fat, bow-legged boy with thin curly brown hair.

"What you doing in this neighbourhood far from your jungle?" Another hooligan pushed his way forward, spat skank at Melvin. This thug had his right hand in his jacket pocket. A forehead scar told Melvin he'd almost bumped into the goon in a school corridor earlier. Trying to guess what the punk had secreted in his pocket, Melvin backed up two steps, and then the youth flashed a knife. Melvin sprinted off, convinced that the gang would not have flashed the blade if they'd had a flashier gun.

As he ran through an alley, he spotted a turning to his left a little bit ahead of him. He approached the corner, swearing, panting. He had been in this same nightmare situation often enough for his fear to dissipate. He was impatient for the ordeal to end. He slowed down to turn the corner after hearing the goons' footsteps approach. He wished he could stop and listen to ascertain if their number had shrunk enough to risk tackling them single-handed. *No*, he thought, *bad odds*. Turning the corner, his knees buckled when he realized he was at bay in a junkyard. He willed himself to run the hundred yards or so to the farthest end of the barbed enclave. Dropping to the ground, he sidled under a cannibalized car, and tried to muffle his loud breath. He could hear the gang in cursing pursuit, but he was now sure that they were fewer than the six or seven who'd first waylaid him.

Peeking from underneath the stripped-for-parts, grey Buick 6, Melvin counted his stalkers: Just four. Then, he brought out the gun he had bought just that afternoon. Costing the seventy five dollars he'd saved from his pizza delivery job, the weapon must now save his life. Luca, who sold it to Melvin, told him the gat was as easy to use as a water pistol. "Just aim and squeeze." Although Luca assured Melvin that the chamber held bullets, Melvin didn't think to check. He did not want Luca to know that he had never touched a gun, let alone used one. Now, bringing out the revolver, he regretted being so vain. *If I could only be sure I've bullets enough to put down all these animals hunting me.* He shimmied out from underneath the car and turned the gun around in his hand, trying to decide whether to try and run back the way he came because he could not spy any of the junior Klansmen. He began walking with his middle finger closed around the trigger when, suddenly, one of his stalkers pounced on him from behind. The boy grabbed hold of the back of Melvin's hood. Melvin tugged the trigger, and the early evening was pierced by a gunshot stabbing the air. A pimply, paleface lout pushed Melvin back, screamed, "Son of a bitch's got a gun!" As startled as was the pack of thugs by the banshee blast, Melvin assumed nevertheless a tactical, crouching position, but grinned ecstatically at seeing the speed at which his foes fled, scampering.

"Who's the dawg now?! I'm the dawg, man!" he said aloud, congratulating himself on his victory. Shifting his bulk into a sitting position, he felt he was safe, for now.

Years later, he could not resist wondering how different his life might have turned out if he had only chased his assailants that night. What would his life be like if he had not waited where he had, straining to hear if his attackers were regrouping? His sense of calming refuge was, he'd soon realise, a form of fateful self-deceit.

Finally assuring himself that all was okay, he stood. But just as he was shaking the dust off his pants, a police siren shrieked through the dusk. Quickly, he tossed aside the gun, and kicked it under the junked Buick 6. He then turned toward the barbed fence of the abandoned yard with the intention of climbing or crawling out when a new voice barked: "This is the police! Drop the gun! Drop to the ground with your arms stretched out in front of you where I can see them!"

Melvin knew the police would not have to "sweat" him for the gun because, from where he was lying in surrender, the tip of the middle finger on his left hand could almost touch the life-taking, life-saving firearm. He sighed, and his mind found itself wandering, of its own accord, back to his aunt Florence, wondering if she would be back home from her janitor's job in the engine assembly plant. Momentarily, he could not remember what shift she was working that day.

"I didn't do nothing!" he pleaded in his best American accent.

The two officers, guns unholstered and aimed at his head, raced up to him, kicked his downed body, hard, then dragged him to his feet.

Melvin groaned. "I was just walking by, minding my own business, when this gang jumped me. I didn't do nothing! They been after me ever since I moved here. I didn't do nothing!" he screeched, even though he really meant it to be an appeal.

One of the policemen bent down and, feeling about in the gloom, soon retrieved the gun. "Is this your gun?" The tone of the officer's voice made it clear that he already knew the answer.

Melvin tried to lie anyway. "Nah," he muttered, even though the fact that he was not wearing gloves hit him when he saw the officer slide the gun into a plastic bag.

"I got it from a friend … Know what I'm saying? It ain't really mine."

***

Melvin blinked at the radiance of the midday sun. He shielded his eyes with his right hand, trying to pick his aunt Florence's old Ford Escort out in the distance. He was shocked to see how right his cellmate Marty was when he described what the outside would look like on his release from the prison. "It doesn't matter what kind of day it is. The world always looks bigger and brighter. Even if it's a snowy day, the snow will look whiter than you can ever remember."

Melvin had smiled, wondering why Marty did not try harder to stay out of jail since he seemed to have such fond memories of the outside. However, he did not risk saying such "sissy" thoughts aloud.

Melvin could not have asked for a better cellmate. Not only had Marty protected him, but he was also lucky Marty was not a "bullerman." Instead, Marty was kind enough to give the impression that Melvin was his bitch. In return for this preservation of his anus, Melvin was glad to play the "submissy" in every way except in bed.

When Melvin picked out Florence's figure, he could not believe how much she'd aged in eleven months. The drive from Detroit to Saginaw Correctional Facility was too long for her to risk visiting often in her rickety flivver. Besides, she toiled for too many hours—sweeping and mopping—at the motor factory, so could not manage to visit him more than twice. And her pay was too paltry to allow her to aspire to own one of the new cars that the plant helped to produce.

He felt guilty because he had not noticed how fast she was aging—no, the right word was "deteriorating."

He fast-stepped toward her to save her the trouble of walking his way. She hugged him, wrapping her scarf around him as if a shield. He shuddered, then giggled awkwardly at the memory of another embrace, so similar to this one, the morning after his parents were slain.

Cruelly for Melvin, Michigan was one of those states where prosecutors could bump juvenile cases into adult courts—especially if the accused youth was black. In February of the year following Melvin's arrest, he was sentenced as an adult. The gun he had bought to protect himself had been used in a robbery, and although he could not be linked to the crime, he was tried as an adult. He received what the judge explained was a "blended sentence," which would combine adult-level incarceration with juvenile rehabilitation. In other words, a "delinquent" would be thrown to the tender mercies of the lifers.

***

The euphoria of finally getting to America with his aunt, as refugees, was, for Melvin, as ephemeral as snow in the Sahara. His accent helped to swiftly erode his elation, for it marked him out as a foreigner immediately. When they first tried to settle down in Charlottesville, Virginia, he tried to fit in, but had no success. He was walking home one day when he was stopped at a pedestrian crossing by a traffic light. An oldster with platinum white hair under a red-and-blue face cap driving past in a truck, pulled up, slid down his window, then hissed, "Nigger, go home!"

After the man vroomed away, Melvin was too shocked to be upset by the stranger's hateful, threatening words. He peered about, trying to see if other pedestrians could tell that he was a foreigner. He was perplexed by how they could tell since he did not open his mouth and did not look any different from other African-Americans. Naively, he assumed that the man who cussed at him had somehow detected that he was not an African-American.

Melvin, who thought he knew all about slavery, had never heard of racism—despite being an Americo-Liberian—before coming to America. He speculated that it was his mother's Mandingo blood in his veins that diluted his American-ness. It had to be what made him exotic and unacceptable. He knew his father's family did not believe in mixing with native Liberians, whom they considered bush and uncivilized. Even as a child, he was starkly aware that there had been some unpleasantness when his father, a purebred Americo-Liberian, wed his mother. Still, a truce had soon been reached when the members of his father's family were won over by his mother's eagerness to be assimilated into the Oliver-Turner family.

Several months after the incident with the trucker who called him "Nigger," Melvin witnessed an African-American schoolmate being cussed by another paleface driver. Then, he knew that all blacks were targets for profanity and bile.

It took his aunt Florence much longer to come to terms with their "strangeness" in America. For months after they first arrived as refugees, she felt dazed. She was flabbergasted because people could not understand her Liberian English. She was confounded because her parents, who were proud Americo-Liberians like everyone else in their circle, took immense pride in their Kreyol and their Yankee heritage. Although she had never met any African-Americans before landing in the US, she had expected that her American background would gain her easy acceptance amongst "her people."

At first, Florence blamed herself for disregarding her genealogy. All she knew about her ancestry was that her people came from Virginia. Family lore even claimed kinship with Nat Turner, and fancied a link to other famous Turners, such as Ike and Tina.

Florence and Melvin moved after spending two years in Virginia, where no job paid a living wage and they remained utterly isolated despite Florence's efforts to explain her ancestry to anyone she could get to listen. They moved to Detroit, Michigan, where she finally found janitorial work in a dying Rust Belt factory.

In Detroit, Melvin's life remained complicated by the teasing he received from peers in the inner-city school. It bruised his spirit. It did not make a difference whether he was targeted by African-Americans, Chicano-Americans, Caucasian-Americans, Latino-Americans, Arab-Americans, or Asian-Americans. Teasing was teasing, and though he expected it since he was a new boy, he loathed equally all of his multicultural aggressors.

USA – 2005

Melvin

Melvin's tears finally ran out on a surprisingly light and airy spring day. It was several years after his prison release. He was standing in line at the Office of Immigration and Assay, awaiting his turn to face an officer. Carmen, three months pregnant, wrapped her left arm around his waist as if to chain him to her. She was more annoyed than fearful, and it was her rage as she clung to him, looking just about ready to slug anyone who dared to separate them, which unleashed the gut-wrenching, soul-draining surge of tears for the final time in Melvin's life. Once his tears dried, gone also was his anger. He was too anxious to plead, beg, or crawl—if necessary—just to be spared deportation from America for a crime he committed when he was not quite fifteen, and for which he had already paid his debt to society.

Lying together in bed earlier that morning, trying not to think about how it might be their last time together, Carmen expended her own tears. She blamed herself for talking him into applying for status to remain in America so that she could get permanent residency through him. Like him, she had been brought to live in the US as a minor, but her Mexican parents were economic refugees, unlike his Aunt Florence. It was because Melvin tried to apply for American citizenship that the Office of the Assay latched on to his criminal case so many years after the fact. Neither Melvin nor Carmen even knew that such a law existed that had developed more teeth since 9/11. The Illegal Immigration Reform and Immigrant Responsibility Act (IIRIRA) of 1996, was passed by a Republican Congress and signed into law, without a word of protest, by a democrat, President Bill Clinton, who was preoccupied with his dangerous liaison with—"that woman"—Monica Lewinsky. IIRIRA stripped immigrants who were convicted of crimes and had served their time of their right to argue their case in front of a judge before being deported. To make matters more draconian, the American Congress chose to exponentially expand the range of crimes that made convict immigrants eligible for deportation. Legal immigrants, including green card holders, could also be deported if convicted of a broad range of offences. The crimes did not need to be violent, and these measures could be applied retroactively. Any illegal immigrant who was apprehended within one hundred miles of the border also fell under the IIRIRA. IIRIRA required the government to jail immigrants before deporting them "by any means necessary." Naturally, this clause made it substantially harder for them to retain lawyers.

The law also allowed little leeway for a successful appeal. None cared that Melvin had tried to stay clean after serving time for pulling a gun, as a teen, on "nigger-bashers." He was still ordered to return to Liberia, which was now deemed "safe" because massacres were fewer. Quite apart from the thought of leaving Carmen and their unborn child behind, Melvin was terrified by the idea of being sent back to the place he had left as a child. Whatever fond pre-war memories he might have gathered during his life there died with his escape from the horror that had propelled his departure. That he knew no living relatives there did not matter. His aunt, who might have identified some remote extended family, died from cancer the year after his prison release. She had unwittingly nurtured the disease in her breast, probably due to the use of carcinogenic cleansers for so many years. Florence's death complicated Melvin's life in many ways. He never even tried to find his way through the maze of getting proper resident status until he met and fell in love with Carmen, who happened to be an illegal immigrant from Mexico.

PART TWO: MIGRATION:
JOURNEY TO A PLACE WHERE DREAMS GO TO DIE?

Jamaica – 1990

Iona

IONA FELT INSTANT terror when she turned the corner of their street and saw the crowd before the tiny bungalow that she shared with Selina, her grandmother. By the time she ran downhill and into the house, she realized that Selina had been body-bagged and removed.

Mrs. Jenkins, their neighbour across the street, worked with Selina at the factory in the Kingston Free Zone sewing jeans. For reasons most of the proles could not fathom, they were made to sew made-in-China labels on the denim. Mrs. Jenkins had not felt well that day and came home early. She thought to check in on Selina because she had noticed her absence from work. Soon, she raised the alarm about her deceased neighbour and co-worker. Her cries brought nearby residents and passers-by scurrying to see what was amiss.

When Iona entered the house after school that afternoon, she heard Mrs. James, their neighbour to the right, whispering in sympathy: "Poor chile, she must've failed to notice that Selina passed in the night before she leave for school."

Iona slipped into the chair by the bedroom door. She was too angry to bother to tell them about how she woke up that morning, sensing that the bedroom she shared with her granny was colder than usual. Reaching her hand across the queen-sized bed to tap her granny, who was lying uncharacteristically face up, Iona was struck by how cold her arm felt. She shook her a few times, but when she did not get a response, she convinced herself that her granny was merely enjoying an uncharacteristically deep sleep. She got up, took her bath, fixed herself a sandwich for lunch, and joined the other neighbourhood pickneys to walk the quarter-hour uphill to school. She convinced herself that her granny would be up and about when she got back from school, because she did not believe her grandmother would die and leave her stranded—abandoned—dependent on the mercies of strangers.

Sitting by the door, watching neighbours fix up the small bungalow for the wake, Iona was more angry than sad. She was mad at Mrs. Jenkins for finding her granny dead. Iona sat sullenly, cupping the side of her face in her right hand. She was convinced that, if only Mrs. Jenkins and the other meddling neighbours had left things alone, she would have returned home to find her granny either gone to work, having awoken from her fantastic, likely rewarding sleep, or pottering about in the kitchen, frying up a meal. Now she was really dead. Because busybodies interfered: ganging up on, nagging, a body!

When Mrs. James walked toward her to pat her shoulder and offer to take her home to live with her and her own grandchildren till Iona's mother returned from Canada, Iona yelled. She was kicking and screaming and cursing them all for ruining everything. The neighbours put her outburst down to her mind-addling grief. So, this once, she was not scolded or smacked upside the head for being too high-spirited or talking foolishness to grown-ups.

After the funeral, Myrna, her mother, patriated Iona to Toronto, where she had recently returned from Nova Scotia. Once their plane landed in Toronto that winter night in 1992, Iona knew that the beautifully dolled-up Myrna was anything but what she imagined a mother would be. The realization was not insight, just recognition. Until her granny passed, she had no need to even remember her mother. Though she could i.d. Myrna in the snapshots that sometimes accompanied the small remittance for her upkeep, she also knew that the photos and money stopped coming after the barrel from "farin" for her eighth birthday arrived. Thus, Selina had had to go and slave in the Kingston Export Processing Zone.

***

As if life was not tough enough for the gawky, eleven-year-old Iona trying to settle into a new school in a new country, her small-boned, startlingly beautiful mother also turned out to be an oddball who preferred gestures to speech. Iona first noticed this when they stood in front of one of the shops at the airport in Kingston. Iona was looking through a glass wall at pictures in a magazine when she turned toward Myrna to find her pointing a can of orange juice in her direction. Wondering how long she had been pointing the drink at her, Iona took it and did not say thank you. It did not matter. Unlike other Jamaican adults who would have boxed Iona's ears for being so sassy, the mannequin-like Myrna just turned and sauntered off to plunk down coins at the cashier.

When Iona was a baby, Clyde Pearse, her father, decided to go off and find himself. He made the decision not long after attending a talk given by a prominent member of the Black United Front (BUF), Mounty James, at the North End Public Library in Halifax. Mounty James and his wife, Connie, were civil rights activists affiliated with the Yankee-bred Black Panthers. The talk was organized to drum up opposition to city plans to build a huge public housing project around Maynard and Creighton Streets in the North End of Halifax that would "relocate" Black Haligonians from downtown homes to suburban rentals.

"It only takes one small action, a commitment on your part, no matter how little, to get our community going. Those small personal commitments build into an ocean of opposition that will stop White people trying to push us out. It will compel them to acknowledge us because we're here to stay, whether or not they like it! We've invested two hundred years in this land. We didn't ask to come here, but we're here now, and we're staying!" Mounty bellowed into the microphone.

Clyde stood amid the clot of souls, listening to Mounty, who at that moment loomed larger than any mortal his eyes had ever beheld. He also noticed Connie, Mounty's wife, who sported a beautifully sculpted afro, standing next to him, handing him notes from others on the high table. Clyde found himself energized to a height he never imagined possible. There and then, he decided to join the Black United Front (BUF) and dedicate the rest of his life to the Black Power Movement. Later in life, Clyde would refer to that talk as a cardinal moment: "Lightning in my eyes, thunder in my ears."

When he returned "up home" to North Preston from Toronto, when it had become increasingly difficult to make ends meet, he moved back to the house his family had occupied for four generations. He now shared it with his wife Myrna, their newborn baby Iona, his cousin Ned, Ned's wife Yvonne, and their brood.

When Clyde got home that night after Mounty's sermonic rap, he found Myrna laying out her clothes for her next day of work as a maid for some White families in Halifax's ritzy South End. She had made dinner and set it out the moment he stepped into the kitchen.

For once, Clyde was not feeling shrivelled-up because he could not find a job. When Myrna looked up at him from her ironing and nodded in acknowledgement of his greeting, then raised her eyebrows, which he knew was her way of asking if he found any odd job that day, he just sat to his supper. He'd decided on the bus ride home across the bridge from Halifax that Myrna was over-committed to the drudgery of her employ. One of the things that had attracted him to her—when they first met at their Toronto furniture factory jobs—was her resemblance to Florence Ballard of the Supremes. He now wished that she looked more like Connie, Mounty's wife.

Later that night, when they were in bed, he tried to explain his newly found passion to her but struggled to find words to recapture his mood at the meeting and his decision to work for the Black Power Movement. He wanted to convince her to join him in his new vocation. She turned away from him, facing the darkened wall.

"Clyde, that is not a luxury either of us can afford, you know?" she said, still facing the slate-dark, slate-blank wall.

"Why not?" he asked, exasperated, while struggling unsuccessfully to turn her cold shoulder toward his warm heart. "Why you need me to explain it to you? 'Cause we have a child?"

He let go of her stiff shoulders and lay back, staring at the flaking white paint of the ceiling. Not white in the gloom, but dingy.

"I need you to stay home and take care of Iona tomorrow 'cos when I'm done cleaning Mrs. Gordon's house, she want me to come in and clean the fur shop in Spring Garden. It's another two hours of pay. It will also give me time to run over to QE II Hospital to see if them are now hiring new auxiliary nurses. Tracy check the files for me, and them still have my application on the pending list." Her words were whisper-soft. Yet, that night, her Jamaican accent—that he usually admiringly said was a no-nonsense way of speaking English—irked him madly.

"I hear the police are hiring more Black men. So, I think you should go down to the station the day after tomorrow and …"

He tuned her voice out, shutting his eyes. He hated her for being so grateful for her menial jobs and for now trying to get him to go and "tom" for the police. The cops had only recently condescended to hire Black men—but only for leading the ass-whuppings of any Black (male) civilians who fell into their clutches.

A few months later, he was damnably disillusioned when he discovered that Mounty and Connie had separated. Mounty was now shagging a White lawyer who backed—on her back—the Black Power Movement. Clyde quit the cadres instantly. He blamed himself for not recognizing Mounty's professional, polished outrage for what it was: Staged blackness that turned mellow-yellow as soon as he downed an offstage beer. He spurned Mounty for "talking black, but sleeping white." Anyway, Mounty was too much of a moderate compared to his newly discovered hero, Malcolm X; compared even to Martin Luther King Jr, whom Clyde considered too temperate. Most distressing? Mounty did not stand a chance of being assassinated, i.e. martyred. He was too inauthentic a radical. More a "tomcat" than a Panther. A lacklustre Black lackey.

One day after collecting his wages at the Halifax Container Terminal, Clyde snuck aboard a ship and stowed away on a ship bound for West Africa. The next time Myrna heard from him, he was in Accra. He wrote her a letter, deeply apologetic and promising to send money for Iona's upkeep. It was a promise he could not attempt to fulfill for a long time because it was a lot harder to find a job in Accra than he had anticipated. Being Black was simply not enough. Being Black had no cachet where everyone was Black!

After Clyde left, Myrna moved back to Toronto, but she sent the baby Iona home to her mum with one of her cousins flying to Jamaica for Christmas. To her consternation, after she sent the baby, she found she had lost confidence in her creed that, if only she worked hard, she would be alright. It was her natal philosophy, and it was why she'd left Jamaica in the first place. When she told her friend about her doubts, Bernice—who had arrived in Canada a few years before her, and worked extremely hard and sent money and barrels regularly and diligently to care for her three children—tried to console her. Bernice's life centred on her job and shopping for stuff to send home. Bernice's barrels overflowed with food items that were rare or scarce on the island or with clothing and shoes much cheaper to obtain in Toronto than in Jamaica.

"You don't know how my children look forward to their barrels from farin." Bernice seemed to derive so much joy from the remittances that she sent home. At first, Myrna was too embarrassed by how she felt. Still, Bernice noticed and consoled her by telling her that she was only missing Iona and upset about that good-for-nothing Clyde. "I almost died from missing my children when I first got here." She wrapped her arms around Myrna to comfort her. "But I promise you, your spirit will rise again. Is only a matter of time."

Soon after, to distract her, Bernice persuaded her, one night, to accompany her to a nightclub. Perhaps it was the strobe lights, or maybe it was the music. It might have been the gin and tonic that Bernice persuaded her to drink to loosen her up. But that night, Myrna discovered what it felt like to simply let go. Not just let loose, but truly let go. She let go of her worries about getting to work on time the following morning because that nightclub was where she wanted to be. When she danced, she could feel the eyes of strange men x-raying her to her "chocolate bones." But she didn't care what bonbons they imagined her flowery, mauve dress might wrap. Bernice, who went up with her to her room to help her select her outing items, had nixed Myrna's first choice. "No, girl, it's too churchy." She went to the rack in the tiny shop off Spadina and picked the sheer, flared, polyester, mauve, sunray dress, which was cut at the waist. When Myrna twirled around and felt the dress rise above her knees at the club, she smiled. She did not even try as she would typically to hold down the front of the dress. She felt mellow enough to allow herself to be whatever the men gawking at her wished her to be.

After her first dance, she never had to pay for booze or smokes at any club again. Men kept offering to replenish her "vices." Myrna went back the next day, alone, but left holding the arm of a moustached man with a "stash of cash." Quickly, she discovered it was much easier to make a buck on her back in a comfortable bed than on her knees, scrubbing and scraping the floors of White ladies' kitchens.

***

After her grandmother's funeral and Myrna's repatriation of Iona, they lived with three different men, which meant Iona had to keep changing schools. By the time she was thirteen, Iona was quite discombobulated about life. Changing schools each time her mother broke up with a man further marginalized her since she was forever a newcomer.

First, being only one of a handful of Black kids in her school, she found herself inhabiting—for the first time—the unenviable position of "minority." Greg, the man they were living with when she turned thirteen, in addition to beating Myrna regularly, also took to spying on Iona in the bathroom and leering at her everywhere else. When Iona first noticed this, she thought of telling Myrna. However, upon going to the bedroom that Myrna shared with Greg, Iona found her lying face up, snoring lightly. There was a half-smoked reefer still burning between her fingers. Iona extinguished the joint, but realized that she would need to stop Greg's peeping herself. She started waiting till Greg was asleep before using the washroom. When she could not hold it long enough for him to go to bed, she stuffed toilet paper in the keyhole.

The first time she did so, she heard Greg cuss sotto voce. Her measure of pleasure? Immense! Yet, one day, she was so pressed that she forgot to plug the keyhole. On sensing Greg leering-peering, she quickly terminated her business. While washing her hands, with her back to the door, the idea was born. Incensed by his lechery, she spilled a dose of liquid hand soap into the toothbrush cup and added scorching-hot water. In one quick unbroken movement, she turned, opened the door and volleyed the mix into the perp's astonished face. She smiled when she saw his pink flesh turn red from the scalding water. His filthy, hippy-style, greasy, long, brown hair now matted to the sides of his head. She spotted his zipper was undone and his embarrassed manhood falling droopingly flaccid. She ran for the front door and knew better than to return that day. She spent the next two days on the streets of Scarborough before the police picked her up. When they traced her mum, they found Myrna stoned out of her mind, so Iona was consigned to foster care.

Just three months after Iona was taken from her, Myrna—now miserably suicidal—died by chugging opioids, booze, and sleeping pills. Iona spent the next seventeen months being passed from one foster home to another, until her father returned to claim her after finding what he assumed was his "lost self." Some of the foster parents she lived with were better than others, but she learned never to trust adults again. They either died on you or were too preoccupied with their own sorry lives to give a rat's ass about you.

***

After stowing away, Clyde had finally got a job teaching English in an elementary school in Koforidua, Ghana. But by then, he had lost contact with Myrna. He left for Lagos, Nigeria, when he heard that opportunities abounded because the oil boom was greasing every outstretched palm. His initial intention was to teach. He enrolled in the University of Lagos after meeting Nkosi, a former South African freedom fighter, who said the Nigerian government had given him a scholarship to study at the University of Ibadan, because he was a political exile.

Clyde managed to enrol in the university, although he could not get a scholarship because he could not justify that he, too, was a political exile, even though he believed himself to be one. The officer at the Federal Ministry of Education in Lagos did not even consider his claim that the blueprints for apartheid had been exported from Canada to South Africa after they had been perfected via the oppression of Indigenous Canadians. While trying unsuccessfully to stifle his boorish yawn, the official shook his head, unconvinced by Clyde's well-rehearsed argument. "Brother, what is apartheid if not the kind of discrimination that has kept Black people economically confined to servitude, and physically imprisoned within specific neighbourhoods of places like Nova Scotia for hundreds of years?" The bureaucrat politely told Clyde that he had other people that he had to see.

What Clyde found most disconcerting was the way the other students at the university perceived him as a foreigner and shunned his presence. He deemed this rude rejection a manifestation of shameless xenophobia. He couldn't comprehend how Nigerians, who had hosted Festac 77—a festival that celebrated the artistic and cultural richness of Africa and its diaspora, and was meant to revive global African identity and political renaissance—could still harbor such prejudice against him. He also realized, to his eternal consternation, that he was about a decade too late to enjoy the benefits of Nigeria's oil boom. He could never fathom how the nation could have been so careless as to let the oil boom become the "oil doom"—the Nigerian neologism.

Luckily, he ran into an illiterate businessman, Alhaji Danbaba, on Broad Street in the heart of Lagos Island. Danbaba was so fascinated by Clyde's command of the English language that he made the expat his personal assistant. Clyde needed no persuading to quit university and move to Kano, where Danbaba had his head office.

In Kano, for the second time in his life, Clyde fell in love with the earth. The first time was when he snuck from the ship on which he had stowed away once it docked in Tema, Ghana. He was so shocked by his emotions upon stepping onto the soil of Africa that first time that he was driven to kneel and place the flats of his two palms on the ground. It was a sweltering dry January afternoon, but the earth felt coquettishly warm and welcoming to his hands as he caressed the soil.

A few weeks after arriving in Ghana, Clyde made his way to Elmina. In Elmina, he was stunned by the contrast in the feelings stirred in him. Elmina pressured him, demanding way too much from him. It pulled him to advance toward a direction that threatened to befuddle his project of finding his true identity. Elmina admonished him to ruminate about how the rain came to beat him, thudding and pelting so mercilessly. Elmina made him angry at the tourists from diverse parts of the diaspora, who stood at the mouth of the door of no-return, overwrought and weeping, but still refusing to know themselves as Africans. Most of all, Elmina set him raging at the tour guide, who reeled off the history of a crime against humanity with a most sordid light-heartedness and disgusting enthusiasm, reflecting his craven eagerness for tips, taking pains to mollify any palefaces who might feel shame or guilt. The guide was despicably hungry to earn his bread, by dipping it in the mash of slain and enslaved Africans' blood and flesh and bones.

But in spite of his experience in Elmina, Clyde fell easily in love with the ancient city of Kano. Though the formerly walled city was missing some of its charms, Clyde was sufficiently impressed by the relics of the gates of the Old City, the Emir's palace and the mosques—old and new. Kurmi was the largest market he ever laid eyes on, and the smell of the old dye pits, many still in use, intoxicated him. He spent days scouring the Old City, Bompai,

Fagge, the Syrian Quarters, and Nasarawa. Sabon Gari was his least favourite part of Kano because, to him, it somehow lacked authenticity. Too touristy, too airbrushed, too bleached.

Initially, Clyde's primary duty working for Danbaba was to correspond with Swiss suppliers of watches. What Danbaba did not know was that Clyde could neither speak nor write French, German, or any of the other languages au courant in Switzerland. Danbaba's company also imported other luxurious items as well as second-hand electronics from various European and US sources. However, barely weeks after he moved to Kano, Clyde persuaded Danbaba that his company would profit handsomely by importing excellent but cheap wrist watches from Taiwan. Luckily, Danbaba heeded his advice, and they struck gold when their first shipment of "brand-name" watches from Taiwan arrived. They cost a fraction of what he usually paid the Swiss for remarkably identical watches. To reward Clyde, Danbaba promoted him to the position of General Manager. However, first, Danbaba explained that Clyde had to perform the Hajj by going on pilgrimage to Mecca. "A big company like ours must not boast a GM who is as ordinary a 'Mr.' as is any infidel."

This condition was no big deal for Clyde, who was already flirting with Islam, Kano's predominant religion. Besides, it seemed a viable alternative to Christianity, the buttress of colonialism and the cornerstone of the Caucasian conspiracy to rule the globe. But Clyde knew nought of the trans-Saharan slave trade, which had transported Africans to enrich Arab traders. Nor that it was the blueprint for the odious transatlantic enterprise, which had shipped his pirated ancestors to the Americas, to line the pockets of European slavers and colonizers.

***

Now a man who had read all he could find written by and about Nkrumah, Lumumba, Mandela, Du Bois, Luther King Jr, Malcolm X had returned to Canada after twelve years. It was, however, not Clyde Pearse who returned but El Haj Malik. He had shed his "slave name" along with his "slave self." Mellifluously eloquent in the many echoes from all the books he read, muting the Indigenous Black Baptist voice deep within, "Malik" landed back in Halifax, Nova Scotia. Nonetheless, like the Bible on which Clyde was nursed, the Koran and Hadith also eluded him, even as he tried to cling to his new religion.

In his search for himself, he forgot to look inside himself for the self that saw him through the deadly winters in Digby, Saint John, the Prestons, Shelburne, Birchtown, Beechville, Hammond's Plains. The resilient self that saw him through the first burning of Africville, which not only survived but rose again like the proverbial king's palace. Which, when torched, not only recovers its original glory, but shimmers with even greater opulence. Clyde did not seek the hardy spirit that enabled him to turn ghettos into some of the most desirable parcels of land in the Maritimes. So much so that Africville became so coveted, it was eventually sacked. Still, its felling had not occurred without a fight. That same spirit of self reignites every July at Seaview Park. Unmindful of the presence of dog walkers, Africville's unbreakable spirit wrests possession, if only for a few hours. It is a spirit that knows that the value of that land lies in its beauty. A beauty impregnated and made rich by the umbilical cords and afterbirths of so many generations who gardened, fished, and orcharded there. Clyde forgot to spelunker deep within all of that self, which, though wounded time and time again, was indomitable, omnipotent.

That self that learned to take the pain and bunch it up, then hurl it back in the robust laughter of folks "up home." That pain that was smelted down into unfettered tears so many times, but at other times had been refined from within and set free in the form of the matchless, unstoppable contralto of the likes of Portia White. And sometimes, even now, that self appears in the stories bellowed in belligerent, raucous voices that descend as whispers into the ears of newborns. It is the self that has kept all those home places alive in spite of and not because of …

Clyde failed to grasp that his missing self did not reside in a tangible place. He forgot that no matter how heavy a bird's meal is, so long as it is a bird with the natural ability to fly, it cannot be anchored to the earth, cannot be grounded. The bird will fly no matter how heavy the content of its stomach. Clyde forgot to look deep within himself, and thus mostly wasted was his African odyssey, becoming as hazy in meaning as an out-of-focus photo.

Unlike the ram, which only backs up to consolidate his strength, Clyde had thus hastened to return to Africa. A continent which had been reconstituted by his ancestral self's significant departure, his significant absence. Clyde failed to acknowledge the impact of the fissure occasioned by his ancestral self's significant departure, his significant absence. Just as he undermined the extent of his fusion to Canada, the "Canaan" to which his ancestral self had been brought, and how much his spirit had reconstituted the Great White North. Clyde, the alagemo's spawn, has forgotten that he is a chameleon. Simply by being born, by coming into being, he is alagemo. He is not a chameleon-in-waiting, waiting to be taught how to dance. He is the spiritual heir to Olduvai-Gorge Lucy, Mitochondrial Eve, the Sphinx, and the creators of human consciousness.

He left Kano after Danbaba died in a car accident. After Danbaba's death, his thirty two children by his four warring wives and seven mistresses could not agree on what to do with his firm. Clyde—no, Malik—flew again to Canada, but he did not return single. El Haj Malik returned with a new wife: Beautiful, delicate Naima. She of the cultured, knowing, but averted gaze. Demurely, she had surrendered to Clyde her own name, "Margaret," as well. She was not even sure how she'd come by the name. Her grandmothers—Scottish on her mother's side and Maroon on her father's side—were both named Margaret. She was never able to ascertain from her elusive mother for which of her grandmothers she was really named—or if she had, indeed, been named for either or both. In yielding her "slave name," Naima felt that she honoured Malik by allowing him to rename and brand her in his own image.

It was not a major sacrifice on her part, for she knew from the very first day that Malik stepped into her classroom in Kano, where she worked as a Peace Corp teacher from America, that she would anchor her life to his if he would have her. He had come on a mission to ask permission for one of Danbaba's sons to be excused from school. The moment she cast eyes on his brawny, babanriga-clad, six-foot-three-inch frame, she knew she loved him more than she had ever loved any other human being. Her love might not have been willing to lay itself on the ground and die for him, but it was almost as strong. Her love was partly pure passion and part-atonement for her mother and all her mother's ancestors, in the hope that it would assuage the generations of degradation that his spirit had suffered at their hands. Neither Malik nor Naima had the capacity to challenge the incongruity of an attempt by one person—on behalf of so many countless generations of their own DNA—to remedy the wounds inflicted on others of the same generations. Blood for blood? Agbedo! But the fatuousness of this abominable notion was as confounding for them as was the Tar Baby for Br'er Rabbit.

The first time Malik made love to Naima, as he entered her, he found himself conflicted between the worship of her almost-ivory-white inner thighs and loathing of the strength of the muscles of those thighs, which enveloped and engulfed his manhood both in welcome and capture. His thrusts were irregular. Sometimes the thrusts probed. Sometimes they caressed. At other times they attacked. Occasionally, they were attempts at retreat. And when he sighed at the moment of orgasm, it was a combination of surrender and self-loathing, so his cry of ecstasy erupted from his throat in the form of a growl.

Naima noted the guttural sound but chose to read it as the pain that a man, fearful he is being strangled, might emit. She, therefore, pledged her own desire to keep him safe from that edge of misery. As she, too, climaxed, she shut her eyes. But the delicious, indelicate spasm also confirmed horribly a suspicion her adolescence had cradled: She was exotic to both White and Black men.

***

"No, Naima, I don't want to tell you why I pushed the fucking guy." Iona's voice was calm.

Naima could feel herself going tense with seething just beneath the veneer of her skin-deep calm. She pressed on softly in her most maternal voice. She used the same tone to calm Ahmed, her toddler, whenever he staged a tantrum. "Look, Iona, if your teacher even looked at you in an inappropriate manner, it might be enough reason to insist that he provoked you. It might get the school to reconsider suspending you."

Iona reached beyond Naima to open the fridge, brought out a milk carton, and ignored the mug that Naima quickly pushed across the work island. She drank straight from the carton, spilling white dribbles on her tight-fitting, faded emerald-green and yellow t-shirt. As she gulped, making exaggerated noises, she stared at Naima, watching to see if she would wince. Iona was forced to concede credit to Naima, who gazed at her with sad, veiled eyes.

Finally, Naima looked away as if suddenly discovering a thing of interest caught in the frilly, red, gingham curtain above the sink. Without turning to look at Iona again, she asked, with genuine care: "Why won't you let me help? Why do you get so much pleasure out of hurting me?"

"Because, like I said to you from day one, I don't fucking need a mother. I had one, and she died. Not that she was of much use to me when she was alive." Iona spat the words, then strode out of the kitchen on her way upstairs.

"Can we at least be friends? You know I was a teacher. I know how the system works. I can—"

"Just stay the fuck out of my business, and we'll be just fine!" Iona shouted from halfway up the stairs.

When Iona first came to live with her dad and his wife, it had not been too difficult for her to figure out that, though Malik had set himself the task of dominating Naima, she was a very eager "submissy." Iona was present when he suggested that Naima don the hijab. Though she was still very young at the time, Iona was not convinced by the paternal attempt to imbue the veil with "feminist" principles. But she also observed how Naima fashioned her first veil out of drapery, a sheer one, so that she remained elusive yet tantalizing. As seductive as specious shyness is. *Why do they both engage in these charades?* Iona wondered.

After Iona exited the kitchen, Naima sighed. She was grateful that Ahmed was out in the garden with Anne, who was puffing a cigarette. Naima worried about Iona's influence on Ahmed—now learning how to talk. The night before, she'd heard him grunt a monosyllable that sounded uncomfortably like Iona's favourite four-letter word.

"You can't just let her walk all over you. You need to be firm with her," Anne said, her voice barging into Naima's thoughts.

"I'll thank you, Mum, for letting me run my own home," Naima said.

"That's just the problem. You're not running this place like it's your home. Isn't it bad enough that you let Malik push you around? Do you have to take this kind of crap from his bratty daughter as well?"

Although Naima's lips said, "I do it because I know that the teenage years are complicated ones, and I'm trying to make allowance for the poor girl," the way she enunciated her words, plus her staccato tone, revealed her stressed-out "tolerance." What she was actually saying was, *Unlike you, Mum, I'm committed to putting my family before my politics and myself.* The driving force in Naima's life was her determination to avoid ending up anything like Anne.

Her resolve was not just because she wanted to punish Anne for being so different when she was growing up and needing a mother who was no-drama maternal. It was, however, an important part of her motivation. All her adult life, Naima struggled with trying to bring herself to forgive Anne for failing to see how difficult it was for a pubescent girl of mixed parentage to fit in without always needing to disavow the titillating spectacle of a mother who exposed her politics everywhere she went by never wearing a bra.

While Naima glanced elsewhere, Anne studied her forensically—and with an exaggerated, rueful smile. Anne would stand by her dogma. A card-carrying member of the National Organization of Women (NOW), her brand of feminism was evangelical. After all, she had worked her vocal cords raw for the lobby founded by her heroine, Betty Friedan.

Even after Naima exited, Anne continued to stare long and hard at the spot where her daughter had stood, as if she possessed the power to immobilize and transfix a subject, not unlike Medusa.

Anne began to sway unconsciously when Bob Marley's "Crazy Baldheads" wafted down from Iona's room. Anne could never resist reggae. It was what first drew her to Jamaica on holiday. It was to the threnodic rhythm and swooning melody of "Many Rivers to Cross" by Jimmy Cliff that Naima, her only child, was conceived on a beautiful rainy night. After she heard him drumming for one of the teeming reggae bands in Kingston, making love to Winston was no rebel act. She found him so seductive that she came even before he penetrated her. She came again and again, in waves and rushes, hours after the intercourse had melted away. She was not surprised when she discovered she would breed, just days before she was due to leave the island. Her choice to have and keep her "love child"—as she proudly explained her impending maternity to her Ivy League comrades in Cambridge, Massachusetts—was her act of rebellion. In her mind, it was one more nail in her father's coffin, the bourgeois scion of plantation-owning brigands. Soon, she left Radcliffe and set up home with Megan, a nightclub guitarist. But after three months, she decided that, while fun at first, lesbianism was boring without a goad. She smoked ganja until moments before her baby was born because she was convinced that it was a medicinal herb, despite what Yank' propaganda would have the world believe. Besides, her baby was a Jamaican child, but a potential U.S. president being born on its constitutionally sacred turf.

Horny from having been starved of sex for almost six months, Anne packed up her three-month-old girl and took her home to her father. Though still incensed and scandalized by her lifestyle, Anne's father was smitten by the sight of his cute granddaughter. Anne's stepmother contacted the family's old nanny, Aida, who was retired but willing to tend the baby. Anne's father and stepmother were sure that the infant Margaret was better off with Aida, copacetic and coloured. They believed the girl would be "happier with her own kind" and were very generous in rewarding Aida.

After abandoning her daughter, Anne tried to forgo her family's wealth, pledging only to take money from her trust fund until her daughter was a little older. She planned—in a fresh frenzy of fancy—to find a job and eschew the paterfamilias's wallet. When that failed, she opted to attempt modern dance—"to combine Josephine Baker and Isadora Duncan."

But before trying to enrol for a dance course, she jetted back out to Jamaica. She downed every drink she was offered in first class to calm her nerves, because even she could not explain her compulsion to go back and find Winston. When she got to Montego Bay, she checked into a five-star hotel. She would have immediately gone searching for Winston in the club where they first met because she had no other address for him. However, on stepping out of her hotel suite, she ran into another gorgeous "hunk" that she had coveted when she was checking in: The hotel bellhop—a Lumpenproletariat, yes, but "lumpy and bumpy" in the right spots. Three hours later, lying spent in the crook of his arm, Anne realized that Winston was not unique in his sexual dexterity. Thus, she dallied two days before heading to the club to seek her baby daddy, Winston.

Unfortunately, Winston no longer played at the club where they first met. Having fallen out with his old band, he set up his own and rehearsed in the yard behind his mother's house. Anne felt lucky when a buddy at his old club volunteered to take her to her ex-one-night-stand. When they got to his mother's house, the old woman was busy cleaning vegetables in the front yard, humming along to the music floating out from the backyard. Anne introduced herself, and was pleasantly surprised that Winston's mother was named Margaret, like her own mother, who died when she was a child, and after whom she had named her baby. Uncanny was the coincidence in the naming! She made her way eagerly to the backyard, where she beheld Winston looking exactly the same as he had the first time she saw him. Then again, "Black don't crack." She knew instinctively that, while he thought she looked familiar, he could not recall her name or where the hell they'd hooked up. Too proud to put him to the test, she said, "Yoo-hoo! It's me, Anne Stockade!" Breezy, jocular was her voice, and she was grateful when he played along.

"Me know, mon. Wa gwan?" Perhaps it was this single act of politeness that made her sleep with him again that night, but afterwards, she wished she had not. Much as she tried, the magic of their debut coitus could not be invoked. When she finally revealed that she had a daughter by him, but would not pressure him into taking on any fatherly responsibility, his response was the classic, "What's a man to do with that type of info?" He rolled off his stomach and stretched his hand across her hotel bed to reach for his half-smoked reefer on the side table. He left her hotel room an hour later, after downing his breakfast, never once showing any curiosity about his child. Anne assured herself that she was neither upset nor mad. She was, after all, "liberated." It was the last time she saw him. He was also the last Black guy she ever fucked.

***

Upstairs in Malik and Naima's house, had Iona known the pleasure that Anne derived from the music she was playing, she would have promptly turned it off. As far as she was concerned, Anne represented the proverbial crazy baldhead she wished could be chased not just out of town, but off the face of the earth. She rummaged through her closet, flinging clothes here and there and stepping on a skirt she had left lying on the floor for days. Her room was like a backyard after a windstorm, with clothes littered everywhere. Eventually, she found a clean blue and grey shirt with thin stripes and wore it over her t-shirt. Dispensing with the idea of buttoning it, she dropped to her knees to look under the bed for the black sandals lying beside her almost-exhausted stash of marijuana. It had fallen there the night before as she'd struggled out of her stretch jeans. Without even glancing once at the mirror, she left her room and almost ran smack into her father.

"Is it true?" Malik asked.

"Is what true?" she said.

He let out a deep, impatient breath. "That you've been suspended again?"

"Yeah," she replied, gliding toward the staircase landing.

"And where are you going?"

"To the mall," she said, hissing, without pausing to hear his response and rushing to vacate the house. *Come to think of it, I don't need a fucking father either*, she thought. The only reason she tried to be civil (albeit standoffishly) to Malik was that he provided her with a roof, a bed, and a table.

Much as she liked playing a mallrat with her friends, unlike most of them in middle-class Vaughan, who still thought being a street kid could be "cool," Iona knew better after her two-night stint on the Scarborough thoroughfares when she was thirteen. After watching Iona leave, Naima waited downstairs for a while to give Malik some time to cool off. She then went upstairs to give him a chance to talk if he felt so inclined. Naima stepped gingerly on the stairs like a prowler, fearful she might awaken the owners of a house she was about to burgle. Quietly, she let herself into their bedroom, where she found him sitting on the edge of the bed, watching TV with the sound muted. Though he did not glance her way, when she entered, she saw from the stiff, upright way he was sitting that he was pent up and ready to explode. Checking her urge to rub his shoulders the way she used to, to help him sleep when they first met, she went over to the bureau and withdrew her rosary before leaving the room. She would do her ablution in the bathroom downstairs and say her Isha in the living room where she would watch television, waiting if he came for her. If he did not—and she was almost sure he would not—she would sleep in their son's room. There was a large old prayer mat there, which she would spread on the carpet.

After leaving her house, Iona changed her mind about "slacking" at the mall like usual. Instead, she boarded a bus, then changed to the subway and went for a ride, changing lines every now and then to avoid getting noticed. A few hours later, bored and hungry, she emerged at Spadina to hunt for cheap Chinese takeout. At the corner of Willcocks and Huron, she encountered a gathering of mostly Black youths.

"We're no longer gonna beg for equality like our parents did!" a voice rang out, startling the Queen's "peace."

"We're Canadians like everyone else, and we're not gonna be apologetic about being here. We're here, and we're here to stay on our own terms. We don't even have to go palsy-walsy just to fit in. Heck! We don't have to fit in with anybody! Let them try and fit in with us for a change, eh? I agree with the brother who spoke just now that education is the way out of the kind of nine-to-five, dirty-job rut that trapped our parents, who ended up acting apologetic about being here, who humble down and beg for factory drudgery and slave wages. And we don't have to be so eager to be like White people. Hell, no! We don't have to toil at break-back jobs they don't want just so we can move to the suburbs and get snubbed. We've got a right to equality and justice just like anyone else. And how do we make this a reality? Education! By sitting next to them in class and kicking their saggy asses. Beat them at their game! With education, you'll be taking your fight for equality to where it really hurts the oppressor the most: His pocket! When you hit his pocket, you crush his balls. Take them cushy jobs away from them and then barge on into Parliament Hill!!"

Suddenly, Iona found herself applauding with the rest of the hip, chic, Black, finger-snapping, poetic-with-profanity crowd.

The electrifying stump orator was a University of Toronto undergrad. An African accent, which she could not immediately place, graced his words. Iona guessed that he must have been brought to live in Canada as a child.

His words bored through Iona's formerly dulled mind and splashed her awake. Here, at last, was a cause toward which she could channel all her pent-up anger. Outrage at her life, rage against her father. She was hooked, and school ceased to represent conformity, but an opportunity for guerrilla intellectualism. No more unconscious obeisance, but hyper-conscious defiance. Still sassy to teachers, she no longer shirked her schoolwork, but studied extra hard to disprove racist, pedagogical theories.

That day, Iona fell in love for the first time. Still, the realization did not come until almost two years later, after she ran into Salim, the speaker, again. By then, she was a first-year student at the University of Toronto and was an activist in the Black Students Taking Charge (BSTC) movement. She found herself working closely with him when she realised that she had fallen in love with him.

He'd arrived as a child refugee in Canada after war had again shattered, bled, and starved Somalia. He was just starting his postgraduate program in engineering at York University when Iona entered the University of Toronto. She dated Salim for nine months but fast outgrew him when she saw that equality for him did not mean equality for all. He could neither resist the adoration of "ladies," who, like Iona, were seduced by his oratorical prowess, nor could he help taking them for granted. However, unlike the other women in Salim's orbit, Iona knew Naima, who had sacrificed her self-esteem to bolster her father's ego. She broke up with Salim when she saw how much like her father he was when she caught him sternly admonishing—for a minor infraction—a female student who was helplessly infatuated with him.

PART THREE: HOME PLACE:
A HABITAT THAT IS CARRIED IN ONE'S SOUL

Canada – 2005

Timothy

THAT SATURDAY MORNING, on the subway to work at the Discount Plus Grocery shop, near Jane and Finch in Toronto, Timothy was searching for apt words to speechify his complaint. He'd have to talk back if his supervisor sent him out to stack shopping carts again. It would be his tenth day in a row sweltering outdoors in the hot July sun, even though the jobs outside and inside the air-conditioned grocery shop were supposed to be rotated. Rotation would let other boys taste the heat outside while he took his turn "chilling" indoors.

After checking the rota posted on the sidewall of a cubicle behind one of the checkout counters, his spirit fell on seeing that he'd been assigned to "Sahara detail" again. So, he made a beeline to the supervisor's office. Relatively small for his age, Timothy was conscious of hunching—to shrink himself even smaller—when he rapped ever so lightly on the supervisor's glass door. Not hearing a response—but first donning his most congenial smile—he let himself in.

"Good day, sssi …" he greeted Donny McDowall, stopping short of saying "sir." He hated himself for not getting used to addressing authoritative figures, especially White ones, without the customary "sir" that was mandatory when addressing superiors back home.

"Yes, Timmy, what can I do for you?"

"It is about my duty today."

"Yes?" Donny looked impatient to get back to the figures he was studying.

"I'm to work outside again today?" Even as he spoke the words, he wished he'd voiced an exclamation, not a question.

"Off you go then! The last time I checked, they were almost out of carts in the shop." Donny dismissed him, resuming his sums and subtractions as a crestfallen Timothy slouched from the room. Once desperate, he was now downcast.

Outside, Timothy found another young man already stacking carts, with ennui amounting to despondency.

"Hi, I'm Wale. You must be my partner," he said, gesturing for Timothy to help guide the long serpentine chain of carts that he was pushing. "Is this your first day here?"

"No, it's my tenth day in a row doing this," Timothy replied, thinking the other boy was inquiring whether it was his first day as a stacker.

"Well, welcome to the snake pit, bro."

"It's not fair."

"And then you die!" Wale answered airily, thus flummoxing Timothy. "Whoever said life was fair? If it was, my brother, you and I would not even be here. If life was fair, you and I would not have been born Black."

"Whaaat?" Timothy did not quite know what to make of the tall, gangly young man, so obviously the spawn of Black-White coitus.

"Yeah, like, bossman took the trouble to explain that he assigns me to stack carts because I'm from Africa and therefore should be used to the sun. He said being Black, I also don't have to worry about getting sunburn. It doesn't matter to baas that I was born here, and I've never been to bloody Africa."

Timothy's head swivelled from side to side, cussing his fate out his very lungs. Although he was almost Vantablack, he did not know just how dark he was until he moved to Canada and found himself a hundred percent blacker than ninety nine percent of so-called Black people. He hated his distinctiveness. His blackness felt as toxic as lead-based paint. It weighed him down like an anchor.

Back in the Kakuma refugee camp in Kenya, where his boyhood was spent dodging UN pedophiles, peacekeeper predators, and fellow refugee camp tyrants, he'd credited his religion with both limiting him and making him a target of the Arab Muslim Janjaweed, who made him an orphan. However, having been raised on stories about the sufferings of Biblical martyrs, he waited in vain for God to intervene. As he matured, he began to doubt that his religion was the problem. Then he got to Canada, where eighty percent of the citizens claimed to be Christian, yet resolutely seemed to shun or disprove of his unrelentingly dark skin. Convinced that his colour was offensive, he sought a chemical cure.

First, at Jane and Finch Mall, Timothy found an African store which stocked skin-lightening creams. He strove to bleach his skin, to annihilate the melanin. It was a slow process, and the result was uneven. His struggle to lighten his complexion was soon compounded when a workmate laughingly advised that he was coming to resemble a "raccoon." When he checked the word in his pocket dictionary, he had to agree that the stubborn dark circle around his eyes gave him a raccoon-cum-harlequin look. So, he reluctantly gave up the skin-lightening creams that were so atrociously wallet-lightening.

He laboured in scorching heat all day. After leaving work that Saturday night, he wished he could go somewhere other than his Driftwood Avenue apartment, too stuffed with second-hand furniture and hand-me-down clothes, the largesse received from over-generous Torontonians when Timothy and his friends first landed in Canada. Unfortunately, he did not know Toronto that well.

So, he trudged home, where he found his roommate, Daniel, recounting his day at court to their other roommate, Hezekiah.

"… Me, I looked as stupid as I could, and I asked, 'What is a ticket?'"

Timothy winced when Daniel and Hezekiah's jollity shook the two-bedroom apartment's walls, irritating the cockroaches.

"And the judge, what did he say?" Hezekiah asked, their guffaws subsiding to chuckles.

"He carefully explained to me that 'It's a piece of paper that says how much you have been charged for a parking offence. Did you not find one on your car on the 16th of May?' Me, I tried to look even more stupid and said, 'It is possible it was on my car, sir, but as I did not even know what a ticket was, I must have failed to pick it up.' So, the judge said, 'Ignorance of the law is no excuse, but I'll give you benefit of the doubt this time.' He then said I should pay the original fine and waived the pe-nal-ty!" He broke the last word up into syllables, the way he had committed it to memory. Daniel worked in a factory two hours from their apartment. He also worked odd hours and had been compelled to buy a rickety Saturn—pure rust held together adulterously by "duck" tape—to save himself the trouble of commuting by the unreliable ghetto bus during winter.

"Ha! These White people and their laws. If we're not careful, we will die penniless in this country. They won't give us good jobs, and they won't help us go to school and learn a trade to help us get good jobs," Hezekiah said wearily.

Daniel nodded his concord with Hezekiah. "They take all our money as tax. If I could turn into a bird, I will fly back to all the refugee camps and warn all the people waiting to come to overseas. I will warn them that, do not believe everything they are telling you about White man's country. It is a hard place to live."

"But it is still better than the camps or even home, given all the massacres there," Hezekiah said.

"True, my brother, true." Daniel nodded enthusiastically. The two of them fell silent. Timothy nodded in agreement with them. He was glad of the pause in the conversation because it gave him a chance to make his announcement. Not sure how they would take the news of his leaving, since it would mean saddling them with the burden of finding someone else to move into the living room to help meet the rent, he selected his words gravely.

"I want to go to school," he said, wishing they had not imposed the rule on themselves to only speak English when they were together. They were all eager to master the language, which they hoped would help them blend better into their new country.

"My brother, we all want to go to school," Hezekiah said in response.

"I have emailed Bol. He is going to university in September."

"Bol Stephen? In … umm …?" Daniel could not recall the name of the city where Bol lived.

"In Halifax, Nova Scotia."

"So that place is better than here?" Hezekiah asked.

"He cut his age. And they let him go to high school. Now he has qualified to go to university with a student loan."

"Bol, Bol! He is always very clever." Daniel could not hide his envious admiration of the enviable, admirable Bol.

"I will cut my age, too. I will say since there is nothing like a birth certificate in Darfur when I was born, that I miscalculated my age before. I told them when I first came to Canada that I was born in 1982. Bol said I can be with him till I can stand on my own legs." Timothy paused, gauging their mood. "I want to go next month." As he spoke, the irony eluded him of how his small stature, the result of his malnourished childhood, would now assist him in paring years off his age. Although he was really nineteen, at only a little over five feet tall, he was skinny and had wide bulging eyes. He had endearingly shocking red lips and could easily pass for a junior high pupil.

"Me and Hezekiah have also been thinking of going to Calgary. They say there is plenty of work there." Daniel's voice met with silence.

Soon, Hezekiah started humming a song in their language, which they'd sung in the refugee camp. Gradually, all sang:

> *"What is home to you?*
> *A place of rest after a long journey?*
> *Not so for me.*
> *Not even so for my father.*
> *Who will ever again call me by my special name?*
> *Oh, when I try to think of my home*
> *I see a lush and luxuriant location.*
> *But I have to remember*
> *That if it is now a fertile place*
> *it is because it is soaked*
> *With the blood of my people*
> *How can I ever find rest?*
> *Oh! that ruined place that I know as home.*
> *What is home to you?*
> *A place of rest after a long journey?*
> *Not so for my brothers and my sisters.*
> *Not even so for my mother.*
> *Who will ever again call me by my special name?"*

Timothy and Daniel became friends as orphans in Kakuma. They counted themselves extremely lucky when they were chosen to leave for Canada at the same time. They met Hezekiah on the plane to Toronto. His home was Dadaab, another refugee camp in Kenya. The lads began to bond on the flight when Timothy bent double due to the sensation of having his stomach churned by the plane. He reached out to grab the hand of the boy sitting to his left—Hezekiah—because Daniel, seated to his right, resolutely kept his eyes shut from the moment they boarded. Being of a sturdier makeup, Hezekiah laughed, saying in English, "Have you forgotten? We are going to White people's country. There, two men cannot hold hands. If they do, people will think they are gays."

His remark brought to Timothy a belly laugh; and didn't the jest neutralize the bile in his stomach?

However, he was still unable to muster the energy to eat the strange airline food. He ended up sharing his portion between Hezekiah and Daniel. Daniel promptly opened his eyes at the first whiff of the promising, steaming aroma. The man sitting across the aisle from them pointed at the creamy yellow substance in a tiny square plastic wedge—which Hezekiah was licking greedily—and said, "That is butter. You spread it on your bread." They all wondered what other weird things awaited them in their new land of hope.

***

A few weeks after moving to Halifax from Toronto, Timothy was moved to reflect that, everywhere on Earth, people like him were either dispossessed wanderers or locked-down have-nots. His friend Bol, who generously invited him to Halifax, either did not mean his invitation to be taken so literally or expected him to have some money saved for his upkeep and to contribute to the rent.

Bol lived in one bedroom, which he rented in a widow's basement on Brunswick Street. Timothy had already outstayed his welcome by the third day following his arrival—which was a Sunday. He made his way to an Anglican church in the neighbourhood. He was the only black face in the massive church housing a predominantly old and sparse population. After the service, he was invited to join other worshippers for refreshments in the church hall. There, an announcer welcomed him, insisting that he introduce himself. He said his name and nationality and explained that he was a refugee, having fled the war in Darfur,

Sudan. He did not miss the suddenly escalated level of interest at the mention of Darfur. It was a charity fixture in the weekly church bulletins.

After his introduction, people mobbed him, bombarding him with questions about his homeland. Some sermonized that they had contributed to goat funds to help people in Sudan and other blighted places in Africa. Others offered charity, asking if he needed winter clothes, beddings, and furnishing. Remembering how the apartment in Toronto had become a dumping ground for rejects donated by equally generous do-gooders, he raised his voice, thanking all who volunteered to bring this or that tchotchke the following Sunday. Then he explained his real need: "I am in Canada to get educated so that I can go back home to make my country a place for living again."

The hall fell silent, and then the smiley-face priest commended his determination to get educated. After expressing how touched they all were by his plight and mission, the cleric intoned that, "It is difficult for any of us to take on the responsibility of your education. These are really tough times, and the system is too complicated." He paused to look at the congregants clustered about Timothy, then said unctuously, "We will ask around to see if there are parishioners who can help you navigate the system."

Timothy damned himself silently. He felt greedy, like an ingrate, for insulting his hosts by requesting aid that was evidently beyond their ken. He decided never to darken again that church.

By Tuesday of that week, things with Bol had so degenerated that he was forced to stop eating for fear Bol might choke him if he caught him handling a fork or spoon. Perhaps it was sheer hunger or the exigencies of schoolwork after he was registered in a high school near Bol's house after declaring himself to be only sixteen. Maybe it was the phone call from Ruth, his older sister, still stuck in the camp in Kenya, who accused him of forgetting her and her poor, fatherless twin toddlers, born to Garang Kir in the camp. Hadn't he only managed to send a miserly two hundred dollars since arriving in Canada? Then again, it could have been a combination of all these events.

Whatever it was, one minute, Timothy was standing at a crosswalk waiting for the light to turn green on North Street. He was on his way to catch the #10 bus at the Halifax end of the Angus McDonald Bridge. The next minute, he heard the screeching of a car as it swerved to a halt. He found himself lying face down in the middle of the road. Thinking he had been hit, he was momentarily happy at the prospect of a hospital stint. To be fed! To luxuriate in a free, warm bed! A respite from misery!

To his disappointment, his self-diagnosis revealed no ache, pain, or bleeding. He began to scheme faking a mysterious, internal injury when a face, which looked vaguely familiar, thrust itself into his line of vision. "You're the young man from Darfur, aren't you? You came to our church last Sunday. I'm Paul Tinkler. I saw you slip on the curb and thankfully was able to avoid hitting you. Are you okay?"

By this time, Timothy was sitting up, and the people standing at the bus stop who saw him fall were now suddenly a pedestrian church.

"You're damn lucky, buddy. This is a blind corner. If this gentleman hadn't been going at a reasonable speed, you'd now be watching a concert performed by angels." The sermonizer stuck his cigarette back in his mouth.

Paul helped him up, installed him in his car, and drove him back to Bol's digs. Then, Paul offered to bring him to his place for dinner the following evening.

After that day, Timothy's life could not have worked out better, even if he had planned it himself. Over supper, Paul, a retired attorney, and his retired activist wife, Mona, who lived in a beautifully furnished house on Duffus Street, were enthralled by Timothy's story. Mona and her best friend, Jane, who was invited along with Valentine, her husband, to the dinner, could not help shedding quiet tears when Timothy told them he was only sixteen. These tears encouraged him to edit the rest of his life in other ways to suit his captivated audience.

"I was away with the other boys herding cattle when one of the older ones who had been placed in a strategic position as our watchmen came clambering down and screaming from his post atop a palm tree to alert us that hundreds of Janjaweed were heading toward our village. We all abandoned our cattle and goats and made for various hiding places behind the hills that we had earmarked as safe places in case of such a raid. We waited until morning and then crept back to the village, dreading what we might find." He paused for effect. Immersed in the story, he was amazed to see how easily he became a part of it.

What did it matter if he was never really such a boy? In the camp, he was privy to too many "Grimm" horror stories about children seeing their parents maimed or killed. That evening, as Paul, Mona, and their friends waited on him, thrilled to share vicariously in his Gothic tales, he felt no qualms about borrowing bits and pieces from the oral memoirs that circulated among camp inmates as common currency to gild with blood their refugee claims.

But his tears that night were honest. He was orphaned, too young to remember his parents, and he knew what it meant to live without them. He knew well refugee camp hunger and thirst, cholera and dysentery. He crossed at Gilo and knew the degradation of living in cardboard shacks, each an isle amid puddles, sans chalk or soap, steady bread or ready water. He knew what it meant to grow without daring to project beyond the immediate moment. The sobs that composed his breath as he regaled his audience that night were genuine.

Paul was proud of Mona for beating their guests to the draw after tabling to-die-for hors-d'oeuvres. Indeed, just before they all made their way from the living room to the dining room, she showed Timothy—and their oohing-and-ahing guests—a free room in their well-appointed home in the exclusive Hydrostone district. Plus, she, an accomplished chef since her retirement, would prepare his meals and tutor him to university. Paul, a lawyer, would assure his due receipt of Landed Immigrant status. Timothy almost collapsed when hearing this news. He could not help weeping in gratitude. From that night on, Paul and Mona Tinkler adopted him in all but name. He had to credit his reversal in fortune to divine intervention.

Had his sister Ruth ever been able to bring herself to narrate—in detail—how their home was raided, he would not have had to fictionalize. He would have told his engrossed audience that he was an un-weaned toddler—hidden under his mother's corpse—and so left for dead by Nuer raiders.

***

The year was 1985 in Darfur, nestled in the western part of Sudan. Thirteen-year-old Ruth, her mother's only daughter and, until a few months prior, her only child, embarked on the daily trek to fetch water. Her blue plastic water container bouncing up and down with each step she took.

Ruth marched on, bare feet stubborn against the cracked earth. Her shadow stretched long and lean in the midday sun that cast a honey-gold hue over the vast arid expanse of what she knew only as home. Dust puffed up from beneath her determined steps, each one deliberate, contributing to the rhythm of her daily pilgrimage for water.

The leather strap of the empty container cut across her forehead, a familiar pressure she hardly noticed anymore. Two miles out, two back. A trek etched into her muscle memory. Ruth's eyes, dark and focused, scanned the path ahead. Here, a rock to avoid. There, a dip where rainwater might linger after the rare storms, hopeful hollows now bone-dry.

In the distance, beyond the reach of her immediate world, the low rumble of conflict rolled like thunder over the horizon. Ruth knew of the war, whispers of it seeping through the cracks of her village's resolve. Yet as she walked, the war seemed another reality altogether. Distant, a backdrop to the pressing needs of the present.

Her task was water. For her mother, for baby Timo, for survival. The weight of this responsibility steadied her pace, lending an edge to her youthful features. An angularity born not of years but of necessity.

She trekked onward, the terrain unforgiving, her mind anchored to the clear, tangible goal that awaited her: The stream, the dipping of her gourd, the return journey with life cradled in her hands. Ruth's thoughts did not stray to the conflicts of men and nations.

Since her mother had lain down her water gourd to cradle baby Timo instead, the task fell solely on Ruth's young shoulders.

The sun, a piercing eye in the sky, watched as Ruth navigated the brush. Thorns and acacia needles threatened, but she moved with practiced ease, her thoughts ensnaring her like the brambles underfoot.

The birth had taken its toll on her mother, leaving her a shade paler, a whisper weaker. Ruth remembered the strength in those arms, the arms that once lifted heavy water with ease. Would they ever do so again?

A memory surfaced, unbidden: Ruth by her mother's side, the two of them like paired shadows at dawn. Her mother's laughter would bubble up from deep within, rich and warm, spilling over the morning's cool silence as they walked together. They shared stories between them, the same way they shared the load of the filled gourds, balancing the weight on their heads, their steps in sync.

"See, Ruth?" her mother had said during one such walk, the horizon just beginning to blush with light. "We carry more than water. We carry life, we carry hope."

Ruth blinked away the recollection as sharply as it had come. Hope felt heavier these days, yet she clung to it, as her mother had taught her. In the rhythm of her steps, in the rise and fall of her chest, Ruth carried more than just the weight of her empty water container. She carried her family's lifeline, her mother's teachings, and the unspoken promise of shared burdens once more.

Her gait was steady, her young muscles already adapting to the increased demands. She had grown taller in recent months, her limbs stretching, hardening like the acacia trees that dotted the landscape. Her skin bore the kiss of the sun, a deep ebony hue that seemed almost burnished at the elbows and knees from her unrelenting labour.

Ruth's eyes, a rich brown mirroring the earth beneath her feet, held a spark that belied her weariness. There was grace, too, in the way she navigated the harsh terrain.

She paused for a moment, not in hesitation, but to survey the path ahead, her breath coming in controlled bursts. Her hair, cropped short for practicality, offered little resistance to the breeze that occasionally swept through, providing brief respite from the heat. It was in this moment, alone with the vastness of Darfur, that Ruth felt the full weight of her role within the family: A sister, a daughter, a carrier of life-giving water. Her brother's arrival had shifted the tides of her world. She was the protector now, the shield against thirst and want.

With a nod to the unseen forces that both challenged and shaped her, Ruth resumed her trek. The hem of her simple dress, faded and frayed, held in place by an equally faded and frayed wrapper, whispered against her calves with each step forward. This was her life now, each day a repetition of the last: Wake, fetch, provide.

Ruth did not allow herself to dwell on the hardships. She drew strength from the image of her mother's smile, from the memory of shared laughter and stories.

A thorny acacia loomed ahead, its hardened branches a challenge to survival. Ruth eyed its silhouette, a natural fortress amidst the savannah. She had grown alongside these trees, their presence as constant as the stars that would soon freckle the evening sky. Now, they stood as markers of her journey, both physical and within.

The acacia's roots snaked across the trail, a network of natural tripwires. A sudden crack underfoot—a brittle twig giving way to her stride—brought her thoughts back to the present. Ruth paused, surveying the terrain for an alternate route. To her right, a series of rocks offered a pathway through a particularly dense patch of brush. She chose her steps with care, leveraging her weight against the stones to propel herself forward.

A sharp sting pierced Ruth's heel. Her foot recoiled instinctively as she stifled a gasp. For an instant, the world narrowed to the throbbing pain at her sole. The vast expanse of Darfur, with its undulating grasses and whispering winds, faded into a distant hum.

Beneath her weathered foot, a large thorn lay embedded in the parched earth—its tip broken off, now a part of her. Ruth winced, steeling herself against the bite of the unwelcome hitchhiker. With practised ease, she lowered her weight onto her uninjured foot, her eyes scanning the immediate vicinity. There, amidst the scattered debris of the bush, another thorn—stout and sharp. She plucked it from the ground, its pointed end promising utility.

Ruth perched on a nearby stone, the water container momentarily forgotten beside her. She wielded the second thorn like a tool, her fingers deft despite the pulsating ache. The first thorn yielded to her ministrations, slipping out from where it had lodged itself. It was a minor victory, each drop of shed blood a small tribute to the resilience that pulsed through her veins.

There would be no outward sign of her discomfort. The plains were not privy to her whispers of pain. In the grand medley of life that unfolded in these parts, such moments were but fleeting shadows. Ruth rose, her gait momentarily unsteady but swiftly regaining its familiar rhythm. She reclaimed the empty container, balancing the weight of her responsibilities once more.

Ruth limped onward and soon the stream shimmered in the distance, a mirage of relief dancing over the horizon's cruel line. She crested the final rise, the ground solidifying underfoot, as though acknowledging her resolve. The water, framed by the sparse acacias and the vastness of the sky, offered its stillness to those who sought it.

Others were there before her. Garang Kir was among those who were making their way out of the stream. His silhouette a slender spear against the backdrop of cattle grazing near the water's edge. He turned, his gaze finding Ruth amidst her solitary approach.

"Ruth Akol," he called out, waving and nodding in respect to the determination etched on her face as he walked away.

"Water waits for no one," she replied, offering a small smile that didn't quite reach her eyes.

Ruth's feet sank into the soft, yielding mud as she waded into the pond, the cool water a refreshing relief against her sore, thorn-pricked foot. She paused for a moment, savoring the sensation, before bending down to fill her scooping gourd. The water was a tad murky, but it carried the earthy scent of life and sustenance. She lifted the gourd to her lips, the liquid cool and refreshing as it flowed down her throat, quenching a thirst she had hardly acknowledged in her focus on the trek.

Suddenly, rain started drizzling, to the delight of the younger children at the stream. The other women and children moved around her, their movements fluid and practiced. Ruth felt a sense of camaraderie in their shared purpose, even though they exchanged few words. The stream was a place of unity, where the burdens of daily life were temporarily set aside in favor of frolicking in the cool water.

Ruth filled her large container with deliberate care, the weight of it promising a heavy load for the return journey. She secured it with a cloth doughnut, tying it expertly around her head. The cloth was soft against her scalp, a comforting contrast to the hard plastic of the container. The weight settled onto her shoulders, familiar and daunting. But she stood tall, feeling the strength in her legs, the steadiness in her stance.

The journey back loomed long and arduous, and with each step she took, the sounds of the stream receded farther behind her. The sun cast long shadows as it began its descent.

As she continued her journey home, her foot throbbed with each step, the ache from the thorn she had removed earlier now a constant reminder of the path's treachery. The recent rains had turned the ground into a mire, each step sinking her deeper into the mud. The once-familiar path now felt hostile, the wet earth clinging to her feet, pulling her down with every move.

As she trudged forward, a sense of foreboding began to creep into her mind. The air, thick with the scent of wet earth and decaying leaves, felt heavy and oppressive. Ruth tried to push the unease away, focusing instead on the rhythmic swaying of the water container balanced precariously on her head. She steadied it with one hand, the weight a constant strain on her small frame, while her other hand reached out instinctively to grasp at the surrounding air, seeking balance.

The sounds around her shifted, the cheerful songs of birds replaced by the distant, unsettling rustle of unseen creatures. Ruth's ears picked up the faint, eerie call of an unknown bird, its cry echoing through the dense foliage. She quickened her pace, her heart beating a little faster, the feeling of being watched gnawing at her thoughts.

Her mind drifted back to her mother's stories of the spirits that roamed the land, tales meant to keep children close to home. Ruth had always dismissed them as mere myths, but now, alone on this treacherous path, she felt a chill that had nothing to do with the cool evening air. She imagined eyes watching her from the shadows, every rustle and snap of a twig amplifying her growing fear.

Her foot slipped in the mud, and she stumbled, barely managing to keep the water container from toppling. The sharp pain in her heel flared up again, causing her to gasp. She paused, breathing deeply, the metallic taste of fear mingling with the earthy smells around her. She steadied herself, her hand trembling as she brushed a stray fly from her face.

Ruth pushed on, determined to reach home before darkness fell completely. Each step was a struggle, the shadows lengthening ominously around her. The once-familiar landmarks seem to shift and blur.

Despite the growing fear, Ruth forced herself to focus. The weight of the water container, the ache in her foot, the feel of the mud against her skin. All these sensations grounded her, reminding her of her purpose. She must reach home. She must bring the water. She must endure.

With each step, she pushed back the fear, drawing strength from the thought of her mother and new brother waiting for her. Ruth's thoughts were a tumultuous mix of worry and determination, her mind conjuring images of her mother and baby brother waiting anxiously for her return.

As she neared the outskirts of her village, a sudden movement caught her eye. A group of familiar faces emerged from the foliage, their expressions a mask of horror and urgency. Panic gripped

Ruth's heart and she let go of the water container as she recognized them: Women and children from her village, their eyes wide with terror as they fled past her. The air was thick with the scent of smoke and the distant sound of chaos, the acrid smell of burning homes filling her nostrils.

"They came," one of the villagers said, breathless with fear. "The Janjaweed. They destroyed everything."

Ruth's blood ran cold. Fears that she had never allowed herself to dwell on were realized in those few, desperate words. She joined the fleeing group, her body moving on instinct as they plunged into a dense thicket. The undergrowth scratched at her skin, the sounds of their hurried breaths mingling with the rustling leaves. The night fell heavy and dark, the group huddled together in the cramped space, their whispers a fragile thread of hope.

Later that night, Garang Kir, along with some of the other boys, braver than the rest, volunteered to scout the village. Ruth watched him disappear into the darkness, her heart a painful thud in her chest. Time stretched unbearably as they waited, the silence around them broken only by the occasional distant scream or the crackle of burning wood.

When the boys returned, Garang Kir's face was a mask of grief. "The village … it's gone. Destroyed. No one left."

The words hung in the air, a devastating blow that stole the breath from Ruth's lungs. For three days, they remained hidden, the scouts venturing out only to bring back news that offered no solace. On the fourth day, Ruth could bear it no longer. Driven by a desperation to find her family, she rushed back to the village, the scenes of destruction unfolding before her like a nightmare.

The once vibrant village was now a smoldering ruin, the smell of charred wood and death heavy in the air. Ruth stumbled through the debris, toward her home, her eyes scanning frantically for any sign of life. Her heart shattered when she found her mother, lifeless on the ground in a hole that she must have been digging. Ruth released the hoe from her lifeless hand. She had to pry her mother's body free to get to the baby that was curled protectively within her other arm.

She was shocked to find that the baby was not only alive but still suckling at her breast, oblivious to the world's cruelty.

Ruth's knees buckled, a raw, keening wail escaping her lips. The grief was a physical pain, tearing through her as she cradled her mother's lifeless form. But there was no time for mourning. Timothy, her baby brother, needed her. Ruth's hands trembled as she strapped him to her back, his small body a comforting weight against her own.

She also had no time to feel herself change, the weight of responsibility and loss transforming her from a child into a woman. She moved with renewed purpose now, her mind sharp and clear. She made her way back to the few remaining villagers hiding in the bush, their faces drawn with fear, hunger and exhaustion. Together, they decided to make the perilous journey toward Kenya, a desperate bid for safety and survival.

As Ruth walked, the baby's gentle breaths against her back, she drew strength from the thought that she and baby Timothy were the only survivors of her extended family, their lives now intertwined with the hope of a future beyond the devastation.

She determinedly banished from her mind the sight of their mother's cadaver laying huddled over Timothy in a hole she must have been digging to shelter him while she bled out. Ruth wanted to believe that he survived by sucking on their mother's lifeless breast. However, at the time she found him, he had blood around his lips. She was never able to ascertain what kept Timothy alive: The residual milk from their mother's limp breasts, or her blood, which was splattered all over her due to the machete chops to her neck? But she praised God that he had survived, so that she was not alone in the world. She kept him strapped to her back as she journeyed alongside Garang Kir and the remnants of their village on the long trek to Kenya.

However, even Ruth could not have unfolded the intricate nature of relations among Sudanese ethnic groups. She knew nothing about the internecine intrusions of Ottomans, Arabs, and eventually the British, or how all these complicated Sudan's history so maddeningly that Timothy had ended up in a womb-like hollow that could have been his shallow grave.

Centuries before he was born, in the land, which was Timothy's home place, some ethnic groups had found it expedient to survive, to become embedded with xenophobic imperialists whilst others were shunned. The peoples got pitched against each other. The Nuer, one of the few African groups that managed to fend off colonial powers in the early 1900s were highly skilled warriors who had occasionally clashed with their neighbours. Such hostilities between ethnic groups were exacerbated after Sudan's independence on the 1st of January, 1956, due to the concentration of the country's wealth in the south, versus the northern desire to control these resources. A common enough scenario throughout Africa. Europe's cartographers were more Machiavellian than Cartesian. Civil war was foreseen. Yet, even as the Sudan People's Liberation Army and allies sallied against the predominantly Muslim/Sudanese/Arab regime in Khartoum, parallel conflicts between ethnic groups raged orgiastically.

***

On the night that Timothy hastily decided that he had finally found salvation with the Tinklers, he made the strategic decision not to pass Ruth his forwarding address and phone number. The story he told Paul, Mona, and their friends did not include a widowed sister. As far as the Tinklers, his saviours, were concerned, he was a lone, forlorn orphan. How could Ruth's existence now enhance his redemption? He was a little conflicted by his "tactical self-interest," but he promised himself that as soon as he made good, he would contact Ruth and make her whole again.

For the moment, his top concern was his education, so he could profit from his situation. Only after could he start wiring Ruth money again. The last time he spoke to her before meeting the Tinklers, when he tried to explain his dire situation in Canada, she snapped at him, going on as if she had compiled the names of every other ex-refugee-camp lad in America and Canada who, in spite of paying tuition fees, managed to dispatch money orders to their needy, overseas kin. She also accused Timothy of not calling often and even suggested that he borrow money to send to her so she could start selling firewood in the camp. She extracted his promise, even though he knew he did not stand a cat's chance in hell to acquire such a loan. However, though he was not speaking to her in English, he could not find words adequate enough in his native tongue to describe how drastically Canada dashes the expectations of hope-strapped refugees. These economic desperadoes dreamed that going to America or Canada or anywhere in the over-developed world was to enter an Oz of riches and a Utopia of paved roads and potable water.

Once Timothy joined the Tinklers, he had a room of his own for the first time ever. Crucially, too, it was the first time since coming into consciousness as a human being that he did not have to worry about where his next meal was coming from or when it might materialize.

Surprisingly, the state of comfort in which he found himself thanks to the Tinklers was so deceptively seductive. He quickly settled into the luxury of a room of his own, the assurance of three square meals, a fridge laden with snacks at his beck and call, the freedom from not worrying about his sister and her children, and the receding memories of his friends who were still waiting at Kakuma, praying for their refugee applications to be stamped "ACCEPTED."

Upon joining the Tinklers, however, Timothy faced an unusual dilemma in the form of the obese family feline, Timmy. It was not just the cat's name—a derivative of his—which irked him to no end, but the Siamese was precisely his own age. Timmy was nineteen, and it seemed especially proud of its seniority since Timothy had to dial back his own age. Timmy was also annoyingly territorial, having spent its entire nine feline lives in the home of the childless Tinklers. Moreover, the animosity was mutual. Whenever Timmy was curled up on a chair, Timothy had to abandon any idea of sitting anywhere near because Timmy would snarl, baring its fangs in sharp annoyance until Timothy vamoosed. Often, that meant no TV and/or no snack. Timothy was also beleaguered by the notion that the Tinklers expected him to accommodate their pet's peccadilloes and eccentricities; after all, they had a history with the de facto child. What worried Timothy most was that he could never muster the courage to face down Timmy by testing how the Tinklers would react if he refused to be timid or timorous before the cat's hissy fits and space-hogging bullying.

Then, a disorienting thought struck Timothy one evening. After he silently said grace before dinner, his eyes caught the packet of Timmy's carnivore feed which read, "All natural, with four high-quality meat meals: Chicken, Turkey, Lamb, & Fish." Timothy's eyes then alighted upon Timmy's dish with the hardly touched portion, ignored beside the stove. Then the unsavoury fact sucker-punched him smack in the pit of his stomach: *All that time, during all those years of my life when I did not know where my next meal was coming from, Timmy just got fat! Timmy never had to worry!*

PART FOUR:
CAN DRY BONES LIVE AGAIN?

Halifax, Nova Scotia, Canada – 2008

Iona frowned at her image in her compact mirror, tucking the brown Pashmina tightly around her head with her other hand. She squinted when she saw that the freckles around her nose remained defiant despite all her attempts to vanish them with makeup. She sighed and then strode briskly from her office toward her class. In the lecture room, some of the students were still milling around the door, but on spotting her, they dispersed to their desks. She waited for their attention before making her announcement. Though she felt a tad nervous, she rifled through the notes from her meeting with Dr. Atkins and assured herself that she could handle the class.

After completing her first degree in political science at the University of Toronto, Iona opted to evacuate that discipline, concluding that to attend circumspectly to Plato, Aristotle, Hobbes, or even Marx, or any of the other modern philosophers and political theorists, was gross naiveté. Her thesis? Hegel's postulations when he correlated a hierarchy of civilizations to a hierarchy of races generated the schema for modern racism. Without Hegel, there would have been no Hitler.

Thus, she was easily seduced by feminism; so she registered to do a master's in women's studies at York University, but became irremediably irritated by the preoccupation with the body and sexuality, and the way everything seemed to be hyper-deconstructed into inconsequentialities. She was profoundly outraged by how the issue of race—the bane of her life—was relegated to being just another "visible minority issue."

Indeed, she feared that racism itself was being deconstructed into a non-problem by White girl—"raceless"—feminists. However, even before she completed her master's degree, she had become fanatical about the ecosystem, and so registered for her doctoral program in International Development Studies at Dalhousie University. She was also drawn to Nova Scotia because she hoped to reconnect with some of her father's relatives. So, she jetted back to Dalhousie, where she was now a sessional lecturer.

"As some of you might have heard, Dr. Atkins delivered a healthy baby girl three days ago," she said, trying to jest about the premature birth of the baby, occurring almost three months before her due date. Though happy to try to direct a course for the first time, Iona was genuinely glad to see that both mother and child were doing really well when she visited them in the hospital that very afternoon.

"Dr. Atkins will not be back with us this term, so you're stuck with me for the semester." She was no comedian, and so was relieved that some students tittered at her self-deprecating remark.

"First off, many of you have not yet signed up for the Community-Based Learning portion of this course. Need I remind you that participation in this exercise constitutes fifty percent of your grade? So please, if you haven't signed up yet, come see me after class." She made a conscious effort to catch the eyes of the two Black male students. Scanning the class list, she noticed that one student, Timothy, signed up for the program, but had not shown up to pick up the necessary forms needed to commence his Community-Based Learning. The other, Siaka, had not bothered at all. Typical of Black folks, she thought, recalling a TV documentary about a group of high school juveniles who went from London, Ontario, to build a school in a Kenyan village.

Even though she knew the students in the documentary scrupled to take up a collection to fund the trip and had gone there with the best intentions, the whole idea was nauseatingly toxic. Of the twelve or so students, only one was Black. And even then, the "visible minority" girl was hardly given any airtime in the documentary. Iona now figured that, more than the poor Kenyan students, the Canadians would gain the most from the experience. Then again, the "First World" always puts itself first. Iona deduced from the interviews conducted after they returned to Canada that they were now even more appreciative of their privileges as citizens of "the developed world"—Wall Street and the White House acting in concert with NATO. Watching them interact with their Kenyan counterparts, Iona could not help screaming at her TV screen because she read a sense of superiority into every gesture the Canuck students made. She was incensed by the fact that not once in the hour-long documentary was any attempt made to unravel the mystery behind Kenya's poverty other than to allege that, like with other African countries, Kenya's destitution was due to corrupt leadership. Thankfully, the only other Black student in her class, Eni, whom Iona found unusually quiet, had not only put her name down for the Africa Project but also emailed the professor to make an appointment to have her form signed.

Siaka shifted in his seat when Iona's glance absorbed his visage. While he was glad she was now his instructor, because she always gave him a friendly smile, he felt uneasy because he had no interest in signing up for the Community-Based Learning.

Iona Pearse wore faded jeans and a matching jacket that sported wear patches at the elbows. Underneath, she wore a black turtleneck. He could not help noticing that, whenever he had seen her around campus, she was always dressed in turtlenecks and wondered if she had a scar or a tattoo on her neck and what she would look like once summer came. He ogled her five-foot-eight-inch frame, which was tamed into submission by what he suspected was a compulsion to run. The first time he eyed her was in the grad students' lounge, where he had gone for lunch soon after moving to Halifax for his grad program. Somehow she seemed familiar, but from where and when? Then, a few days later, he drove past her, running as if her life depended on it, on a street not far from the Quinpool Road apartment he shared with another student. He hoped she was not one of those overzealous T.A.s who would make them work extra hard just to prove herself—even if she had a "Dr." prefix and a "Ph.D." suffix to her name. He made a mental note to check the academic calendar to see if it was still kosher to drop the course. He was more at home with numbers and had only registered for the class because he assumed that the community-based part of it would mean little or no writing.

Timothy, who had not quite decided where he would go for his Community-Based training, also had half a mind to cut the course. When he registered for this elective, he did not expect the community training part of it would be mandatory. He also wanted to explore the possibility of taking other less demanding courses, even if it meant waiting another term because he was not really keen on any form of social work that could devolve into pissing matches between bickering egos. He decided he would just sign up initially and then email to indicate he was quitting, if he found something better.

"Excuse me. How long before those of us who signed up for the Africa Project find out if we've been selected?" a buff young man with a blond crew cut and multicoloured tattoos on his pink neck asked. Iona remembered him from the first class when he showed off pictures of his three-month stint in Ghana on a teen sports program.

Iona picked her words carefully to shroud her anger at his unconscious, blithely proclaimed privilege.

"I should have a shortlist of people by next class. But don't worry. I'll also list other worthy projects around Nova Scotia for those who don't end up going to Africa." She smiled, finishing her response to the crew-cut lad. She did not add that she had stressed to the sponsors the need to encourage African students to participate in this project. Seventy five percent of the class had indicated interest in drilling wells and latrines as part of the Africa Project. This was why she talked to the organizers to work out some selection criteria. Part of her agenda was also to urge students who were so enthusiastic about going to "help poor Africans" to take more interest in working in poor communities in Nova Scotia for a change.

To her surprise, the organizers saw her rationale. Thus, they gave her free rein in selecting the participants from her school. They also invited her to be part of the three-week project in Ile Ifa, a tiny, multiethnic, but little-known West African country. Iona and her chosen few would be part of a billionaire philanthropist's entourage, while groups from two other universities would join them one week into the project.

"But it won't be the same," a girl with half of her brunette hair dyed flame-red said. She was the reason Iona was wearing her thick hair, which she was grooming into sister locks covered in a Pashmina scarf. She'd almost slapped down the ditz the week before when the girl ooh-ed over her hair, even asking to feel the hair extension because she had assumed it was synthetic.

"I know, but let's not forget that the Africa Project is not supposed to be a holiday." Iona tried to hide her irritation.

"What's wrong with killing two birds with one stone, hey?" the girl insisted. Her classmates chortled.

After the class, Iona was pleased to see Eni waiting alongside the other African students. Briskly did Iona attend to other students so she could turn her full attention to the Black students.

Eni looked stunning in a thick baggy turquoise blue shirt with a white camisole underneath. Her large, bronze, gypsy-style ear loops with blue stones matched the Egyptian scarab on her neck. She had grown into a petite, slender, young woman. Her complexion had paled to light-brown after all the Canadian winters she had endured. But her lips remained noticeably dark. Was she or wasn't she wearing the cocoa-brown lipstick that she favoured? When viewed from certain angles, and depending on how she wore her natural, thick, curly and untamed hair, her round, large-eyed face could look too wide for someone so slight of frame. Yet, she retained the same air of mystery that had fascinated all who'd first eyed her on that Victoria Day when she was found on the street in Halifax.

"If there is a problem with accommodating me on the Africa Project, I can find something else to do here," Eni said.

"No, that's not the case at all. You were one of the first to sign up. Actually, I'm glad you all are here. The project organizers are particularly keen to have African students participate. So, I was wondering if I might interest you two in signing on as well," Iona said, looking at Timothy and Siaka, who were standing side by side.

"I don't know," Timothy said, "but my parents have also been encouraging me to volunteer for this project."

"Your parents are involved with this project?" Iona was ecstatic at the idea of real Africans participating.

"They are really my foster parents."

"Oh." Disappointment tinged Iona's voice.

"Okay, I'll sign up," Timothy said. Ever eager to please, he misread the reason for Iona's dejection. "I'm only reluctant because it will take three full weeks of my summer when I could be working and earning money."

"I don't expect the trip will be all work and no play. Although you should all be prepared to put in more than the thirty hours minimum, which the course requires," Iona said, reminding them.

"See, that's why I don't think it's fair. We'll be getting the same marks as those who do community work here." Perched on the edge of a desk, Siaka sounded like he was talking to himself.

"Will it make it fairer if instead of the full ten-page paper, five describing your activities will do?" Iona was determined to persuade them.

"Sign me on then," Siaka said, his face like iron. He felt no nostalgia for a continent of omnipresent oppression. He had also never allowed his mind to dwell on the images conjured by his father's assertion about his ancestral relationship with Nova Scotia.

Ile Ifa, Africa

On the day of departure for Ile Ifa, Iona got to the airport late, late, late. She'd wanted to get there early to assure her students of her professionalism and her care for their wellbeing, but her cabby was irritatingly tardy. She fumed all the way to the airport but choked her seething rage. Then, dragging her suitcase to the check-in counter, she ran smack into a network cameraman. Next, a local TV newsman shoved a microphone in her face. "Iona Pearse?"

"Yes?"

"Is this your first trip to Af—"

"Do you mind?!" she yelled, while sidestepping the nuisance.

Alan Steiner, director of the Africa Projects Foundation, strode to her side. He gave a thumbs-down to the reporter, who signalled his cameraman to stop shooting.

"I apologize for the—" Alan started saying.

"Why are they here?" She cut him off.

"Can we talk over there?" He noticed how the people on the check-in queue were listening intently while feigning disinterest. Iona looked at her suitcase and then back at Alan. Should she haul the baggage along? He gestured to a short, skinny man standing beside him to watch the bags, and Iona walked alongside her patron.

"First, I want to apologize that we did not give you a heads up on this matter. It's a snafu on the part of my P.A. He should have alerted you that a video crew would be accompanying us to Africa."

"But what for?"

"They're shooting a documentary on the Bicentennial Anniversary of the end of slavery, and they're interested in the work our foundation has been doing in—"

"I'm sure you mean the end of the transatlantic slave trade."

Alan paused for a moment, miffed by how Iona kept shorting his sentences. He could not immediately figure out what the hell she meant but thought it best to agree.

"Yes, of course." He tried to hide his pique.

"Don't you need some clearance from the university ...?"

"We got their permission to approach the students for their consent."

"Oh?" Iona now knew that the lack of notice was no oversight.

"Look, we don't mean to pressure anyone into participating. I'll remind the crew that they can't shoot anyone who doesn't okay appearing on camera."

She sensed that he had read her body language correctly. Although she was undecided about showing up in the documentary, Iona refused to consent too hastily.

"Yes, please do that. I'll think about it and let you know."

She waved to Eni, whom she spotted walking away from the check-in counter, followed by Siaka. She joined the queue again and, after collecting her boarding pass and saying a prayer for her trundled-away suitcase, approached Eni, Siaka, and Timothy, who were sitting, waiting for the rest of the team to finish up before navigating airport security.

Iona also saw Alan's wife Doris and a woman in her early twenties, their daughter Charlotte, whom she recognized from celebrity gossip snaps. She stopped to greet the botoxed Doris and the airbrushed Charlotte, but was grateful when a plump woman wearing a khaki shirt and shorts—as if ready for a safari—breached their assembly to coo at the Steiner femmes. Iona was thankful for the interruption, for an awkward silence had befallen their trio after she shook hands with Charlotte. She guessed that Alan had told his wife and daughter about her response to the videographers but, well, too bad.

Iona took a seat beside Eni. This act represented what she called in her mind a "congregation of the tribe." Ordinarily, so-called "political correctness" would have forced her to avoid a conscious show of Black unity. Still, that morning, she was preoccupied with riling the "system," which made her seek out other Black people in crowds. The "system" that morning meant "ofays" like Alan.

Thankfully, Timothy, who had met Doris and Charlotte through the Tinklers, and who seemed smitten by Charlotte, noticed her trailing her parents' group. He bounded to her Fashion Forward side.

"So, did you guys give your consent?" Iona felt dutybound to ask her students.

"Yes, it's to mark the end of slavery," Siaka said, nodding.

"Actually, the Bicentennial only marks the coming into law of the Abolition of Slavery Act," Eni explained.

"Thank you!" Iona beamed to salute Eni's response. Yet, she noticed that Siaka looked confused.

"What's the difference?"

"Slavery continued for many, many years afterwards. In the U.S., it took another sixty years and a civil war for domestic slavery to end." Eni knew her stuff and didn't mind strutting her knowledge.

"And I'd even argue that slavery is still very much a part of the world today," Iona said.

"As in human trafficking and child labour?" Siaka asked.

"Of course. Besides, just because you don't see the chains, it does not mean they're no longer there." Iona launched into a spontaneous lecture on global economic architecture, tying it to how workers in the economic South suffered brazen exploitation. She illustrated this point by describing how her late grandmother worked in a so-called Export Free Zone in Jamaica, which was just a glorified plantation. Indeed, the only difference now was that the "produce" was designer jeans for consumers in the North. The trade reaped enormous profits for so-called investors here. She ended her "teachable moment" when she noticed Siaka fiddling with his iPod. *Was Eni's listening also only politeness?*

***

On the private jet, Iona went sleepless because the Steiners were being loudly interviewed. Chatterbox Doris was explaining how she came to be involved in Alan's philanthropic work.

"I confess that my reasons are a tad selfish. My work in Africa is part of my salvation. It rescues me from a mundane life."

Iona craned her neck toward the aisle, but could not see Doris's plastic-doctored face to ascertain if she was smiling into the camera. But few would-be saints deign to smile. Tears are the best policy.

"Your life? Mundane?" the interviewer asked incredulously.

"Let me rephrase that. What I mean is … it rescues me from a self-centred life. I feel honoured to be able to serve, to work to better the lives of these poor people, and I'm glad that my daughter has adopted the family tradition of doing charitable work. We had our moments of anxiety about her, but last year, she toured some East African countries with some friends—"

"We also went to South Africa. It was a safari." Charlotte blurbed herself into the give-and-take.

"I was coming to that next," the interviewer said. "How does a young woman like you, who has had an easy life, everything you've ever wanted, go on a safari to Africa and come back eager to aid poor Africans?"

Doris's pride in her daughter oozed like jelly from every treacly syllable.

Iona saw the journalist's head bob up and down as he adjusted his position so that the microphone favoured Charlotte.

"I can't really put it into words. I've been going to Africa since I was a child," Charlotte said, peering into the camera, then lowering her eyes, so humbly. One-part debutante, one-part ingénue.

"You know the Ile Ifa property has been in the family for four generations?" Alan, who had been rifling through *The Financial Times*, asked rhetorically. "It was given to my maternal great-grandfather, Edwin Stuart." He noticed the questioning look on the journalist's face, so continued. "He was a Briton, posted as district officer to Ipeja Village. Ipeja is the seat of the traditional ruler. A few hours' drive from Abula, the capital."

"Apparently Alan's ancestor was a benevolent D.O. Adored by all. The O- y-o-f-a of Ile Ifa ... Alan, am I saying the title properly?" Doris, who had reinserted herself into the interview, asked.

"No, dear. Even I can't quite remember how to say it now. I spent so many holidays there as a boy that I could almost speak the language. But no more. Anyway, that's the title of the traditional ruler."

"Here, I've written it out the way Alan's father taught me, with all the inflections and what-have-you," Doris said, presenting the paper she'd written on. "The present ruler of the place is a great-nephew of the one who gave Alan's ancestor the land."

"How big is it?" the reporter asked.

"Do you mean the country or our land?" Alan asked.

"Your land."

"Oh, it's a lot smaller now. Only about a thousand hectares or thereabouts. Less than a third of what we used to own. My father gave most of it back." Alan sniffed—to remark the grand gesture of a saint.

"You've skipped your grandfather William's bio, Alan," Doris said. "William migrated to Canada but kept the connection to Ile Ifa. An enthusiastic hunter, he was a confidant of Prince Edward."

"I don't understand," the reporter said.

"Not the present Prince Edward. The late Prince of Wales."

"Of course. You must mean the abdicator. The royal who abdicated the throne when they wouldn't let him marry a two-time Yankee divorcee," the reporter said, so they would not deem him utterly bankrupt of all history not headlined on supermarket tabloids.

"Precisely. The family lore is that William Stuart built the hunting lodge in Ipeja, so his friend, the prince, could escape from his stressful, regal duties," Doris explained.

"Amid his unconstitutional dalliance with Mrs. Simpson," Iona said under her breath as she sighed. She shifted in her seat and muttered, "Stressful? My ass! She can't be saying that, except for that scalpel-straightened face! The bloody hunting lodge was most probably where the bloody prince and his randy cohorts went to get their freak on."

"Even after it was built, most of the land remained fallow, which was why Alan's dad gave a huge chunk of it back," Doris said.

"He also wanted to benefact the people. Being predominantly illiterate farmers, they had over-farmed most of what was left of the village," Alan said, adding to his wife's impromptu infomercial.

"Fortuitously, the land came into the hands of Alan's ancestors. Otherwise, the whole village would have starved in the early '80s if they did not have the land—returned by Alan's dad—to fall back on."

"But what about the diamond?" the reporter asked, feeling genuinely bamboozled.

"The diamond was only discovered a few years back. Here is everything you need to know about our operations in Ipeja." Alan handed him some papers.

"It was not the newness of encountering Africa that awoke something in me." Charlotte's voice sounded impatient, as if she had been waiting for the reporter to turn his spotlight back upon her ready-for-prime-time face.

"But it was your first time without us, dear," Doris had to say, to placate her camera-hogging daughter.

"Yes. Anyway, my friends and I insisted to our tour guide that we wanted to see and experience the life of an African village. Although it's really not allowed, he arranged for us to visit his village one evening. It was a life-changing experience. They had nothing. No pipe-borne water, no electricity, no school, no hospital. Yet the people were so happy. So poor, yet so happy, and so grateful! I found a group of children playing a game which reminded me of 'Ring a Ring o' Roses,' and I joined them. At the end of the evening, I gave them all the money I had with me."

"You should never do that, dear. It might cause a rift. Never hand beggars money. Also, never give the children candy. It's bad for their teeth," her mother said, chiding Charlotte mildly.

"Anyway, when we were leaving, all the village tots lined the road to watch us drive past, chanting our names. They had even made up a song with my name because I played with the children. Imagine, they made up a song about me ..." Her voice petered off, and she sounded as if she was overwhelmed by tears brought on by the recollection.

Peeved, Iona reflected: *Her rich White gal gift of penny candy won her the reward of a chorus-line hymn to her name!*

"I think I fell in love with the continent instantly, and it seemed such a shame that so many people there are poor," Charlotte said, finishing up, sounding a bit like Leni Riefenstahl, sobbing over Africans after having fawned over Hitler.

Iona imagined Doris patting her daughter on the cheek, her smile blending pride and indulgence. She heard Doris preen. "Isn't she priceless? Our daughter, who expects nothing but the best and has always got it, yet has room in her heart to care for others. How sweet. She came home and said, 'Mum, I've decided what I want to do with the rest of my life. It's unfair that so many Africans are poor.'"

"How did that make you feel as a mother?" The question was appropriately awe-filled. The journalist was interviewing saints.

"First, I asked her, 'Who told you that life was meant to be fair? Anyway, that's why there are people like us. To fund latrines for sanitation and provide wells for fresh water ...'"

Having heard enough, Iona brought out a small bottle of Jamaican rum, bought at the duty-free. Her virgin flight on a private jet, how could she know what kind of service to expect? She glanced behind her to see if others were also eavesdropping, and saw Siaka sleeping.

Siaka had snoozed off as soon as his head hit the headrest, because, upon boarding, he had taken the tranquillizers gifted him by Angela. Timothy, sitting to his right, also did not hear the interview. Boarding the plane brought back to mind his first flight, and the memory was its own turbulence. He focused on reminiscing about his departure and the friends who came to visit him the eve before he left the refugee camp. He remembered how full of hope for the future he was—and the joy in his friend Matthias's eyes when he came to help him pack. Joy tinged with envy because Matthias was still waiting for his luck to change. He interspersed virtually every sentence with his secular prayer, "I hope I get a sponsor soon." He also recalled Matthias's gratitude when he divided up his raggedy clothes between Matthias and Mark. He smiled ruefully at how they joked and argued playfully over who would get what, even though Mark, unlike his cousin Matthias, and Timothy, was quite tall. As Timothy played the benevolent peacemaker, Matthias peered up at him from where he was kneeling beside the nylon bag containing the used garments.

"Don't forget your brothers. Don't forget who we are when you get there."

"What stories will you tell the White people when you get there?" Mark asked.

"I will tell them about the conditions here. I will tell them about you, my friends, my brothers, and all we have gone through together."

"Don't forget how we were shot by our enemies at Gilo River," Matthias said.

"How can I forget that and our ways? I am going there for a purpose. I will get my education and come back because it is important for me to come back and help," Timothy pledged in a shaky voice.

"Well, when life becomes sweet for you over there, the sorrow here will be as if it never happened," Mark said.

"How can life ever be so sweet that I will forget this place? When loneliness awaits me over there? I'll shrink. I won't be able to grow fat even if I eat good food." Timothy tried to lighten the mood.

Now seated on a private jet, he turned his wrist over, trying to measure if it was fatter or had stayed the same. He shut his eyes. The lean years had turned fat, yes. But was he still lean? He felt guilty because he had not thought of his friends and kin for so long, but it was not due to his life being "sweet and fat" that he forgot them. Forgetting them was how he'd survived—psychologically, emotionally.

Eni surfed through the impressive in-flight entertainment without finding anything to arrest her interest. She then left her screen on the channel with the miniature image of the plane, which was inching its way across the electronic map toward Abula, the capital city of Ile Ifa. She rose, retrieved her carry-on baggage from the overhead compartment, and fished inside for her notebook. She sat down again and began to scan its pages. She had a notebook for almost every year she lived in Canada. She was unwavering in her resolve to sort out the confusion about where her present life began and her past life ended. She must have had parents and possibly siblings at one time or the other before she surfaced on the Haligonian street under Victoria's fireworks. Even if she was an orphan, which was her way of reconciling herself to the fact that no one had ever turned up seeking her. She had to make sense of her origin. It was one of the reasons why she'd volunteered speedily for the project in Ile Ifa. She closed the notebook and resumed watching the tiny image of the plane.

Soon her thoughts turned to the many horror stories of corrupt customs officials and throngs of conmen that she had read about during her research on Ile Ifa. She looked forward to seeing Abula, the country's capital, one of its oldest cities, which had started out as a small town. In the forty years since Ile Ifa was granted independence by the British, Abula had grown into a megalopolis with almost half the country's twenty-three million citizens living there as bustling, hustling inhabitants.

Siaka was feeling well-rested after sleeping through the all-night flight. Any apprehensions that Siaka had about returning to Africa dissipated once he cast his eyes on the verdant view as the plane approached the city of Abula, which rose to meet his eyes in sync with the rising sun. To him, Abula looked like a haven infused with energy, tempered by impressive modern buildings, and an unwieldy, spaghetti-labyrinthine network of roads.

As the aircraft touched ground at Abdullahi Mamood International Airport, the young morning sun illuminated the expansive cityscape, skyscraper-shadowed shantytowns.

Like the others on the entourage who were first-timers in Ile Ifa, Iona did not notice that the airport was eerily placid as they were swiftly ushered through customs and immigration by a

Canadian High Commission posse. The speed at which they were being processed through a typically onerous exercise alerted the local press, who started snapping away with reckless abandon. The students, Iona, and the videographers could not know that their breezy passage through the airport was no mean achievement. In fact, their way was smoothed due to the American dollar being a rare and coveted commodity. The Ile Ifa dina traded at roughly twenty eight hundred to the Washington, available solely via the black market. It was sold by machine-gun-wielding currency merchants who carted local currency notes around, cruising the streets in neon-flashy bullion vans.

The airport was normally a virtual war zone because local hoodlums targeted foreigners. Thus, Alan's company had arranged with the Canadian High Commission to engage the best security outfit in the country to be their guides. Had the students known this, they might have wondered why they should need any kind of armed escort since they were in the basket-case country to do good.

The most corporate-efficient and brazen thugs virtually running the country were dubbed the "Area Boys"—youth gangs who mugged, kidnapped, carjacked, and invaded public buildings and homes to tote off bundles of thousand-dina notes. The Area Boys hit the jackpot when they moved out of commercial motor parks, which they had looted for decades, to capture major markets. A few years back, politicians leagued to exploit their mafiosi expertise by hiring them clandestinely as political gangsters. Soon, the Area Boys wised up and installed a top cadre as governor of Abula state, where Abula city is located. Their candidate quickly wrangled his way into the presidential office, replacing his crony, a retired military general. Now the Area Boys were above the law because they were the law.

There were no credit cards in Ile Ifa because no major, global bank wanted anything to do with the Ile Ifa dina. As such, private citizens were forced to haul cash around, mainly in the side panels of cars and/or in their bulging pockets.

As the Canucks navigated Abula in a stretch Hummer, sandwiched between Land Rovers carrying sunglassed-flak-jacketed-AK-47-toting details, Eni witnessed higgledy-piggledy roads, fields, skyscrapers, and tin shanties. To the north, the interlocked isles of Victoria Ville, Plantain Island, Ecos, Papaya, and Ikokia, congested with high-rises, boasted impish, crude, garish opulence—like gold nuggets scattered amid trash.

Abula's frontiers now sprawled into lush, adjacent jungles and marshlands due to Chinese money floating gimcrack, brazenly tall skyscrapers. The entourage had to avoid deadlocked traffic through the city's main thoroughfare because overnight a building under construction collapsed, killing twenty nine people.

The imploded pile was one of the many hollow hotels and bling-bling casinos jerry-built thanks to Chinese cash. As a result, the manic collapse of structures was endemic in a country lacking construction codes and government support for labour. The twenty nine people who died were men, women, and children, all sweated for a pittance, i.e., slave wages. They were some of the squatters on the building site, sleeping and eating in shelters made of discarded cement bags and rickety bamboo props. They died asleep when, just before midnight, rain washed away the poorly finished foundation, and the multistorey heap toppled onto—crushed into mud—snoozing, exploited clans.

Having studied Ile Ifa, Iona was alarmed to read that the Ile Ifa All People's Congress, which had been in power for close to eight years, was as unconcerned about the spate of building fails and other problems as its so-called opponent, the Ile Ifa People's Development Party, which had been ousted after twelve years of draining the treasury. Yet, no party vowed to regulate industries. No party heeded the public interest. The resource-laden state was essentially under the stranglehold control of one party, which had strategically divided itself into two camps so that only a handful of men and women could perpetuate themselves in power. Like carpetbaggers, politicos shuttled from one party to the other to suit their personal ambition, while ensuring that the hundreds of other parties remained inconsequential. Governance depended solely on cronyism, kickbacks, and baksheesh.

Tragically, even the so-called free press had lost its voice and any sense of objectivity. The media jostled to sing the praises of whichever of the "two" leading parties was funding its barefoot journalists and often blacked-out media houses. China, Russia, and the G7 states seized the opportunities fostered by the ensuing mayhem to pump money into the hands of professional non-governmental organizations, partisan bagmen and women, and other bigwigs. These ultra-rich and missile-bristling countries would then send observers during the next election, a few months away, to pronounce it "free and fair" as usual. If pressed, their representatives in Ile Ifa would go on TV and declare that the elections are "free and fair enough" so as not to warrant cancellation or a rerun. That way, the business of robbing the country of its resources through their multinationals and the connivance of paid-off politicos proceeds quietly. Pin-stripe, photo-ops-backed, with soldiery shows of force.

Iona wondered why the shoestring press and equally beggared Ile Ifa eggheads (those who hadn't joined the brain drain to the well-armed, well-off G20) did not question why Chinese investment in the country jumped from a couple of hundred million dollars a year to several billions. Were they too famished to link the burgeoning Chinese influence to their government's failure to enact building codes and/or to pursue policies independent of Chinese approval? Iona knew that a lot of the "White noise" from America and Europe was nothing but whining about the rise of China. She smiled ruefully when she recalled how the Western (i.e., white Supremacist) press had been claiming that the reason why the EU, NATO, and G7 nations withdrew their so-called preferential trade agreement was due to the Ile Ifa government's crackdown on human rights and minor politicos—those without followers, but with loud mouths. However, she had studied and uncovered the fact that the preferential trade agreement had really been nothing more than a tool for keeping "independent" Ile Ifa servile.

She had also taken the trouble to find some Ile Ifa newspapers and had been bemused when she read how, basking in the newfound romance with China, the regime countered the accusation by the "the White powers" by saying they were just jealous because they could no longer rival Chinese investment. She, however, did not realize that what such government propaganda hid was that Ile Ifa's establishment had steered the country into a tight corner where they had no option but to do whatever China said, since it had bought off the political class to plunder—sans protest—what was left of Ile Ifa's resources. Essentially, China held the country as a vassal state in all except name. The U.S., infamous for doing the same thing all around the world, kept screaming that China was planning to militarize Ile Ifa to gain a stronghold around the sea surrounding the island nation. Thus, the U.S. kept a gunboat cruising menacingly just offshore.

To avoid the infernally stalled, downtown traffic, the Canucks limo'd down sideroads. Their convoy meandered through posh districts, where drug merchants, political kingpins, and other plutocrats lived in mansions behind bizarrely decorated high walls. Walls that were protected by bulletproof gates and lined with broken beer bottles and other anti-burglary devices. These compounds were sometimes interspersed cheek-by-jowl with stubborn ramshackle sheds, and improvised stalls abutting open, putrid gutters.

Despite Abula's size and gilded prominence, its terrifying repute and a dearth of touristy sites compelled foreigners to pass on by. Instead, foreigners would typically make their way to Ile Ifa's oil-drowned areas around its Tiga delta region.

Ordinarily, the traverse from the airport to Ipeja Village would not require a three-hour drive. However, halfway through Abula, the convoy ran into a traffic jam on streets flooded from the rainstorm that had almost drowned half the city the day before. The backed-up traffic was also hindered by vendors who hawked everything from hardboiled eggs, raw meat, and live chickens, to cigarettes, made-in-China toys, and second-hand, "new" Italian suits, to scrap motorcycle parts.

Had the passengers in the Hummer been able to see the streets in that neighbourhood without the knee-deep flood, they would have been shocked by its filth and desolation that contrasted sharply with the areas around the airport, which were populated by three-star hotels. The grand filth and grandiose desolation would have struck them dumb. Shocking anyway was the mob who jolted each other as they waded through the sewage flood on foot, vulnerable to vermin, injury, and disease. Despite the country's oil wealth, the citizens had woken up that morning to yet another fuel shortage. The Canucks witnessed pedestrians skipping over what resembled a log of wood sticking out of the murky water at a street corner. How could they know that the object was the remains of a policeman caught trying to snatch a woman's handbag? Some of the people who now leaped across the body had looked on approvingly as one of the people who'd stopped the thief threw an old tire around his neck while another sloshed him with gasoline and set him ablaze.

The Canadian entourage also did not realize that another log of misshapen wood was the corpse of a seven-year-old boy, who was tortured to death after being denounced as a witch by his stepmother. She was the dirt-poor family's only breadwinner. His wasted body floated—bloated—in a gutter alongside a mountain of toxic, gutted computers. The steeply sloping garbage was colossal enough to rival Ghana's Agbogbloshie. Young, able-bodied, unemployed Ile Ifarians dotted the mound, scampering here and there, too desperate to care about the risk to their health. How else would they extract aluminum and copper from the dumped electronics shipped from the rich, White West?

Five and a half hours later, when they reached the outskirts of Ipeja, the convoy split up. The crew went to one of the guesthouses belonging to Alan's mining concern. The students, Iona, and Alan's family, proceeded to the hunting lodge. When their car neared the walled compound, its beautiful hedge of flowers and walls, newly painted, intimated a mirage. The reality had boots-machine-guns-and-sunglasses guarding the gates.

The compound was a horticulturist's dream. The sprawling bungalow—the oasis to which they had come—conjoined two humungous ranch houses. The exterior walls were constructed out of enormous laterite rocks in various shades of grey. Iona could not help imagining how bereft the mountain from which the rocks had been quarried must now be.

The garden was exquisitely sculpted by the foremost landscape architect in Ile Ifa during Alan's father's life. Although the lodge had been constructed by Alan's grandfather, in the family lore, it was Alan's father who was fondly remembered as its architect. He had impeccable taste and indulged his beaux-arts aesthetic in all his residences around the globe.

In sharp contrast to the benighted, surrounding village, the compound was brightly lit by state-of-the-art generators tucked very far away in the hundreds of hectares behind the house. It was impossible to hear the grinding hum of the polluting engines. Lying languidly to the right of the bungalows was a saltwater pool.

At the southern corner was a stable that held Arabian horses.

Inside, the walls were done up in Italian marble, and was centrally air-conditioned.

Alan's visitors were struck by its imposing opulence. Most impressed was Timothy, whose memories of Africa were of misery, massacres, and mud. Even Siaka, ordinarily more reserved, could not resist touching a marble column to see if it was real. Timothy was acutely aware that his feet were being caressed by lush, white carpet. In the vast living room, there were scattered islands of Persian rugs, while the walls floated life-sized stuffed heads of lions, an elephant, and even the extremely rare African black panther.

"Wow!" Iona exclaimed, both awe-struck and riled. "Wow!" she exclaimed again as she tried to identify which of the many heads belonged to extinct or endangered species.

"I must apologize for my ancestors' tastes. Which is why I've been most committed to preservation …" Alan felt compelled to say. "I assure you, none of these heads is younger than about fifty years old. And wouldn't it be a waste to throw them away since they were already here before we, I mean the world, realized the dangers such hobbies pose to the ecosystem." He tried to jest, but his guests ignored him. They were preoccupied with touring the show-piece house.

"It's also why we've been looking for a museum to take them on," Doris said. "Please make yourselves at home." She waved her hand—like a magic wand—to materialize the expanse of the palatial room, before hurrying to catch up with Iona, who was wandering through a long corridor to the far end of the estate. Doris was followed by an ascetic-looking man in a long-sleeved white French suit who'd led a drove of servants to welcome them when they spilt from the louche limo. "Dear Abdul will show you to your second-wing quarters. Abdul has been the manager of this place for …"

"Twenty nine years, madam." Abdul, who now stood ramrod beside the door, filled in the vital statistic.

"And still going strong!" Alan said, who recollected faded memories of a boyhood spent with Abdul, when they'd frolic in the woods behind the lodge. They'd tumble carefree together in fields overgrown by elephant grass. Eyeing the two men just then, it was impossible to imagine that Abdul was only nine months older than Alan. In contrast to Alan's figure, so trimmed and tamed by rigorous exercise, Abdul's was thin from the exigencies of managing an army of four wives and seventeen children on his salary. A salary undoubtedly generous but which, given the size of his family, could only go so far.

They ate a sumptuous meal of coconut rice, fried plantains, chicken peri-peri, and groundnut sauce, prepared by an army of local culinary experts tucked out of sight in the ultra-modern gourmet kitchen. Doris went dutifully to personally thank them for the delightful meal before returning to her guests, all sipping postprandial coffee and tea.

Ever the businessman, Alan was anxious to catch the local news. Since the non-family members were not strictly guests, he did not think it rude to take his coffee in the entertainment room; which included a cinema with a seventy-two-inch plasma screen TV. Just in time, he ogled a news item covering their arrival. Even he was impressed by how quickly his touchdown had made the headlines. He was surfing the channels when the others joined him. They all fell silent and focused on the TV when they saw how engrossed he was by the news. It was a news item that seemed to enthrall Alan.

The camera zoomed in on a map of the Democratic Republic of the Congo (DRC), highlighting the eastern region. The voiceover continued:

"Overshadowed by the global economic crisis, the ongoing plundering of the Democratic Republic of the Congo's valuable resources persists. Eastern DRC, home to some of the world's most abundant reserves of minerals, metals, natural gas, and oil—including ten percent of global copper reserves and thirty three percent of global cobalt reserves, alongside vast deposits of diamonds, gold, silver, timber, uranium, and zinc—has long been a target for exploitation by rebel factions, foreign militaries, and multinational corporations seeking to enrich themselves. While other African conflicts have been fueled by diamonds and gold, in the eastern DRC, columbo-tantalite—or coltan—has emerged as a highly sought-after commodity. With the DRC possessing eighty percent of global coltan reserves, it is the new black gold."

A montage of images, showing rebel factions, foreign militaries, and multinational corporations vying for control over the abundant reserves of minerals, metals, natural gas, and oil, played as the voice over continued. Then, as the camera panned over a crowded and chaotic coltan mine:

"Coltan is a crucial component in the production of heat-resistant capacitors used in cell phones, laptops, and other advanced electronics. The escalating global demand for technological innovation has led to a surge in the demand for coltan, prompting miners and traders to intensify their efforts to extract it. In September 2001, coltan reached a peak trading price of almost four hundred dollars per kilo." Shots of workers labouring in dangerous conditions flashed across the screen as the voiceover mentioned their low pay.

"With coltan miners earning ten to fifty dollars per week—five times higher than what most other impoverished Congolese earn in a month—government and rebel forces have imposed taxes on miners for access to the mines, resulting in fierce and often violent competition for control over the mines and surrounding areas. Despite the perilous conditions in the mines, which have led to countless fatalities, there is no shortage of workers."

Images of child miners are shown as the voiceover notes their involvement in this lucrative trade. "And tragically, an increase in demand for coltan has led to an increase in child labour, with approximately thirty percent of school children forced into mining work at the expense of their education."

The news segment ends with a sombre tone as statistics on lives lost during the conflict are displayed.

"The struggle for control over coltan mines remains a central factor in the conflict in eastern DRC, a conflict that has tragically claimed over four million lives in the past decade. Whether it's Apple, Samsung, Tesla, or other multinational companies, a Hutu militia like the Democratic Forces for the Liberation of Rwanda—or the DFLR—which fled Rwanda after the 1994 genocide, a Congolese rebel group like Nkunda's Tutsi rebels, or the Congolese army itself, each entity has a vested interest in the lucrative coltan trade."

Timothy and Charlotte had instantly lost interest in the news and were both whispering as they flipped through celebrity news on Charlotte's phone. Eni shifted uncomfortably in her seat, feeling the weight of the suffering playing out on the screen. She glanced at Iona, who sat next to her, her eyes reflecting a mixture of sadness and anger at the senseless violence. Beside them, Siaka remained unreadable, his gaze fixed on the TV.

***

As Eni stepped into the room that had been assigned to her that night, she caught a faint whiff of lavender, which must have clung to her clothes that she had earlier hung up in the wardrobe. It was the scent of her favourite candle that she always burned when she needed to relax and centre herself. She reached for her backpack that was beside an ornate nightstand and brought out her notebook.

The silence in the room was only broken by the sound of her soft breathing as she began to rifle through the pages. Her fingers began to lightly trace over her words, feeling the slight indentation of the pen on the paper. Her hand would occasionally pause, a slight shiver running through her as she remembered some of the events she had written about. Eni continued to rifle until she got to a page about the remembrance of a life in the DRC. She had recorded that memory soon after she started to write her visions.

She began to read it without much alarm. She had long come to terms with the horrifying realization that, no matter who the main characters in her nightmares were, she was always one with them. In order to stop herself from getting too sucked in by the many horrors she had recalled, whenever she had to read through her entries, she would tell herself she was a mere observer of these past traumas. Even when she started to refer to the characters in her nightmares in the first person.

As she read, she could feel the cold stone floor beneath her, smell the musty air, and see the desperation etched into every scratch on the walls. But even as she relived this memory, she willed herself to remain calm:

I am sitting on the bare floor of a dark, putrid-smelling cell. All around me, the plastered mud walls are covered with scratching. Some are deep and frantic while others are lighter and more desperate. It was as if the former inhabitants of this hell hole had been driven by their isolation to the point where they tried to scratch their way out through the plastered mud walls. The floor is cold and rough under my bare feet. Concrete and dirt scratch my skin with every move.

I take a moment to let my eyes adjust to the darkness surrounding me. The only light seeping into the cell comes from a small, barred window near the asbestos ceiling, casting faint shadows across the damp walls. I hear the distant echoes of muffled wailings and shuffling footsteps, a constant reminder of the presence of others in this hellish place.

As I shift my weight on the hard ground, a sharp pain shoots up my leg, a reminder of the beatings I have endured. The memory of rough hands and cruel laughter haunt me, fuelling a deep well of anger and defiance within me. But in this moment, as I sit alone in the darkness, that defiance starts to waver, threatening to give way to resignation.

I trace a particularly deep scratch on the wall in front of me, feeling the rough texture under my fingertips. Each mark tells a different story of suffering, desperation, and shattered hope. In these etchings, I see not just cries for freedom, but also resilience.

Why was I arrested? *I kept wondering, as if my freedom depended on the answer, even though I knew it did not. Was it because they had found my letter to Pierre about my willingness to sacrifice everything for our cause, like Ndeko Patrice Lumumba? Was I just one of the many people that the Belgians, Americans, and their Congolese collaborators, Kasa-Vubu and Mobutu, rounded up in order to stop the uprising that had erupted at the news of the assassination of Ndeko Patrice Lumumba and the other comrades? I refuse to let my mind dwell on Pierre, bolingo na ngai. I do not want to allow my mind see his body butchered and then burned by acid, the way we were told that Ndeko Lumumba and the other patriots were killed. Instead, I will my mind to wonder over to Ndeko Lumumba's speech on the day of his inauguration as our prime minister. The day I knew that it was up to me and others to turn around the course of our country. I steel myself, even as I sit in this cell, awaiting my execution. My faith in my country and my passion for a Congo free to manage its resources after such a terrible history is like an armour.*

I concentrate my mind on the air outside the Palais in Léopoldville, which was thick with anticipation on the day of the declaration of our independence. The smell of sweat and dust mingled as I stood among a large crowd that had started gathering the night before. My heart was pounding in my chest as King Baudouin of Belgium's voice beamed through the many megaphones that had been fitted around the building for the occasion.

Each word sliced through the air like a knife. He spoke of his ancestor, King Leopold II, whose agents had cut off my grandfather's hands for failing to harvest enough rubber. My stomach churned as this king of Belgium continued to speak with a shameless reverence for his evil ancestor. His praise for Leopold's "genius" felt like a slap in the face, a cruel mockery of the suffering we had endured. Leopold, the man whose hands were stained with the blood of millions, was now being heralded as a visionary. The crowd shifted uneasily, the collective anger like simmering volcano ready to erupt.

Baudouin's words painted colonial rule as a benevolent mission, a civilizing endeavor that had supposedly uplifted the Congo. I could almost taste the bitterness in my mouth, a bile that rose with each patronizing sentence. The king's speech was a basketful of lies, an attempt to maintain the façade of Belgian superiority and goodwill. The scent of flowers from nearby gardens seemed almost offensive, too sweet compared to such bitter words.

When Kasa-Vubu took the stage, his speech was not a stark contrast—short, polite, and uncontroversial. His gratitude toward Baudouin for his attendance and well-wishes was met with some timid applause. It felt hollow, a mere formality in the face of such blatant disregard for our pain. Few in the crowd clapped mechanically, devoid of genuine emotion.

Then, unexpectedly, Joseph Kasongo invited Ndeko Patrice Lumumba to speak. A murmur of surprise rippled through the crowd, followed by a tense silence. Ndeko Lumumba, our voice, our hope. As I imagined him stepping forward, his presence commanded our attention even though we could not see him. The air seemed to crackle with electricity, the atmosphere charged with unspoken words and repressed fury.

I glanced around at the faces in the crowd—eyes wide with anticipation, jaws set in defiance. This was our moment. Ndeko Lumumba began to speak, his voice a powerful current that swept through the crowd, lifting our spirits, igniting our resolve. The scent of sweat and dust faded into the background, replaced by the intoxicating aroma of possibility and change. As he spoke, the chains of our colonial past seemed to loosen, the dawn of true independence breaking through the darkness of oppression. The air became thick with the scent of sweat and anticipation, mingling with the faint aroma of street food being sold nearby. My hands clutched the edge of my thin, worn dress, damp with perspiration. We had all come to witness history. We did not know that the day would be made more triumphant by hearing the voice of our struggle articulated by our leader, Ndeko Patrice Lumumba.

Where we stood outside, I could not see his face, but in my mind, I see his face crowned by short hair parted unevenly, wearing glasses and a bowtie. He has a moustache and is dressed in a suit. His expression is serious and focused. I had memorized his face the day I went to see Pierre in their office where he worked as one of Ndeko Patrice's assistants. I could not believe how ordinary he looked when he walked past me. Later that afternoon, when Pierre was walking me to the bus stop and I remarked about Ndeko Patrice's ordinariness, Pierre smiled and said that was what made him such a great man: His simplicity and his willingness to die for us if need be.

As Ndeko Lumumba began his speech, his voice cut through the noise of the restless crowd. His words resonated deep within me, speaking directly to the heart of every Congolese gathered there. He didn't just address us; he celebrated us, praising our hard-fought independence as the culmination of our collective struggle, not a gift from the Belgians.

He spoke of the personal suffering we all knew too well: The forced labour, the relentless discrimination, the land snatched from our ancestors, the wealth disparity that left us impoverished in our own homeland. His voice carried the weight of our shared history, each word a witness to the injustices we had endured. I felt the roughness of the earth beneath my feet, a reminder of the land we had been denied.

Ndeko Lumumba's promise was a balm to our weary souls. Independence, he declared, would end our suffering. Through our own democratic institutions, we would finally see social justice and fair wages. The vision of a Congo free from racial discrimination, where repression was a relic of the past, filled my heart with hope. He spoke of our nation becoming the pride of Africa, a beacon for the pan-African movement. The scent of blooming flowers from a nearby garden that now drifted through the air was no longer sickening. It was a sweet symbol of the new beginnings he promised.

He called upon other nations, especially Belgium, to support our journey, emphasizing the need for mutual respect between two equal and independent countries. But his appeal to us, his people, struck the deepest chord. He urged us to abandon tribal divisions, to unite for the future of our Congo. The crowd around me murmured in agreement, a collective acknowledgment of our shared destiny.

As he concluded, Ndeko Lumumba's words were a rallying cry. He called on every Congolese to make sacrifices for our nation's future, to respect the rights of non-indigenous settlers while firmly warning that those who violated our laws would face exile. His final declaration, that our independence was a decisive step toward the liberation of the entire African continent, sent a shiver down my spine.

"Long live independence and African unity! Long live the independent and sovereign Congo!" His exclamations were met with a roar from the crowd, our voices merging into a powerful chorus. As I raised my hands that I had clenched into fists—feeling the rough calluses of hard work—and joined in the chant, my heart swelling with pride and hope, I noticed an old man standing next to me raising the stumps left of his hands. He reminded me of my koko ya mobali who died a few months ago. Unlike my koko ya mwasi, my tata and mama, who had died from the hardship

of working the rubber plantations, my koko ya mobali had survived to tell his stories of torture. He had been rewarded by seeing the hope of a truly free and independent Congo that was happening right before my eyes as I listened to Ndeko Lumumba's speech that day. I reminded myself that this was the moment that my parents and ancestors had died for. It was actually happening before my very eyes. As I continued to punch the air with my fists, my heart beat with joy for this moment, our future, our Congo.

These are the memories that I allow my mind to dwell on as I wait in that cell for the executioner to come for me. I am afraid to die but I believe that my death, like that of Ndeko Lumumba, my Pierre, my ancestors, and so many others, will not be for nothing. Our independence had been unleashed, and the future, for those we were living behind, will be bright no matter what happened to me.

Eni put aside the book, sighing as she realized that those aspirations for Congo had not been met. As she settled into bed to sleep, she knew the night would be riddled by nightmares. Although she had never had any other dreams of her life in the DRC, she had assumed that it was because she was executed after her confinement in that cell. She yawned, wondering if she would dream of her execution after reading that passage. Nothing could have prepared her for the nightmares that invaded her sleep that night. For the first time, she dreamed of a future. A life that she was yet to live, and it was no less harrowing than all the many nightmares about past lives that she had lived through.

Eni found herself wrestling with herself as she fell asleep. First, she did not feel the usual detachment that she had learned to feel whenever she was plunged into her nightmares since she had come to realize that her trances were things of the past. That night she, felt like an intruder, a voyeur. In this dream she saw a boy, backing her as he tended to his sick mother.

Eni could not immediately see his face but there was something, both familiar and unsettling, as she watched him lift his mother's head off the cloth-stuffed pillow on her makeshift bed and began to coax her to drink some gruel from a badly chipped enamel cup. The interior of the modest, sparsely furnished room had walls made of unplastered bricks. The floor was dirt and, to the right of the bed, there was a small area with scattered charcoal pieces and a metal container, possibly used for cooking. Some daylight filtered in through the small gaps in the brick wall; and the sparse, functional arrangement of the space highlighted the austere living conditions. Eni's eyes continued to make a sweep of the tiny room and she shuddered in her sleep when she saw the year on an almanac on a wall close to the door of the room: 2023. It was the future. She watched as the boy finished feeding his mother and then tucked the cover with tiny fish patterns around her to make sure she was comfortable.

"I think I will be back early today," he says as he turns away from the bed. Eni can see his face for the first time. It is her face. Not any of the other faces she had seen in her nightmares, it is the face she sees in the mirror every day since she emerged on the street of Halifax. He has on a pair of tattered green underpants and is naked from the waist up. Eni caught her breath as she recognized the scars on his body, his two navels are as familiar as hers. He bends down and picks up a red t-shirt from under the narrow bed, where his mother is lying, and puts it on. The t-shirt features a green and yellow cartoon character that reminds Eni of Peter Pan.

"Is it today they are coming?" his mother asks through wheezing breath.

"Yes. Noko said I should wear my best shirt because the White television people are coming to ask us questions."

"Stay close to him. Tell him not to let you talk to them where the security people will see you." She sounds anxious.

"Don't worry. You know Noko will not let anything bad happen to me."

"Will Zeke and Mukoshi also be there when they are talking to you?"

"I don't know, but they are so young. What can they say that I can't?" The boy sounds like an old man but looks no older than nine or ten.

Eni follows the boy out of the shack. Dawn has barely broken over the horizon, casting a pale light over the sprawling landscape of a mine. He trudges forward with a resigned determination, a small figure against the vast expanse of dirt and rock. He moves with a practiced familiarity, his bare feet navigating the jagged terrain with ease. The air is heavy with the scent of earth and sweat, mingling with the faint, metallic tang of minerals unearthed from the depths below. Eni is enveloped in the cacophony of shouts and the clinking of tools striking stone.

The boy walks up to a man with a hardened expression, who is waiting with two young boys who look no older than seven and five.

"How is your mother today?" the man asks.

The boy shrugs as they resume walking. The two younger boys fall in line as they try to keep up with the determined strides of the older boy and man. Eni concludes that they are a team, bound by blood and necessity, each carrying their share of tools and burdens. The older man leads the way, his broad shoulders hunched under the weight of a heavy sack, his eyes scanning the horizon for the day's labour.

As they continue walking, they catch up with other groups and others also fall in line behind them. Eni takes in the expanse of a mine, which looks like a maze of pits and tunnels, each one a potential death trap. The ground is a patchwork quilt of activity, with men, women, and children alike disappearing into the earth and re-emerging, covered in grime. As the boy and his group approach their designated spot, he glances at a deep, narrow hole, and Eni concludes they must have worked there the previous day. The gaping hole seems to beckon with a dark, open mouth, promising both sustenance and danger.

The boy's face is set in a mask of concentration. Eni is desolate as it occurs to her that this is no place for daydreams or distractions. Every moment demands his focus, every movement a calculated risk in the unforgiving environment of the mine.

The boy drops to his knees, peering into the darkness of the pit. The man hands him a makeshift tool, and without a word, he begins to dig. The older of the two younger boys is not far behind, watching and mimicking his actions, small mirrors of determination and toil. The rhythmic sound of digging is punctuated by the occasional sharp crack of stone, a reminder of the mine's treacherous nature.

As the day wears on, the sun climbs higher, casting harsh shadows over the landscape. The heat becomes oppressive, and the smell of sweat grows stronger, mingling with the earthy scent of freshly turned soil. The boy's movements slow, his young body pushed to its limits, but he presses on, driven by an unspoken understanding of the stakes.

By about midday, Eni spots a camera crew, made up of a blond woman reporter, her cameraman, and a third man holding a file. The reporter smiles as she waves the boy and his group toward her, away from the treacherous pits and tunnels.

The group hurry to put aside their tools and walk over to the TV crew.

"We thought you were working at the other end of the …" the reporter starts saying.

"No, they closed that pit. It collapsed two days ago," the man explains.

The reporter and her crew look mortified, but the boy and his group show no emotion at all. Eni concludes that they must have seen too many of such incidents.

"So, which of them is the one whose father and brother died in the pit that collapsed last month?" the reporter asks.

The man points at the older boy. "This one, Dekya. His mother is my younger sister. It was his father and older brother who …" He swallows unable to complete his sentence.

"The pit ate them," the boy says matter-of-factly.

Eni's heart goes out to the young boy as he stands barefoot on the dirt path, his legs covered in mud. His bright red shirt adorned with a Peter Pan character, standing in stark contrast to the human devouring earth around him. The boy looks unfazed as he engages in conversation with the blond woman, who crouches in front of him. She takes pictures with a still camera and looks up at him with a focused expression. To her right, the third man in her crew is writing in his folder as he takes in the scene, while the video cameraman crouches next to the woman, capturing the interaction. The boy's uncle and cousins stand behind the crew waiting for their turn to be questioned.

"I want you to tell us your name and age." The reporter's voice is kind and concerned.

"My name is Dekya Swaze. I am twelve years old."

"Do you go to school?"

"No."

"Why not?"

"I have to work and earn money so me and my mother can eat."

"Why is your mother not working?"

The boy looks into the camera, thinking for a fleeting second.

"My mother went to school to be teacher but there isn't work. My father, too, went to school for bi-o-lo-gy and che-mis-try," the boy explains, faltering over the unfamiliar words. But his pride in saying them is clear to Eni. "But we came here from Lubaya in Kabango because there was no work for them. I have to come and work here, because my mother has a bad chest from working here, and now there is no one to look after us. I am the only one who can."

"So what happened to your father and brother?" the reporter asks.

"My father and brother were digging underground when a big rain started to fall. They were unable to get out before the pit swallowed them."

The reporter looks from the boy to his uncle and his two young children, then clears her throat before speaking.

"This whole operation sounds like a death trap. We've been told that a tunnel collapses every month."

The man remains silent, looking away from his sons and nephew and focusing on the ground as if the answer was written there.

"It is our work and we are in God's hands. So we pray, go down the pit, and do the work, hoping that we will live to see tomorrow." When he finally looks up to face the reporter, he seems to have shrunk before Eni's eyes.

"The relationship between us and the owners of these mines is like slave and a master." His voice is a whisper.

Looking almost as embarrassed as the uncle, the reporter turns to face the boy again. "So what do you think about at night just before you fall asleep? What do you dream about becoming in future?"

"Me?" He looks surprised by her question.

She nods, smiling to encourage him.

But he just shakes his head slowly from side to side. "Nothing. I do not dream about any future. I am too tired. I can only think about the work I will do here tomorrow." He spreads out his hands to take in the expanse of the mine and the sun seems to catch the smiling face of the Peter Pan character, which now looks like an alien on his t-shirt.

The reporter signals to her cameraman, who pans to focus on her as she begins to speak. "Are you still in doubt about the real cost, the human cost, of our addiction to cobalt, coltan, and all the other natural resources that this land seems to be …"

Eni was sobbing so heartrendingly that she jerked awake.

***

On the flip side of town, in the real Ipeja, another group also digested the news. Theirs was a smaller screen, and their atmosphere was not nearly as sumptuous as Alan Steiner's. They were impressed by how quickly the mine owner had become the day's top news. A motley group of die-hard dissidents, these men disdained Alan Steiner as a safari-suited carpetbagger. Though descended from local royalty, Hafiz, the faction's leader, had no respect nor affection for the current O'yo'fa of Ipeja. The traditional ruler of Ipeja, His Royal Highness Ademowo II, was his maternal uncle. Still, Hafiz denounced the "puppet" for accepting Steiner's so-called "generous" offer to allocate thirty three point three percent of the proceeds from "his" diamond mine to Ipeja village. Because the land had been bestowed free of charge, Hafiz believed that Alan owed the villagers a much larger percentage of "his" profits. Also suspect was Steiner's largesse to the current ruler, which Hafiz believed had seduced the O'yo'fa to accept Steiner's profiteering. Steiner had given scholarships to four of the ruler's seventy children to study abroad. He also employed two other princes in the diamond mine. He made the favourite queen, a hardly literate seamstress, a member of the mine's board of governors. The O'yo'fa had also been spotted bumping about the pothole-pocked roads in a gleaming white Rolls Royce, yet another gift from Steiner.

At first, Hafiz tried to reason with the O'yo'fa by pointing out the town's nihilistic poverty, the dilapidated schools, the lack of potable water, the erratic electricity supply, and other signs of wanton destitution. He insisted that the formula for diamond-mine-profit-sharing was lopsided. He argued that if Steiner were truly honourable, given that the land was a gift, he should have ceded the mine to the town or granted villagers a much more significant royalty. After all, why should individual greed trump community need? The O'yo'fa pooh-poohed his nephew's complaints. He reminded Hafiz that, being the offspring of a woman, he had no say in the kingdom's governance. He then threatened to run him out of town if he did not cease and desist his "too-bookish, too-unrealistic rabble-rousing".

Hafiz thus chose to imitate his heroes. They were billionaire dissidents active in the Delta region of Nigeria, whose adventures he followed religiously in the tabloids. He commenced his militancy by co-opting school dropouts and disgruntled, unemployed youths to form a cadre that he christened the Liberation of Ipeja Movement (LIM). He settled on the convoluted name so as to have a pronounceable acronym.

The one group member who was not an Ipeja citizen was Melvin—Hafiz's friend and fellow dropout from the University of Ile Ifa. He met Melvin when they agreed to share a room as "brother" students. Even after Melvin was rusticated once the university discovered his forged O-Level results and false citizenship papers, the pair remained friends. So, Melvin stayed with Hafiz, who, being the head of the student union, was allocated a hostel room all to himself. Hafiz also had an office in the student union building. Their bond began just before the diamond was discovered in Ipeja, and being an indigent student, Hafiz found succour in the like-minded companionship. After a bloody riot, during which the vice-chancellor's house was burnt, Hafiz, too, was rudely rusticated. Thus, he was back in Ipeja, trying to engage in local politics. The idea of forming LIM only came up when the mother-lode of diamond was discovered in Ipeja. The LIM sextet lived in two bedrooms in his late father's compound, which Hafiz had inherited.

As they eyed the news, Hafiz, occupying the only armchair in the gloomy room, whistled when the newscaster read another item following the puff-piece about Alan's cavalcade. "The Swiss government has announced that it will pay six thousand five hundred dollars to any Nigerian living in Switzerland illegally who is willing to return home."

"You see! This is what I love about Nigerians. They know how to stand up to these motherfucking White folk," Melvin said.

One of the things which Hafiz liked about Melvin was his accent. When they first met, he'd mistaken Melvin for an American. Melvin had held on, as if for dear life, to the American accent, which he had tried so hard to cultivate before his deportation from the U.S. His accent had now rubbed off on Hafiz.

The two other members of LIM in the room raised their fists, hailing the Swiss government's offer as a victory for illegal African migrants all over Europe. They tuned out the rest of the report about the brutal living conditions Europe offered African migrants. They missed the footage of shantytowns in the middle of cities like Rome and Paris or the virtual prisons that were "holding camps." All but Melvin failed to see the clip of an interview with a young man in his early twenties in the Spanish city of Ceuta on the coast of Morocco.

"I know they don't want us because we're Black. But we're just begging them to let us in. Let them give us a chance, too, so we can have a useful life," the interviewee pleaded, staring into the camera. When the camera panned to reveal the razor-wire-topped barricades surrounding the little-known European enclave, Africans were seen pressed against the fencing, desperate to enter the EU—an appalling and ironic replay of the Middle Passage, now reversed, as Africans in their prime sought to spend their lives laboring for Europeans.

Melvin was actually hypnotized by the televised eyes of the desperate interviewee in Ceuta. He tore himself away from the TV, exited the room, and entered the corridor that gave access to all the rooms in the house. Here and there, beside doors behind which whole families stuffed into single rooms resided, were kerosene stoves, mortars, pestles, and other kitchen utensils. The utensils marked the areas beside each door as each family's kitchen.

The young man's televised eyes were eerily familiar to Melvin. He recalled the eyes of a man that had intrigued him outside the U.S. Embassy in Lagos. Melvin had wound up in Nigeria after the U.S. deported him to Liberia, where, for two harrowing years, he endured all of his worst fears about trying to make a life in Monrovia. It was a city trying in vain to dust itself down after a long, drawn-out war that had left more than blood stains and bomb craters. Melvin moved to Lagos when he heard that Liberians were able to buy Nigerian passports—for the right price—and, with these, were acquiring visas to go abroad. Since he had been deported as a Liberian, he reckoned that he could sneak back to the U.S. on a Nigerian passport. It was not the best laid-out plan in the world, but he'd been desperate to rejoin Carmen and their daughter, born a few months after his deportation.

The first time that Melvin noticed the man with the disturbing eyes opposite the U.S. Embassy was the second time he went there to apply for a visa, armed with his third Nigerian passport. Ignorant about the man who was quite famous in Nigeria due to several newspaper accounts of his plight, Melvin thought it odd that the gent did not queue up like the other hopeful visa applicants. He sat across the road from the embassy, observing the comings-and-goings of applicants and rejects—as if he were at a cinema.

Melvin was able to put the man's story together when he heard two women discussing him. "Poor man, seven years! Can you believe it?" one said, shaking her head slowly.

"Do you mean he's actually been sitting there for seven years?" the other woman asked. She was pregnant, but she kept trying to conceal her stomach with a large black shawl.

"Every day, without fail, he arrives at four-thirty AM, and sits there until the embassy closes. The embassy even tried to bribe him so he'd stop coming, but he refused. He just wants to return to America. His wife and children are there. I read his story in *Lagos Life* last year."

"But the wheelchair, how did he …?"

"That, I don't know."

"I think one of the newspapers said that he developed some health issues and ended up in the wheelchair after his deportation," an eavesdropping man chimed in, shrugging.

After that day, Melvin, who kept going back with new passports and identities because his visa applications kept getting turned down, ignored the man. That was until the day after his fifth application was turned down, and he was crossing the road to find change for bus fare. He found himself face to face with the "brother" who sat holding up a multicoloured umbrella with one hand. A slight drizzle had started suddenly. The man held the umbrella away from his face to favour the direction of the rain. When Melvin caught his eyes, he was startled by their emptiness.

When Melvin finally gave up on his visa applications, it was not due to the rudeness of the security guard—whom he suspected was being deliberately vindictive because he was probably only working as a guard because he could not afford the cost of a visa. Melvin, who had spent much of his life cultivating an American accent, immediately recognized a kindred spirit the first day he heard the guard speak. The guard seemed to have invested a lot of time studying American films and loved to lavish on visa applicants all the abusive lingo he'd thus acquired. "Get the fuck away from this gate, you motherfucking nigger!" was a favoured expletive. Even though he seemed to target Melvin from the get-go, and Melvin had to smile and find words to placate him each time he spat curses his way, he was not the one who finally caused Melvin to stop trying to reapply for an American visa. It was not even the expense of procuring one Nigerian passport after another that stopped him in his family-reunification mission. Neither was it the condescending attitude of the American interviewer who, on the day of his last visa application, when he tried to fathom one of her trick questions, had snarled, "I did not ask you for the story of your life. An honest, straight answer is all I require." She smirked cynically. "Application denied." She stamped his passport without even raising her head to snicker.

Nor was it the overwhelming presence of U.S. Marines in full combat gear, menacingly patrolling the vicinity of the embassy in Lagos. It was also not the frenzied prayers of Nigerians milling around him when he stood in line for six solid hours in the heat in the shed-like reception area. None of these really ruffled him because he had grown accustomed to all that.

It was the eyes of the bloated man with the umbrella who had been sitting in "protest" in that wheelchair for over seven years that finally did it for Melvin. That day after he saw the vacant look in the man's eyes, as Melvin shambled away from the U.S. Embassy toward the bus stop at the end of the long street, which housed several other embassies, he could not help wondering, with alarm, *When did this man die? Why had no one noticed that he was expired psychically?* In truth, he did not want to find out. Still, he could not shake these questions from his mind and could not make himself go back ever again. After that day, he could not continue believing the several stories he made up for himself about why he had lost track of Carmen and his daughter. He left Lagos and made his way to Ile Ifa, intending to attend university there.

"Why are you sitting out here in the dark?" The question startled Melvin out of his reverie.

He had been sitting on a low fence in the yard outside Hafiz's family house alone for several minutes, not even noticing that the electricity had blacked out again. Startling him was Taofik, Abdul's son, also a LIM comrade. Taofik was returning to the house following a mission. Melvin did not answer but traipsed after Taofik. They found Hafiz and the other men in the now candle-lit room, drinking garri soaked in water. One man passed around a bottle of roasted peanuts.

Since the food riots earlier in the year, in Ile Ifa and several other West African countries, imported rice and bread—which had, over the previous two decades, become staple foods—were ever more expensive. But rather than alleviate the situation, the riots only elicited a draconian response from the government, embarrassed by the unrest that broke out while a joint mission of the IMF, World Bank (locally known as "Imperial Mother Fuckers" and "World Bandits"), and African Development Bank were "in country," plotting new ways to loot the destitute without sparking rebellion or triggering a spat with China. Troops unleashed to quell the riots slew over a hundred protesters by bullet and/or bayonet.

However, the grifters, the grafters, the governors, had reason for glee: General elections were imminent, and everyone knew that the "Natural Governing Party" would recycle basically the same candidates "elected" consistently since independence. The cutthroat Area-Boy-turned-backslapping-president had cut duties on food and cement imports. A fifteen percent wage increase—the first such hike in a decade—was promised for public sector employees. The president also vowed to review fuel prices, telephone rates, and bank fees. The people of Ile Ifa, who had heard it all before, were, unfortunately, still naïve enough to be optimistic. They assumed some promises would be kept because the IMF had endorsed the policies. Through a P.R. at a Wall Street press conference, the IMF proclaimed, "Noting the concerns of the people of Ile Ifa, we're pleased that the government is poised to institute structural adjustment programs to alleviate worry."

Hafiz rose as soon as Melvin and Taofik stepped into the room. "Well?" he said, wagging his forefinger playfully at Taofik. Taofik looked crestfallen fleetingly, then broke into a smile before digging into his shirt where he had concealed a large sheet of paper. All the others gathered around the wobbly rattan centre table. Hafiz began to unfold the blueprint to Alan Steiner's ranch house.

"I can't believe your father came through for us," Hafiz said, studying the blueprint.

"He said we have to let him know when we plan to attack so he can make sure the domestic staff sneak out before we arrive." Taofik beamed proudly as he spoke.

Turning to Melvin, Hafiz, also smiling, said, "O' ye of little faith!"

"I admit I was wrong, my man. I totally misread Mr. Abdul. I thought he was too much of an Uncle Tom to betray his massah." Melvin tried to joke about his apology, but the others were too engrossed with planning their ambush to indulge his Malcom-X-wannabe wit.

***

In the morning, Enilolobo was awoken by the familiar song of a laughing palm dove. Although she could not recall where she'd previously heard the song of the beautiful tiny bird, she repeated its name, which was like its clarion call.

"O'dere ko ko! Odere eee ko ko. Odere koko, odere koko!" She tried to stretch but her body felt like lead. Frowning, she realized that she did not look forward to the rest of what she had thought would be a lovely day.

For the first time since she had resolutely started recording her dreams, she could not bring herself to jot anything in her notebook. She kept going over the future she had seen to try to make sense of it but she could not. She gave up and went to the dining room, where Alan, Doris, Charlotte, and the two boys were already finishing breakfast. They urged her to hurry because they were set for a tour of the town and then a visit to some of Alan's projects before paying a courtesy call to the O'yo'fa.

"Where is Iona?" Eni asked, noticing that she was missing.

"Oh, she's skipping the rounds this morning," Doris said sweetly, but managed to imply by rolling her eyes and making a gesture with her hand as if drinking, that she thought Iona was hungover. Not wanting to delay the others, Eni volunteered to stay and keep Iona company.

Holding a cup of coffee, Iona breezed in to join Eni, as soon as the others left, after promising to send a car for them later. Iona wished that Alan and Doris would plunge Hummer-first down the diamond-mine shaft. "I still can't believe this place," she told Eni, who smiled a non-committal smile. After the group left the hunting lodge, their first stop was a hospital where Alan had built a well and to which he regularly sent drugs—badly-needed, but always short-in-supply. He had also constructed two new wings. One was an infectious diseases ward, rapidly crammed due to the surge in the incidences of AIDS and its opportunistic infections. The second wing was a male-only psych ward. Doctors and nurses lined up outside to welcome Alan and his family and show their appreciation for his open wallet. In the mental ward, Charlotte caused a stir. Her golden shade of blond hair enthralled many patients. Pointing at her head, one begged her for some strands. Charlotte giggled, basking in their adulation, but her mother walked stiffly up to her and ushered her outside.

"You don't want to encourage this kind of attention, dear. These men have probably not been in the company of any women for a long time. It can be dangerous," she said mildly, admonishing, even as she quivered, imagining a Black hand slapping her own "tits."

***

The ambush occurred just after midnight. Although the LIM could field only its six fully pledged members, Hafiz and the others easily mustered eighteen jobless youths. Having studied the compound's blueprints, they knew how to avoid the CCTV cameras that had been installed the year before. The youths crept up on the armed detail at the lodge, who were caught totally unawares. Efficiently, the youths overpowered and tied up the bored, lazy-ass guards. To prove that they meant business, they slit one guard's throat. Not sport or theatre. After that, they faced no resistance from the rest of the security team, who did exactly as they were told by disarming the elaborate alarm system.

Although Ile Ifa had witnessed its fair share of unrest and solo guerrilla attacks, these mainly troubled the Tiga Delta, which was far enough from Ipeja for the gun-toters at the hunting lodge to feel a false sense of personal security. Besides, the value of the diamonds in Ipeja had not yet hit the populace. Oil was still the primary interest of anyone craving a quick, violent grasp at a slice of the national cake.

Shod in neon trainers made in China and wearing black t-shirts and baggy jeans sagged to the max (some revealing boxers with cartoon characters), the young attackers moved swiftly to surround the two interlocked buildings. After taking secure and strategic positions, Hafiz rained several shots into the innocent night sky.

Hearing the gunfire, Siaka's blood rushed to his head. He was at once transported back to a time and place he had scrupled to forget, but which had haunted his dreams. Like a panther, he glided out of bed and slid on his stomach toward the door, which was ajar. He continued to crawl, propping his bulk with his elbows on the lush carpet all the way down the corridor. He stopped when he saw Timothy, looking deranged, run out of his room speaking in his native tongue.

"Down!" Siaka ordered him, surprising himself at how fast he had slipped back into combat mode. *I guess it's like riding a bike.* He almost smiled at that realization. Together, they slid toward the other end of the wing, where they found Iona and Eni huddled behind an antique armoire just inside Eni's room. Siaka had no problem persuading them to drop to the floor so they could all crawl through the adjoining corridor to the wing that Alan's family occupied. In front, Siaka was about to slip through a door and back into the corridor when they heard another shot followed by a bellowing voice.

"Alan Steiner! If you value your family and friends, come out here! We want to talk to you. We need to renegotiate the profits from our diamonds!" To the party huddled in Eni's room, the voice sounded a little—but perilously—inebriated.

"They don't sound like robbers," Eni said, baffled.

"We can't trust them," Siaka stated, resuming his shimmying exit.

"Wait!" Iona could not hide her excitement.

The other three turned to face her.

"I … I think I want to go out and talk to them," Iona said.

"Are you out of your mind?" Timothy screeched.

"Maybe." She tried to smile. "But then again, maybe not. Listen, why should we risk our lives for Alan and his family? Why should we take sides with him against these people who only want what's rightfully theirs in the first place?" She grimaced nervously, scanning her students' faces in the hope that they were won over.

"No way. I'm not getting involved in any battle that does not concern me," Timothy said. Then, because he was sitting close to Iona with his back against the wall, he shifted his bottom to glide away from her. Eni began to weep quietly.

"I'd like to stay and discuss the dangers of your way of thinking with you, but I have a life to preserve: Mine." Siaka was calm. He recommenced his crawl from Eni's room without looking to see if either Timothy or Eni were accompanying. Timothy scrambled after him.

Before Iona got up, she raised her hands and shouted, "My name is Iona Pearse. I'm coming out. I have no weapons. I'm raising my hands so you can see that I'm unarmed. I just want to talk to you."

She looked down to flash Eni a reassuring smile, but Eni was sitting against the wall with her head bowed and her arms around her legs bent double against her belly. Her face rested on her notebook. She had been trying to write in it when the first shot rang.

On the other side of the hunting lodge, Alan heard Iona. Thinking she was going to negotiate on his behalf, he raised his voice, too, cautioning her not to take any undue risks. By this time, Siaka and Timothy, who continued to snake through the long corridor toward Alan and his family, were near a window and heard the indistinct voices of the attackers. They paused to listen, trying to make out what they were saying or if Iona was making any headway with them, but gave up when they could not.

Outside, Hafiz's group aimed their guns at Iona, who approached them steadily, smiling extra broadly (because her life depended upon it), her sphincter contracted, too ready to shit involuntarily while her legs trembled uncontrollably. Her arms were raised in surrender.

"She's nothing but one of those American bitches. She thinks she can outsmart us," Melvin whispered to Hafiz. He labelled her Canadian accent as American. When she came close enough for them to see her face clearly, Hafiz could not help smiling wryly.

"You'd better be one hell of a fast and smooth-talking bitch, or you'll soon be drawing your last breath," he said, still smiling.

Iona gulped hard, but her sphincter relaxed a tad, though her legs still felt like rubber. She kept her lecturer voice as calm as she could; she had to back her tongue with spine. "I hope you know this can't go on for too long. Alan has a radio link to the mine, and I'm sure he's got trigger- happy goons on call. Perhaps the mine has contacted the cops and troops by now."

"So? What business of yours is all of that?" Melvin shouted at her. Glad he'd held fastidiously to his American accent, so he'd not feel intimidated by this flinty twig of an American woman.

"It's my business because I think it's insane that in this day and age, any White man should continue to grow rich and fat off of Black folks." She prayed hard that her classroom rhetoric had traction with these cutthroat hotheads.

"So, what else is new?" Hafiz asked, doubting her sincerity.

"Listen, man. I know the place pretty well. I've also spent the last two days in close contact with folks inside. I know how they think."

"So? What's in this for you?" Melvin asked.

"I'm not sure. All I know is, this is where I want to be. This is the side I'm on. I believe in what you're doing. Besides, three of the people in there are my students, and I'm responsible for their being here."

"You're a teacher?" Hafiz asked incredulously.

"Sort of. I'm a post-doctoral researcher, and I teach part-time. I'm Iona Pearse," she said, folding her arms over her breasts: A buffalo stance to back up her professorial lip.

However, lacking the ability to see her humanity, strength, and passion for her principles, Hafiz looked her over as though she were a used car he could buy.

Though the way the eyes rolled over her body was discomfiting, Iona was determined to succeed, to survive. Just then, though she felt as if she was at a precipice, it was as if all her childhood, her teenage rebelliousness, her studies, all of it had been geared toward getting her to this time and place. It dawned on her that the sensation she was feeling, about taking life by its horns, about taking charge of the course of destiny, must be akin to what men feel when they opt for war. With this thought, trembling became muscle flexing. It was not an altogether uncomfortable feeling for Iona who had been fighting all her life.

Hafiz was enthralled by Iona's beautifully sculpted body: The firm breasts atop a flat stomach, which curved out into voluptuous hips. He saw the fire in her eyes and was flattered because he thought it matched the sensation growing steadily in his groin.

His head reeled with a desire to possess her, body and mind, and the fact that she stood there levelly meeting his gaze beguiled him. Signaling to Taofik to keep watching her, he called Melvin aside.

"Bro, she is nothing but baggage to us," Melvin, who had read Hafiz's intentions correctly, said.

"Easy, man. Let me handle this."

"I know she's a tasty-looking chick, but—"

"Just who is running this show? You or me?" Hafiz's voice only needed to drop an octave to make Melvin shrink. The latter was acutely conscious of his outsider status despite shoring up LIM since its inception.

"Can't you see she could be worth something to us?" Hafiz pretended his lust was politic.

"How? What does she know about the place that's not in the blueprint Taofik's dad sent us?"

"As a hostage, stupid."

"You mean …?"

"I mean, let me handle this my way," Hafiz said. His eyes shot a sly glint that Melvin caught.

"Besides, can't you see that the babe is not offensive to even x-ray scrutiny?"

"My man!" They clicked the barrels of their guns together twice in a macabre salute before turning back to strut toward Iona, who had been studying their body language. She felt strangely calm—as if she were Nanny-of-the-Maroons reborn.

"At ease," he barked at Taofik, who was looming over Iona. Taofik stepped back.

"Break down the situation inside!" Hafiz commanded. Iona decided to ignore his irritating tone and began to describe the Canuck compound.

Inside, Siaka and Timothy, having snuck to the other side, heard muffled voices that led them to the door to the study where

Alan and his family were holed up. It was, of course, locked. Alan, who had striven unsuccessfully to scan the compound via the malfunctioning security monitor, realized now that Iona had decamped. Fearful that knocking would give away their position, Siaka whispered frantically for Alan to let them into his de facto "panic room."

"Why should I trust you?" Alan's hiss was a stifled whimper.

"Because we're here." Siaka fell quiet, scheming, then said in a chillingly calm voice. "You're safer with us under your eyes." Lying next to Siaka, Timothy could see his eyes turn into fangs. "Trust me, man. You don't want me on the other side," Siaka said, turning to lie face up. He listened intently to Alan confer with a panicked Doris. Only the clattering of Timothy's teeth rattled the otherwise deathly stillness.

"Why would they want to kill us?" Alan asked. His voice came low from behind the door.

"Because they're Black, like them." Her words squeezed through clenched molars. Her dread? black hands slapping white "tits."

Siaka and Timothy heard Alan pleading to persuade Doris. But he sounded unsure of his own position. An investment strategy may pay dividends, but not help to preserve one's life.

"You're talking as if these are normal people. Well, they're not! Who would have thought? After all we've done for them ..." Doris was perplexed, flummoxed, and close to pissing herself.

"Dad, did the man at the mine get the high commissioner yet?" Charlotte's voice was high, more of a whispered screech.

"Look, calm down both of you!" Alan commanded—or pleaded. Moments later, Siaka and Timothy heard footsteps, the door clicked, then it slithered open. Alan did not notice Siaka's calmness, his ready stealth, as he lay there in the corridor. Alan gestured frantically for the supine pair to enter. Siaka stood and stalked into the room as if he owned it, like a soldier. He went straight for the window, sneaking a peek without moving the curtain. Just as he expected: Pitch darkness. Turning to Alan, he demanded, "What kind of ammo ya' got?" Without waiting for an answer, he stepped calmly forward, ogling the gun in Alan's hand.

"May I?" Needing no reply, he plucked the gun handily from the paralyzed Alan. He turned it around in his hand, whistling in approval. Then Siaka followed Alan's eyes, which dashed toward what looked like a large liquor cabinet with a bunch of keys still in its lock. He leapt toward it and swung wide its door. He eyed the superb and gleaming guns within, ignoring Alan and Doris, their eyes dazed.

"Looks like you've been expecting our friends out there for a while. Have any of you ever handled any of these?"

Alan nodded and made a move toward the cupboard when he noticed that Siaka had him square in his sights.

"You need to be careful with that," Alan started saying. He felt shamed by his suddenly squeaking voice. "Have you—"

"Let's get one thing straight: I'm the bossman here," the former—and clearly unreformed—child soldier said, his gat trained on Alan's heart.

"Oh my God!" Charlotte exclaimed. Her sphincter puckered.

"I warned you!" Doris's eyes shot daggers at Alan. Her mind was frantically plotting to slit her throat before ever having to see Charlotte raped by these brutes.

"You didn't think that after hearing you guys confer before letting us in, we'd be stupid enough to put our lives in your hands, did you?" Siaka hissed.

"Excuse me ..." Timothy said, his voice still high-pitched.

"You, sharrap!" Siaka ordered. "Now listen up. All of you. I don't know how this will end, but I was a soldier long enough to know that in situations like this, the gun is God. It determines who lives and who does not. And the person holding the gun is even greater than God. So don't any of you even think of messing with me." As he spoke, he transformed. His mannerisms, his voice and his face altered beyond recognition. He was Malcolm siamesed with Mao: All power flows from the barrel of a gun.

"Good. Now, I want to leave this place alive. Which is why, Alan, I can't let you get us killed."

"But … we didn't mean to offend you by what we said …"

"It's not just that, man." Still swinging his "piece" from target to target, including at hand-wringing Doris and ready-to-piss-herself Charlotte. Siaka lectured, "You've got too much baggage, man. Way too much to be a reliable soldier." He said this as if contemplating a way of making Alan a better soldier, then seemed to change his mind. He motioned for Alan to open the cabinet. Nodding, he gestured for him to get a gun. Then he turned to Timothy.

"You ever handled a gun?"

Timothy swivelled his head east and west.

"Good." Siaka smiled at Alan's puzzled look.

"Now, Alan, load your weapon."

They all saw Alan's hands shakily slot bullets into the weapon. "Uncork it and hand it over to Timothy. Now, Timothy, there is no need to be so nervous. Just point the gun at Alan." Everyone gasped.

"Relax. Especially you, Timothy. Now you all heard Timothy say he's never handled a gun before. So, we all know that any surprise or shock might make him pull the trigger." He spoke as if instructing kindergarteners.

"This is uncalled for!" Alan shouted, his voice imitating a wheeze.

"Really? Do you think I'm stupid?"

When Alan did not answer, he asked again. This time louder. "Do y'all think I'm fucking stupid? Just moments ago you were going to leave us at the mercy of those killers because we're Black like them! Y'all the enemy, despite your good grammar and bright, white smiles!"

"Oh, God! Oh God! Oh God!" Doris wailed.

"Shaarrrapp!" He shouted at her, and her hand came up to her mouth as her bowels shat into her panties. This maternal reaction gave Charlotte the permit to befoul her underwear too. Perfume could not countermand the foul aroma wafting from the bawling twain. Alan just shook, unable to render any assistance or comfort.

"It's true. Siaka is right," Timothy said, suddenly calmer, and ignoring the tear-gleaming females.

"Good. Keep the gun aimed at Alan at all times, but don't shoot unless you have to. Don't even wait for my order." He turned to address the women. "Any false move from either of you, and Daddy's dead."

Doris whimpered. "Can we at least clean ourselves? I don't want to die like this!"

Siaka's mind flashed back to all of the grisly, dirty, stinking deaths he'd witnessed—and perpetrated—and now here were these entitled people expecting to die "clean."

Still, he told Timothy to take the women into the WC and shoot them if they tried anything. He turned back to Alan.

"Alright. Now you, Alan, I want you to go to the window and start offering them whatever they want."

"But all they want is for me to go outside."

Siaka paused, thinking. "Go to the window and just start talking. Promise them your wife, your kid, your mine … I don't care what else. I need some time to figure out how to smoke 'em out—and then smoke 'em if I have to."

Alan wondered if the absent Eni had sided with the guerrillas too. Sounds of crying and sniffling and running water came from the WC as he shuffled to the window—his eyes a-flood, his crotch sodden.

***

After Siaka and Timothy left, Eni waited for what she knew not. She remained in her room, hoping that the deadlock would miraculously end peacefully. Then, realizing that her peril was real, she crept stealthily from the house through the door nearest the pool. She felt compelled to play diplomat. Still clutching her notebook, she felt calm as if she had faced danger many times before. Her unshod feet felt reassured by the cold tiles lining the pool area. How incredibly quiet it was. The warm air outside the air-conditioned lodge kissed her face and embraced her thinly-clad body. She took one, then two steps toward the direction where she heard Iona treating with the LIM, when she was conscious suddenly of eyes watching her from within the lodge, just as she saw the group outside trying to make out who she was. Almost as if on cue, both sides began to fire. Each side having concluded the other was trying to sneak up on them, failed to recognize her.

***

One minute, I'm walking, clutching my journal. I'm tiptoeing, really, because I fear I might falter and slip. Then the next minute, I'm up in the air, flying. At first, the familiar pain burned me like fire, but by the time I hit the water in the pool—still slightly warm even though the sun had gone to sleep several hours before, I feel nothing except the caress, the sweet caress. I look up when I hit the bottom of the pool and see my notebook floating on the surface. I try to surge upwards to touch it, to take it, to retrieve it, but somehow or other, I have once again become one with water, land, and the clouds. I watch my words streaming out of the pages of my notebook in the various colours of ink with which I have recorded my mind over the years. I see the colours merging into black, floating one way while my blood makes patterns that flow in the opposite direction. I shut my eyes, wondering which side the bullets that killed me this time came from. But it does not matter. All the sides are parts of me. Black blotching white; white bleaching black. Sunlight always shadowed …

EPILOGUE? WHAT IS PEACE WITHOUT EQUALITY?

Ti Olúwaa ni ilẹ̀, àti ẹ̀kún rẹ̀,
The Earth is the Lord's, and the Fullness Thereof

A FEW DAYS after Enilolobo died, Iyin let herself into her apartment at Warden and Finch. Though she had worked a full shift, she felt refreshed because she decided to walk leisurely home from work at the Scarborough Grace Hospital instead of taking the bus as usual. Once home, she found her mother watching a Yoruba movie in the living room.

"Kabo, Oko mi, Iyabo, Durosinmi," her mother said, welcoming her.

Iyin could not help smiling as her mother called her old names. She still remembered how hearing her mother call her old names used to infuriate her. She sat close to her mother on the sectional couch so she could wrap her left arm around her and ask how her day had gone.

Her mother assured her, "I have been blessed to live long enough to eat your food. I have no complaints. I am grateful." She pointed to the dining table. "I made eko and efo riro. I know you only like to eat light when you come home from your afternoon shift."

Iyin got up and quickly went to her room to change into something comfortable before returning to the sitting room. She found her mother standing up.

"Should I turn off the TV?" her mother asked.

"What about you? Have you eaten?" Iyin asked.

Iyin collected the remote from her mother, who assured her she had eaten when she finished cooking the meal. "You know my stomach does not allow me to eat anything too late nowadays. But I can sit with you while you eat if you want me to."

"No, I'll pop in and see you before I turn in for the night."

Iyin changed the TV channel to the news. She then made her way up the two stairs to the raised area of the living room where the dining table was. As she began to eat, half-listening to the news, she reflected on how much she had come to enjoy her mother's company. She knew she had come a long way since Tosin died three years earlier.

She met Tosin, a pastor, a couple of years after moving to Toronto. She could hardly believe how easy it was for her to fall in love with and to be loved by the young, firebrand preacher. He was a pastor at the largest Toronto branch of her Pentecostal church. They got married just six months after they met. She was flattered that he picked her because she knew that there were many single sisters in the congregation who fancied the handsome gent. She smiled when she recalled how caring he was. Even after the first year of marriage and she was still not pregnant, he didn't once express any anxiety.

"Did I not tell you there was nothing to worry about? O' ye of little faith," he said, teasing her as they left the doctor's office the day they went to hear the results of the barrage of tests they had taken. Iyin had pestered him into seeing a doctor because she yearned to start a family. She hugged him, relieved that the doctor said he could not find any reason why they could not have a baby. He asked them to give it some more time and then come back to discuss options in a few months if they still had not become expectant parents.

Cruelly, Iyin's idyllic marriage ended in a heartbeat. Seven weeks after their consultation, Tosin died in a collision on Highway 401. He'd been en route to preach at one of the new Pentecostal branches when a drunk cop rear-ended him, forcing his car into a ditch and crushing him against his steering wheel. The cop staggered away, unscathed; his drunk and dangerous driving charges expunged by judges biased in favour of police officers.

Despite this tragedy, Iyin's faith was unshaken, until one Sunday, when the senior pastor of their church preached a sermon that made her question—for the first time since becoming a Christian—her blind belief in miracles and the guarantee of a life without tragedy.

"Look, let's not kid ourselves," the pastor, who spoke in an American accent, bellowed into the mic. "The Bible does not lie when it says, 'Truly I tell you, if you have faith as small as a mustard seed, you can say to this mountain, "Move from here to there," and it will move. Nothing will be impossible for you.' How can you claim to be the child of God and die of cancer? How can you say you love God but cannot overcome? How can you say you have faith and remain childless?"

Iyin fidgeted—squirmed—in her front-row seat. As she listened, images started to dart across her mind. She saw Tosin, bowing unfailing every morning to commit his life to God before stepping out into the world. She saw him kneeling by their bedside on the day of his accident, and she remembered every word he said in prayer as he led their devotion that morning. As a nurse, she had also seen far too many good people, even innocent babies, die of cancer. So that preaching, that day, didn't sit well with her. There were miracles, there was salvation, and still there was death for all. Fate rarely keeps faith with faith.

She spent the whole of the next day in bed poring over verse after verse of the Bible to bolster what she recognized as her suddenly wobbly faith. By the evening of that day, she philosophized that, if prayer, fasting, and holding tight to one's faith were sufficient, she'd still be a wife and likely a mother, not a widow.

How shockingly light and free she suddenly felt!

For the first time since becoming a born-again Christian, when her mother called her the next morning and greeted her by calling her old names as she had persistently done, Iyin did not flinch.

Neither did she go back to sleep or resay her daily prayer as she once would. Instead, she let her mother's affirming voice caress her soul.

"Eseun Maami," she'd said, thanking her mother. Then, to her own surprise, she shared the Pentecostal pastor's dread words. Her mother, noticing that she was weeping, begged her to come home for a visit.

Instead of going home for a short visit, Iyin applied for a visa to bring her mother to Canada. Time for a mother-and-child reunion.

"I can only come for about ten days because of my work, but I need you for more than ten short days," she explained when her mother—afraid to fly—hesitated when Iyin first floated the idea.

With her mother at her side, Iyin grew stronger daily in the company of this woman that she had tried so hard to shun. Ironically, it was her mother who helped to renew her Christian belief.

"So what if God does not work miracles?" Her mother stunned Iyin by asking her this question one day after watching an evangelical miracle service. "Would He stop being God?"

"But you also believe in miracles. You and Baba believed that it was Ifa … "

"And if you had not been born, would that have stopped Ifa being Ifa?"

Iyin's jaw opened to produce a counterpoint, but she had no words to respond to her mother's question.

She returned to her old church, but because she stopped running away from who she was, she could dismiss whatever misstructured notions the brimstone-and-fire-preaching pastors spewed. She ran their words through a mental sieve—her bullshit detector—and kept the good.

As she was about to finish eating that evening, Iyin's eyes

surveyed a scene playing on the TV of people on a dinghy pitching perilously upon sky-high water. She raised the volume of the TV to hear the report.

"Italian coast guards and naval vessels tried unsuccessfully to intercept and forcibly return a boat filled with African migrants on the high seas today. They did not do any screening to ascertain if any of the passengers were vulnerable people seeking asylum or needing protection. The boat had over a hundred people from troubled African countries—Liberia, Somalia, Nigeria, Ivory Coast, Ile Ifa, and Eritrea. Some of the migrants were sick or injured. There were three pregnant women. Others were families with young children. One of the rescued persons is an unaccompanied boy who no one on the boat can account for. The unaccompanied child, who only answers when asked his name, did not say how he got on the boat. The members of the International Offshore Aid Group (IOAG), a humanitarian organization that rescued the boat before the Italian coast guard could send it back, are appealing to anyone who recognizes the boy to come forward. The medical people on the team think he is about ten years old. They hope someone will recognize him because of the unique marks on his body."

Iyin gasped when the image of the boy came up because she could swear it was the face of the girl who had made her abandon her job and flee Halifax. The camera moved from the boy's face and closed up on his chest, then his back.

"The medical team of the IOAG think the marks on his back and chest are freshly healed and could be bullet wounds. They suspect he might be a victim of child traffickers."

When the camera tilted, revealing the boy's stomach, Iyin screamed. The boy had two navels. Her mother came scurrying. "What is wrong?"

Iyin pointed at the screen.

Her mother understood very little English, so she sat down next to her at the table, puzzled. She, too, exclaimed when she saw the navels, but Iyin motioned for her to wait because the reporter was now asking the boy his name.

"My name is Toluwanile Jagunlabi." The boy practically barked his answer, facing the camera as if ready for war.

"Kabiyesi!" Iyin and her mother exclaimed simultaneously.

"He refuses to answer any other question," the reporter said, finished.

Iyin muted the volume as the news switched to sports scores.

"Two navels, like the girl you told me about?" her mother asked.

"Maami, it's not just the two navels. That is the same face of the girl! That is the exact face of the girl who said her name was Enilolobo!"

Iyin's mother sat pondering and wondering for a few minutes as Iyin sat facing her—as if she expected her to explain the brazen truth of apparent reincarnation.

"But you said the girl did not harm anyone. You said that, when she spoke to you, she was gentle and did not threaten you in any way."

Iyin nodded, and her mother pivoted her head sorrowfully.

"Humph," her mother said, sighing deeply. "This boy that I just saw does not come in peace."

Acknowledgements

I am deeply grateful to the Ontario Arts Council and the Canada Council for the Arts for their generous grants, which provided the support and encouragement I needed to bring this novel to life.

I extend my heartfelt thanks to Adetoun Ilumoka, Ajoke Jacobs, Carole Enahoro, and other dear friends who read early drafts and offered insights that helped shape this work.

Special thanks to George Elliott Clarke, Poet Laureate, for his meticulous editorial guidance and invaluable suggestions that elevated this novel. His support was instrumental in helping me navigate the challenges of publishing in Canada.

I am profoundly thankful to the incredible team at Guernica Editions, for their belief in this project and their dedicated efforts to bring *A Ladder of Bones* to the world.

To my partner in all things, Soji Oyinsan, your enduring patience and unwavering support mean the world to me. To my children and extended family, thank you for your constant belief in me and your encouragement every step of the way.

I am especially grateful to my son, Soji Oyinsan II (Shakes), for his remarkable talent and for creating the artwork for the cover design, which perfectly captures the essence of this story.

Thank you all for being part of this journey.

About the Author

Bunmi Oyinsan is a writer, educator, and cultural producer whose work spans literature, television, and education. She holds advanced degrees from Saint Mary's University and York University in Canada, where her research explored the intersection of Pan African oral philosophies, literature, and film studies.

She has authored novels, stage and radio plays, short stories and children's stories. She has also written and produced compelling TV series such as *Owuro Lojo* and *The Golden Cage*, which delve into the complexities of intimate partner violence and gender-based issues.

In addition to her literary achievements, Oyinsan is a passionate advocate for education. She founded Lekki Peninsula College and Lekki Peninsula Nursery and Primary School in Lagos, Nigeria, to provide quality, affordable education for at-risk youth and children from low-income families. Her innovative curricula incorporate vocational skills and cultural awareness, empowering students to thrive academically and socially.

Through her nonprofit organization, **Sankofa Futures Initiative Center**, and her creative platforms like *Sankofa Stories and Nursery Rhymes* and *The Sankofa Pan African Series* on YouTube, Oyinsan continues to inspire discussions on African history, culture, and social justice.

When she's not writing or teaching, Oyinsan enjoys collaborating on creative projects. She resides between Canada and Nigeria, drawing inspiration from both worlds.

MIX
Paper
FSC® C100212

Printed by Imprimerie Gauvin
Gatineau, Québec